"I suppose I must appoint myself your guardian angel."

Aimee was shaken by the brief crack in his armor, but she disguised her bemusement with a less than delicate sniff. "Perhaps what passed between us in the garden has slipped your mind, but at this point I can't help but think you are the last person who should be watching over me."

He shrugged. "I suggest we both do our best to pretend that never happened. It was a kiss. Nothing more. And I'm willing to put whatever differences we may have aside if it means making sure you stay out of trouble. I happen to think a great deal of your father, and I would be remiss indeed should I allow anything to happen to his daughter because of her obstinacy."

"Obstinacy? How dare you?"

His eyebrows arched at her outraged gasp. "What's wrong, my lady?" he queried mockingly. "Surely if I can survive for a few days under the same roof with you, you can tolerate my company for a short while as well. Unless there is some reason you think you might have a difficult time. Perhaps that kiss meant more to you than you pretend . . ."

Kimberly Logan

Seduced by Sin

AVON

An Imprint of HarperCollinsPublishers

This is a work of fiction. Names, characters, places, and incidents are products of the author's imagination or are used fictitiously and are not to be construed as real. Any resemblance to actual events, locales, organizations, or persons, living or dead, is entirely coincidental.

AVON BOOKS
An Imprint of HarperCollins*Publishers*
10 East 53rd Street
New York, New York 10022-5299

Copyright © 2008 by Kimberly Snoke
ISBN: 978-0-06-123920-5
www.avonromance.com

First Avon Books paperback printing: April 2008

Avon Trademark Reg. U.S. Pat. Off. and in Other Countries, Marca Registrada, Hecho en U.S.A.
HarperCollins® is a registered trademark of HarperCollins Publishers.

Printed in the U.S.A.

10 9 8 7 6 5 4 3 2 1

To Ann, Kathy, and Jan,
who were there at the beginning.
Thanks for showing me the way.
And to Steven, Kailee, Kurt, and Ryan,
for always giving me something to smile about,
just when I need it the most.

Acknowledgments

The last two years have been extremely difficult for me in many ways, and there were times when I thought this book would never be completed. If it were not for the encouragement of a handful of very special people, it is quite possible that the words inside of me would have never found their way onto the paper.

To my editor, May Chen, and the staff at Avon, thank you so much for sticking with me through it all and for your unlimited reserves of patience. It is greatly and sincerely appreciated. To my agent, Paige Wheeler, thanks for fielding my frantic e-mails and talking me down from the ledge more times than I can count. Your support and understanding has meant more than I can say. And a shout-out to my wonderfully talented fellow writers in the Sisterhood of the Jaunty Quills: Anne, Shana, Margo, Shirley, Cindy, Robyn, and Jenna. It's nice to know that I'm not all alone out here in the trenches!

And, as always, much love and gratitude to my family, who love me no matter what. (You too, SkittleDoo!)

Seduced by Sin

Prologue

London, 1823

It began with a dream.

For Lady Aimee Daventry, there wasn't anything unusual about that, in and of itself. In fact, in the ten years since the night of her mother's murder, she had grown rather accustomed to the violent nightmares that so often plagued her slumber. And this one had started out in much the same way as all the others.

She was nine years old again, and she stood in the darkened, first-floor corridor of the Albright town house, drawn from her bed by she knew not what. Her slippers frozen to the carpeted runner and her arms wrapped about herself to ward off the chill that seeped through the fabric of her nightgown, she listened with apprehension to the frantic whispers that drifted into the corridor from the library just up ahead.

One of the voices belonged to her mother, the Marchioness of Albright. The other was a harsh, masculine rumble that Aimee didn't recognize. For some reason, the sound of it was enough to send a frisson of unease slithering its way up her spine.

Who could Mama be talking to at this hour?

Though she strained her ears, she couldn't make out what was being said over the deep growl of thunder from outside. So, one slow step at a time, she forced herself forward on unsteady legs until the door of the room loomed before her. It had been left hanging slightly ajar, and a thin strip of light spilled out through the crack.

There was an unintelligible mutter from within, followed by a gasping sob.

Was Mama crying?

The possibility horrified Aimee, and she reached out with every intention of pushing the panel the rest of the way open and rushing to her mother's defense. But something arrested her mid-motion, halting her in place with her fingers wrapped around the doorknob. Her instincts were screaming at her, warning her in no uncertain terms that if she went into that room, her life would change forever.

From out of nowhere, a wave of fear rose up, sending her heart flying into her throat. She fought her way through it, however, and managed to give the door a small nudge, widening the crack enough so that she could peer into the chamber.

In the faint glow of a lamp, she could see Mama standing next to Papa's mahogany desk, still dressed in the red silk gown she had worn to the Briarwood ball earlier that evening, though her sable hair had started to unravel from its elegant topknot of cascading ringlets. Her beautiful face marred by tearstains, she faced the French doors that had been flung open to the storm-tossed evening, her chin upraised in defiance and one arm extended before her, palm outward, as if in an attempt to keep the man who loomed on the threshold at bay.

The man who held the gleaming muzzle of a pistol pointed at her head.

A brilliant flash of lightning illuminated the library, penetrating the shadows that shrouded his features and revealing a face twisted into a mask of hatred.

"I'm afraid your pleas fall upon deaf ears, my lady," he was saying with predatory softness. "Tonight is your night to die."

It was too much for Aimee. The stranger's terrifying statement, along with the sight of the gun and his malevolent expression, was enough to send her mind into full retreat. The ground shifted beneath her and she mentally withdrew, her vision blurring even as events proceeded to unfold in a jumble of disorienting images that she couldn't quite seem to bring into focus.

A black curtain descended just as a gunshot rang out, and she knew no more.

When she finally returned to awareness, she was kneeling on the floor next to the desk with no memory of how she had gotten there, staring in dazed incomprehension at her mother's motionless form lying a few feet away, a crimson pool of blood staining the rug beneath her head. The French doors swayed *in the gusts of rain-scented air that swirled into the room, but the man was gone.*

Stifling a sob, she looked down into Lady Albright's still countenance, searching for some sign of life. There was nothing. No rhythmic rise and fall of the chest, no flutter of lashes. No spark whatsoever.

Her mother was dead, and Aimee's agony at the realization was staggering.

It was at that moment that the marchioness's glassy eyes unexpectedly blinked.

Aimee yelped, scrambling backward to cower against the desk as that amber gaze focused on her and pinned her in place with burning intensity. And while the rest of her body remained stiff and unmoving, Lady Albright lifted a pale hand and pointed an accusing finger at her daughter.

"You!" Emerging from between blood-flecked lips, the word held a seething mixture of sorrow and despair. "Why do you continue to hide from what you must remember? They all believe it's over, but you know the truth." Her finger shook, and a single, crystalline tear spilled over to trail down her cheek. "You must listen. It isn't over. It will never be over until you remember it all . . ."

With that shiver-inducing statement echoing in her ears, Aimee jolted awake in the darkness of her bedchamber, the memory of her mother's condemning expression emblazoned on her conscience like a brand.

It was a long time before she was able to sleep again.

Chapter 1

"She's beautiful, Maura."

Cradling the pink swaddled bundle in her arms close to her chest, Aimee lifted a corner of the blanket with a reverent hand so she could look down into the red, wrinkled face of her infant niece. Blue eyes peered up at her in drowsy curiosity, and rosebud lips puckered in a faint moue before three-month-old Fiona Elise Sutcliffe yawned and drifted off to sleep with her tiny fist curled about her aunt's finger.

Aimee felt her heart catch at such a trusting gesture, and she smiled in delight as she turned to her sister, who was perched on the garden bench next to her.

"In fact," she continued, taking care to keep her tone at the level of a whisper, "I do believe that you've been blessed with the perfect baby."

Her face alight with maternal pride, Maura Sutcliffe, Countess of Hawksley, settled her loving gaze on her slumbering daughter. "I certainly like to think so. But then, I seem to remember you saying the exact same thing about Jilly's Thane and Roderick when they were born."

"And I meant every word of it." Aimee cast a glance in the direction of her red-haired nephews, who were busy playing with a regiment of toy soldiers in the shade of a nearby elm. "I don't think anyone could argue that Thane and Roddy just happen to be truly exceptional children."

An inelegant snort came from the figure seated on the bench across from them.

"If *exceptional* means stubborn, unruly, and thoroughly incorrigible, then I'm afraid I am forced to agree." The eldest of the trio of sisters, Jillian Daventry Monroe, shook her head with a rueful grimace. "My sons drive their nursemaid to the brink of handing in her notice on a fairly regular basis, and even Connor seems incapable of reining them in. I fear I am ready to declare myself a suitable candidate for Bedlam."

Her exasperated avowal drew a soft burst of laughter from Aimee and Maura, who were both more than well acquainted with the twins' headstrong temperaments.

It was an unusually pleasant September day in London, and the three of them were seated in the garden of Jillian's newly purchased Berkeley Square residence, taking advantage of the peaceful moments they had been afforded to indulge in a sisterly chat. Aimee had been looking forward to this visit ever since she had received Jilly's invitation to tea earlier that morning, and with the cheerful afternoon sunlight beaming down on her, bathing her in comforting warmth, the dark dreams that had haunted her for the past fortnight suddenly felt very far away.

But that was something she had promised herself she wouldn't think about. Not today. So she brushed aside the taunting visions that danced through her head and faced her sisters once again.

"I imagine it's only natural for children of Thane's and Roddy's age to get into a bit of mischief every now and then," she spoke up in loyal defense of her nephews. She had always shared a close bond with the boys and usually found their pranks humorous rather than dismaying. "And they are far more inquisitive and high-spirited than most three-year-olds."

Maura raised a brow. "They are also quite spoiled, thanks in no small part to their aunt Aimee."

Bowing her head, Aimee focused her attention on the baby nestled in her arms. The sight of those small fingers gripping hers filled her with a fierce yearning, making her more aware than ever of the aching feeling of emptiness that seemed to have become her constant companion of late.

"Perhaps I am a trifle overly indulgent," she admitted. "But as it is unlikely that I shall ever have a husband and children of my own, surely I am entitled to dote upon my niece and nephews on occasion."

Her words were followed by a tension-fraught silence, and she looked up just in time to see her sisters exchanging veiled glances.

Drat! She should have bitten her tongue before making such a comment. She knew how protective the members of her family had always been where she was concerned, and that hadn't changed with the passing of the years. Recently, they had all taken to eyeing her with a great deal of anxiety whenever she mentioned her unmarried state, almost as if they expected her to prostrate herself at their feet, weeping and wailing in abject misery due to her sad lack of prospects.

Little did they know that she had long ago resigned herself to her solitary fate.

"I do wish the two of you wouldn't behave as if I had just announced that I am suffering from some rare and fatal illness and expect to draw my last breath at any second," she said wryly. "It isn't as dire as all that."

"We can't help it, darling." Jillian frowned, making no attempt to conceal her distress. "It worries us when you say such things. After all, you are not some aged spinster who is so firmly on the shelf that there is no hope left for you. You are young yet, only nineteen, and you deserve to have a family of your own someday."

Pretending to occupy herself with the task of tucking the woolen blanket more snugly about Fiona's feet, Aimee gave a slight shrug, affecting a casual indifference that she was far from feeling. "I suppose some things simply aren't meant to be."

"Nonsense." This unequivocal assertion came from Maura, who folded her arms and regarded her younger sister with a shrewdness that was unnerving. "That is something you tell yourself because it makes it easier for you to continue on as you always have, hiding behind the walls of Papa's town house."

"I'm not hiding!" Aimee's vehement protest had her niece stirring restively in the crook of her elbow, and she paused, waiting to make sure the infant had settled back to sleep before going on in a much quieter voice. "I'm not."

Maura narrowed her piercing blue eyes. "Aren't you? You spend your days with your nose buried in a book and rarely venture out unless it is to pay a call on Jilly or myself. And whenever you have been given the chance to change your circumstances, you have turned your back on it. I'm sure I needn't remind you of Papa's offer to provide you with a Season the year you turned eighteen. You refused in no uncertain terms."

"Yes, and I haven't regretted that decision for an instant." Aimee shuddered, unable to hide her distaste. "Can you imagine me, mingling with the aristocratic members of London society, attending balls and dinner parties and musicales? I have no idea how to be witty or charming or how to go about flirting with gentlemen the way other young ladies my age do. I would have ended up as one of those poor, pitiful wallflowers that hover about the edges of the room, forgotten and miserable."

Just envisioning the scenario she had described was enough to set her stomach to churning. It was true that she had never been a very social creature, and she often wished that she could be more like her fearless older sisters. Both boldly independent Jillian and regally sophisticated Maura were raven-haired beauties who had inherited their strong wills from their late mother, renowned stage actress Elise Marchand Daventry, the Marchioness of Albright, and it was highly doubtful that either of them knew what it was like to be ruled by shyness or uncertainty.

Aimee, on the other hand, was well aware that she possessed none of the attributes that made her siblings so very striking. Small in stature, with hair of an unremarkable shade of brown and rather ordinary features, she was the plain Daventry sister. The dull and insipid one whose only true claim to attractiveness was a pair of wide amber eyes that were much too big for her elfin face.

A mouse in more ways than one.

As if reading her mind, Jillian leaned forward and reached out to lay a sympathetic hand on her arm. "You give yourself far too little credit, you know. I'm sure you would have handled it all better than you think."

Aimee shook her head. "You know how terribly timid I am, Jilly. Even as a child, I had a tendency to freeze up and withdraw whenever a situation intimidated me. That's just the way it has always been. Ever since—"

She broke off, biting her lower lip, but there was no need for her to finish the sentence. They all knew what she had been going to say.

Ever since the night she had witnessed their mother's murder and had been found crouched beside the body, all memory of the incident wiped from her mind.

Up until five years ago, all of London had believed that the scandalous Lady Albright, notorious for her many rumored affairs, had been killed by her married lover, the Earl of Hawksley, before he had turned the pistol on himself. It had been Maura and the late earl's son who had discovered the truth: that Hawksley had been framed for the crime by a man who had been secretly obsessed with the marchioness.

Jillian exchanged another concerned look with Maura before addressing Aimee once again. "Darling, I know how hard Mama's death was for you to cope with. It was hard for us all, but you were just a little girl when it happened. After the horrible things you must have seen that night . . ."

Her amber eyes dampening behind the lenses of her spectacles, she stumbled to a halt and let her voice trail off, obviously unable to finish.

"What we are trying to say," Maura ventured after an awkward moment, taking up where their elder sister had left off, "is that it would be perfectly understandable if you are having difficulty putting it behind you. But it has been five years since Mama's real killer was brought to justice. Five years since Lord Stratton confessed and cleared my husband's late father of the crime. The man is dead and gone now, and we have all moved on with our lives. Don't you think it's time for you to do the same?"

Aimee felt her heart give a painful throb in her chest. How *could* she move on when there was still so much that she couldn't remember? Her physician had claimed that her memory loss regarding the events of that evening had been her mind's way of protecting her from the trauma of what had occurred, and perhaps that was so. Now that she was older, however, she found her inability to recall any of it a frustrating hindrance.

"I wish it was that easy for me," she murmured aloud. "But as long as my memory is so full of holes, I don't know that it is possible for me to just let it go."

"The doctor said those memories may be lost to you forever," Jillian pointed out gently. "That's something you may have to learn to accept."

But what if I'm starting to remember?

The thought flashed across Aimee's mind, summoning forth brutal images of her mother's body lying on the floor, her head surrounded by a pool of blood.

You must listen. It isn't over. It will never be over until you remember it all . . .

Mama's voice echoed in her head, sending a shiver up her spine. It had been years since she had last suffered from dreams of that night, and they had never before been this vivid or filled her with such foreboding. But though a part of her was tempted to confide in her sisters, to turn to them as she had since she was a child, she resisted the urge. There was no reason to upset them over a few silly nightmares, and she was no longer a frightened little girl who needed someone else to fight her battles for her.

Even if she sometimes felt like one.

Jillian was still speaking, completely oblivious to her youngest sister's preoccupation. "Darling, you must see that you can't go on like this. If you would only make an effort to spread your wings a bit. Perhaps accompany one of us to the occasional social event and allow us to introduce you to a handsome gentleman or two—"

"To what end, Jilly?" Aimee cut in dispiritedly. "Even if I could put aside my insecurities, I'll never be the belle of the ton. I'm simply not the sort of female to turn a man's head or stir him to the heights of passion. Why bother when it all seems like such an exercise in futility to me?"

"How will you ever know if you won't even try?" Maura slanted her a reproving look. "You shun male company as if they were bearers of the plague. If you will recall, I offered to invite several of Hawksley's more eligible acquaintances to the dinner party I am having this evening, but you rejected the notion without a second's hesitation."

Aimee stiffened. Maura's swiftly approaching dinner party was just one more thing she didn't want to think about, for she had been dreading the event for weeks. After spending the past several nights in a row pacing her bedchamber, battling her nightmares rather than sleeping, she was far too exhausted to deal with the added responsibility of making polite small talk with a cadre of would-be suitors. Merely contemplating the notion was enough to have the beginnings of a headache throbbing at her temples.

"I don't suppose you would believe me if I told you that I was feeling a trifle indisposed and won't be able to attend." She eyed Maura hopefully.

"I don't suppose I would, and I will be most wroth with you should you even attempt to fob me off with such a poor excuse."

As if roused by Maura's no-nonsense tone, Fiona chose that moment to give a fretful cry, just as the Monroe family butler stepped out onto the terrace to announce that Lord Hawksley had arrived to escort his wife home.

"It seems that your husband has perfect timing," Aimee said with a smile, brushing a kiss against her niece's downy cheek before handing the babe to her mother. "I'm afraid this little one has had quite enough of me."

"I suspect she is well aware that it is close to her feeding time." Maura rose, lifting her daughter high against her shoulder. "As much as I hate to cut our visit short, I should be off. I don't want to keep Hawksley waiting, and there is quite a bit for me to do before tonight."

Amid laughter and hugs, the three of them said their farewells, and Maura headed off up the path toward the town house, Fiona already nodding off again in her arms. She had no sooner disappeared from sight, however, than Aimee turned to find Jillian scrutinizing her with knowing eyes.

"You may think you have succeeded in distracting me, young lady," her elder sister said sternly, "but I haven't forgotten what we were discussing."

"There isn't anything left to discuss." With an inward curse at her sibling's tenacity, Aimee avoided that perceptive stare by focusing on the twins. Having abandoned their toy soldiers, the two of them were now trailing after a black and white kitten that had wandered into the garden to investigate the patch of grass around the elm tree.

"Dress me up in a pretty gown and parade me before every bachelor in London, but I will still be the Daventry sister that no one notices or cares to know."

"The only reason no one notices you is because you hide behind those protective barriers you've erected to keep others at a distance. But sooner or later, darling, you have to learn to trust people enough to let them in."

A lump clogged Aimee's throat at Jillian's words. That was far easier said than done, she thought dismally. Once before she had made the mistake of letting down her guard, of opening her heart to someone else, only to be left humiliated and devastated by the experience.

From out of nowhere, her mind conjured up a mental picture of a rugged, masculine face, framed by a shaggy mane of dark hair. Slate-gray eyes that burned with brooding intensity were set beneath a pair of high, arched brows, and a pale, angry-looking scar cut an uneven path from temple to squared jaw, bisecting the corner of a firmly chiseled mouth. It was a face of harshly carved planes and angles, magnetic in its appeal and still handsome despite that single jagged mark of imperfection.

The image had Aimee's pulse speeding up in reaction, but she pushed it away with determined force. She had no desire to think about *him* right now. Whatever childish hopes she had once harbored, whatever emotions he had once inspired within her, she had buried them long ago. Why let herself dwell on a man who had made it more than clear that she could never be the sort of woman he wanted.

And who could blame him for that? she wondered, her shoulders slumping. *After all, what gentleman with a modicum of sense would ever be interested in tying himself to such a dull and unaccomplished little mouse with so few qualities to recommend her?*

A cold breeze suddenly wafted against her cheek, stirring the tendrils of hair at her temples, and she wrapped her arms about herself to ward off a slight chill as she finally met her sister's gaze. "Not every woman is meant for marriage and motherhood. As blissful as you are with Connor, you can't deny that you once rather enjoyed being an independent female yourself. Isn't it conceivable that I could be content without a husband?"

Jillian's countenance softened. "Of course it is. But you have so much love inside of you to give, darling. Is it so very terrible that I don't want to see you end up alone, with no one to give it to?"

Her eyes blurring with tears, Aimee fisted her hands in her lap. Her sister's words struck her like arrows, plunging straight to the heart of the girlhood dreams she had once secretly cherished. "Not so very terrible, no," she whispered. "But some people are better off alone."

"Now you sound like Aunt Olivia."

"Perhaps, in this instance, Aunt Olivia is right."

"Aunt Olivia is a very unhappy woman who doesn't know how to exist without making others unhappy as well," Jillian said firmly, her less than favorable opinion of their father's spinster sister obvious in the clenching of her jaw. "And she is *not* right. Not about this."

Getting to her feet, she knelt down next to Aimee and covered her younger sister's hands with her own. "You'll see. I speak from experience when I say that the perfect man for you will appear just when you least expect it, and he'll sweep you right off your feet."

"That's very romantic, Jilly, but not very practical," Aimee said, her voice reflecting her skepticism.

"No one ever said that love was practical, darling." And having delivered that assessment, Jillian gave Aimee's hands a quick squeeze and straightened. "Now, if you don't mind keeping an eye on Thane and Roddy for a while, I have some things I need to attend to before Connor comes home. But I want you to think about what I've said while I'm gone. You deserve love and happiness just as much as Maura and I do, and you mustn't even let anyone convince you otherwise."

Aimee waited until her sister had vanished up the garden path before heaving a tired sigh and letting her lashes drift closed. How she longed to believe in Jillian's assurances. To believe that there was still a chance of a happily-ever-after for her. But her battered heart had yet to heal from the last time she had tried to reach out to someone, and the mere thought of risking that same sort of pain and disillusionment again paralyzed her with dread.

"Aunt Mee?"

The inquisitive voice drew her from her ruminations, and she opened her eyes to meet the curious stares of her nephews. They were standing before her, their identical faces splotched with dirt and their tousled red heads tilted to the side as they peered up at her.

One of them—she was relatively certain it was Roddy, who was usually the more vocal of the two—swiped a chubby finger along the side of his nose and wrinkled his forehead in perplexity. "Are you goin' to sleep?"

The query elicited a laugh from her, in spite of her somber mood. "No, moppet. I was just resting my eyes."

"Oh." He paused for a second, as if mulling over her reply, then scrambled up on the bench to seize her wrist. "But you can't rest your eyes now. We need your holp."

"My 'holp' with what?"

"Kitty runnded up the tree, and he won't come down." This came from Thane, who moved a step closer to her, his expression morose.

Craning her neck, Aimee squinted up at the highest branches of the elm. There, she could just make out a disgruntled feline face peeping out from among the foliage, whiskers twitching in indignation. "And why would kitty do such a thing?"

"Roddy pullded his tail. Really, really hard."

"In that case, perhaps kitty would be better off staying in the tree."

"No!" Roddy's response was emphatic, and he punctuated the exclamation with another tug at her arm. "We want to play wiv him. Please, Aunt Mee?"

And it seemed that she could refuse these two scamps nothing, Aimee thought ruefully. Getting to her feet, she smoothed out the skirts of her fawn-colored day dress and leveled the boys with the sternest look she could summon.

"Very well. But you must promise that you will be nice to kitty and not pull his tail again."

"We promise, Aunt Mee."

Roddy's innocent tone didn't fool her, especially when she caught the less than subtle glance he exchanged with his brother, who giggled before clapping a hand over his mouth to smother the sound. She ignored them, however, and went to stand next to the base of the tree as she tried to decide how best to tackle the problem.

It quickly became clear that while the kitten would venture down onto the lower branches of the elm in answer to her coaxing, it wasn't about to cooperate any further. Especially when its two tormentors were still very much in evidence, bouncing up and down exuberantly at Aimee's side. The animal dug its claws into the limb just above her head and refused to move, its fur bristling.

Obviously, more drastic measures were called for.

Aimee wrinkled her nose, far from relishing the task ahead. It had been years since she had climbed a tree, and she wasn't precisely dressed for the activity. Though she supposed she could fetch a footman or stable boy to do the job, she had no desire to take them away from their work for such foolishness.

So, squaring her shoulders, she reached up to wrap her hands around the branch, getting a good grip before bracing a foot against the trunk of the tree. Then she hefted herself upward. It was a slow, arduous process, and her skirts impeded her progress every step of the way as her feet scrambled for purchase against the rough bark, but she finally managed to climb high enough that she could swing a leg up to straddle the limb.

It was at that moment, however, that disaster struck.

The kitten, offended by Aimee's sudden appearance on the branch it was perched on, let out a yowl and swatted at her hand, claws raking across her fingers. It was enough to startle her into loosening her hold, and she slipped sideways, plunging toward the ground with a panicked cry.

Only to be caught by a pair of warm, strong arms.

Stunned and short of breath, Aimee took a second to regain her equilibrium, barely restraining the urge to wince at the disheveled picture she knew she must make. She was struggling to find the words to explain her embarrassing predicament even as she pushed the tumbled curls from her eyes. But any explanation she might have given flew right out of her head when she looked up at her rescuer and found herself staring into the face of the very man she had just recently dismissed so forcefully from her thoughts.

Royce Grenville, Viscount Stonehurst.

Chapter 2

Her heart lodged in her throat, Aimee gaped up in horrified dismay at the man who held her, unable to believe that this was actually happening. She was speechless, frozen into immobility by the unexpectedness of his appearance when he should have been miles away, sequestered behind the high walls of the Cornwall estate where he lived in virtual seclusion.

What on earth was he doing here? And why did he have to show up now, just in time to witness her humiliating tumble?

For what seemed like a small eternity, the silence stretched out between them. Then Lord Stonehurst angled his head, his usually impassive gray eyes surveying her with what Aimee could have sworn was amusement.

"Well," he murmured, the all too rare humor that tinged his rough voice confirming her suspicions that he was laughing at her. "I believe I have captured a mouse."

Thane and Roddy's giggles prodded Aimee from her stupor, and a heated tide of color flooded into her cheeks. Reaching up with a trembling hand, she gave the solid wall of his chest an insistent shove, her fingers tingling disconcertingly at the contact.

"Please." The plea emerged as little more than a whispered croak, and she had to clear her throat before she could try again. "Please, my lord. You can put me down now."

To her chagrin, Stonehurst's grip only seemed to tighten, and he arched a brow, obviously in no hurry to comply. "You know," he drawled, "I may not be quite as well versed as some when it comes to the mores of polite society, but isn't it customary for a young lady to offer a gentleman her thanks when he has just finished rescuing her from a rather grave and perilous situation?"

Still reeling from the shock of his presence, Aimee took a second or two to register what he was saying. The musky male scent of his skin and the feel of his sinewy arms cradling her so closely had muddled her thought processes to the point where she was having trouble remembering her own name. But somehow she managed to clear away enough of the fog that had clouded her senses in order to attempt a response.

"I do thank you for your intervention, Lord Stonehurst," she ventured, relieved that she managed to address him without betraying any hint of the tension that had bubbled up beneath the surface of her carefully composed façade. "Though describing the circumstances as 'grave' and 'perilous' strikes me as a bit of an exaggeration. Wouldn't you agree?"

He gave a negligent shrug. "Perhaps. I suppose it depends on whether or not you view the bruising of one's . . . pride as an inconsequential matter."

From his meaningful pause and the manner in which his gaze skimmed over her, Aimee doubted that *pride* had been the word he'd intended to use. "Yes, well, my pride is quite intact," she assured him. "And I am perfectly capable of standing on my own. So if you would be so kind as to put me down, I would be most appreciative."

"Of course, my lady. I am ever at your command."

He lowered her without any further hesitation. As he did so, however, Aimee couldn't help but notice the ripple of muscles in his shoulders and back under the superfine material of his coat. The powerful bunch and flex enthralled her, and for an instant she was tempted to smooth her palms over that broad expanse, to savor the tensile hardness and . . . and . . .

And she had to get hold of herself! Heavens, but a few minutes in the man's company and she was already letting her mind wander in a dangerous direction.

Needing some distance from his intoxicating nearness, she took an unsteady step away from him as soon as her feet touched the ground, then stared up into that scarred visage in consternation. All previous traces of levity had fled his expression, and he returned her examination with unnerving stoicism.

A tall and imposing figure, he loomed over her, his stance militarily correct. He hadn't changed in the year since she had last seen him, she decided. The lines around his eyes and mouth were perhaps a bit more pronounced, and his dark brown hair was longer. Its thick, untamed length just brushed his wide shoulders. But the masculine beauty of his features still had the power to hold her spellbound. The contrast between the unmarred side of his countenance and the side marked by the livid scar—a testament to his time with the British Cavalry—was striking.

Aimee had first met Lord Stonehurst five years before, upon Maura's marriage to his friend, the Earl of Hawksley, and she had been fascinated by him from the beginning. Beneath that taciturn exterior, she had sensed a pain and loneliness to match her own, and she had taken to trailing in his wake like a friendless puppy whenever he had visited her father. To his credit, he had been surprisingly patient with her in his own gruff way, and an innocent bond of friendship had formed.

But the year Aimee had turned eighteen, everything had changed. She had awakened one morning to the realization that her childish infatuation with the viscount had blossomed into something more. Powerful new emotions had stirred to life within her, giving birth to all sorts of fanciful dreams for the future, and she had ended up throwing herself at the man's head like some naïve fool, blurting out her true feelings for him.

Even now, she could picture the way his expression had abruptly closed up as he had set her from him. Could still hear his distant response to her shy confession.

I do apologize if I have given you the wrong impression, my lady, but you would do better to bestow your affections on someone who can return them. You see, timid little mice who flinch from the sight of their own shadow hold absolutely no interest for me.

His rejection had wounded her deeply, but what had hurt even more had been the manner in which he had ended their friendship and cut himself from her life. With no farewell or word of explanation, he had simply turned his back on her and walked away.

And now here he was, standing before her once again, peering down at her in a typically inscrutable fashion, as if what had once passed between them had never happened.

She'd been such a little simpleton to believe that someone like him could ever really care for someone like her, she thought bitterly. But all that was behind her, and she had no intention of letting him have the upper hand. All she had to do was manage to stay calm, aloof, and in control, and she just might make it through this encounter without embarrassing herself any further.

"Why are you here?"

The question spilled out before she could call it back, sounding abrupt and far from welcoming. Though his eyes narrowed at her rather unaccustomed rudeness, Stonehurst made no comment. Instead, he simply folded his arms and studied her intently. "I was in town attending to some business affairs, so I decided to stop by to pay my respects. I've been considering making an investment in Monroe's shipping enterprise, and I thought this might be a good time to discuss the matter with him."

"I-I see." Pleating the folds of her skirt with nervous fingers and mentally cursing herself for letting him fluster her, Aimee licked her dry lips and avoided his searching gaze. "I'm afraid Connor isn't here right now. He is still at the office."

"So the butler informed me. I told him that I didn't mind waiting, as I had a bit of spare time at my disposal." He cast a hooded glance about the garden before giving her an inquiring look. "I was under the impression that Mrs. Monroe was out here with the children."

"She was. She had a few things to tend to, but I'm sure she will be out directly."

"Hey!"

The exclamation came from one of the twins, who startled Aimee by bounding forward and seizing the viscount's coat sleeve. Her nephews had been so quiet for the past several minutes that she had almost forgotten they were there.

"Did you bringed us any candy?" the little boy demanded to know, bouncing up and down on the balls of his feet in anticipation. "Huh? Did you?"

"Thane!"

"I'm Roddy, Aunt Mee."

"Of course you are." Positive from the way her face was burning that she must be as red as a beet, Aimee resisted the urge to groan in frustration. It wasn't like her to make such a mistake, and she laid the blame for her error solidly at Lord Stonehurst's doorstep. "Darling, you must know it is rude of you to ask such questions."

"But he always bringed us candy before."

The announcement staggered Aimee, though she wasn't sure why. After all, she had known he still traveled to London on occasion, and she had suspected that he came to see Hawksley and Maura. But it appeared that his friendship with Jillian's husband had become close enough that he had made a point of calling on them as well.

Apparently, she and her father hadn't been deemed worthy of a visit. As usual.

Strangely hurt by the slight, she watched as Stonehurst went down on one knee next to Roddy, his large frame dwarfing the child's much smaller one. "I'm sorry, lad," he said gently. "I was in a bit of a rush today and didn't think to bring any candy. I will the next time. I promise."

Thane joined his brother, his eyes wide and unblinking as he met the viscount's gaze. "You was a soldier," he piped up. "I heared my papa say so."

"Yes, I was."

"And soldiers always keep their promises, don't they?"

"Yes, they do. Or at least they try."

Not to be outdone by his brother, Roddy thrust out his chest importantly. "My papa says that soldiers fight in wars." He jabbed a finger at the angry red line that cut such a vicious path along the viscount's cheek. "Was you hurted in the war?"

Stonehurst lifted a hand to trace the scar in an absent fashion, and his expression suddenly became very far away, almost as if he were focusing on some inner vision that only he could see. For a brief instant, the shadow of something dark and haunted passed over his features, and his gray eyes shone with an anguish that was so raw in its intensity that Aimee flinched.

"I was wounded in battle, yes," he acknowledged hoarsely. "But in truth, lad, I was hurt long before the war."

Now what was that supposed to mean? Aimee wondered, curious in spite of herself. Even when they had shared such a close bond before, the man had always been frustratingly cryptic about his past. She had heard only whispered rumors about what had led to his estrangement from his deceased father and elder brother, and while she was aware that he had received the scar in battle at Waterloo, he had never confided in her as to the manner in which it had come about. Whenever she had questioned him, he had become so withdrawn and moody that she had never been able to bring herself to push for answers.

Feeling a sharp twinge of empathy at his obvious torment, she decided that enough was enough and took a step forward, drawing her nephews' attention.

"Why don't the two of you go and play with kitty until Papa gets home?" she suggested, shepherding them away from the viscount with a slight shooing motion. "I'm sure he'll be eager to see you both after such a long day at the shipping offices."

"Kitty runnded away when you fell, Aunt Mee," Roddy informed her loftily, planting his feet and frowning up at her with the same stubborn intractability that his mother so often displayed.

Of course kitty had "runnded" away. At this point, Aimee almost wished that she could join the animal. "Then why don't you go find Mama and let her know that Lord Stonehurst is here to see her?"

Just like that, wide grins spread over the twins' freckled faces. "Yes, Aunt Mee," they chorused, their delight in being given a job to do superseding their interest in the viscount. Pushing and shoving each other in their haste, they took off across the garden, each determined to be the first to reach their mother with the news.

As soon as they had vanished into the house, Stonehurst spoke up from behind Aimee, his words holding a sardonic edge. "It's all right, you know. I wasn't going to gobble them up."

She whirled to face him, her hands on her hips. "I should hope not," she said with asperity. "After all, they meant no offense. They're just naturally curious."

"I am well aware of that. And whatever you may think, I don't make a habit of raking small children over the coals for my entertainment."

Aimee bit her lip at his less than subtle rebuke. She knew that, of course. But she certainly wasn't going to admit that she had been far more worried that her nephews' probing would cause him further pain than she had been at the possibility that he would lash out at them for their inquisitiveness. "You are right, my lord, and I apologize. It's just that you never seemed to want to talk about your . . . injury in the past. Has that changed?"

He stiffened visibly, then pivoted on a booted heel to stand with his back to her and his head bowed. When he addressed her again after another short and rather awkward span of silence, it was in a coolly remote voice that left no room for discussion. "No. That hasn't changed."

Telling herself that it wasn't disappointment she felt washing over her, Aimee lifted her chin. "Then perhaps we should move on to a different subject."

He glanced back at her over his shoulder, the scarred corner of his mouth quirked upward in derision. "Excellent proposal. By all means, let us don our masks of social civility. What shall we discuss? The weather of late? Your father's health? Yours?"

His mocking comments pricked at her temper, though she managed to rein it in with a supreme effort of will. "Pleasant, quite well, and just fine, thank you."

The viscount gave a harsh bark of laughter at Aimee's succinct response and spun about. The next thing she knew, he had crossed the distance that separated them in a few long, ground-eating strides, coming to a stop before her. This close, he towered over her, and she could smell the heady blend of his cologne. As always, it served to throw her off balance, leaving her scrambling to hold on to her wits.

"My, how polite we are." His unsettling stare never wavering from her face, he captured her hand in his and skimmed his finger over the stinging red mark that the kitten had raked across her knuckles earlier. "You needn't prevaricate with me. It doesn't happen very often, but I can tell when you are angry. Those tiger eyes of yours flash quite charmingly and that sweet little mouth puckers up like a prune. What's wrong, Mouse?"

That did it. Drawing herself up, she leveled him with a furious glower. "Don't call me Mouse," she hissed, tugging at her hand in a vain attempt to free herself.

"Ah. It seems you have grown a set of claws in my absence. You know, I can remember a time when you used to like it when I called you that."

"That was long ago. I've changed."

"Not so long ago. But perhaps you are right and Mouse no longer suits you. I find that I like Kitten just as well. It's most appropriate in the circumstances, don't you think?"

Aimee bristled and opened her mouth, fully prepared to deliver the set-down he so richly deserved. But before she could say a thing, he raised a hand and touched her cheek in a feather-light caress, his thumb just brushing her lower lip. It was like being struck by lightning, for every muscle in her body jolted at the unexpected contact, and the scathing reprimand froze on the tip of her tongue.

"Spit and scratch all you want, little Kitten," he murmured, his mouth curving almost seductively as his head bent toward her, "but I know you've missed me."

Time seemed to stop as their gazes locked, their lips so close together that Aimee could feel his minty breath, warm against her skin. Surely she had to be misreading what she was seeing in his eyes. That couldn't be desire swirling in those silvery gray pools. Not for a plain little mouse such as she . . .

At that moment, a sudden gust of wind whipped through the garden, tugging at her skirts and slapping her abruptly back to her senses. She saw Stonehurst's nostrils flare, and he took a step away from her, dropping his hand.

"I apologize, my lady," he said brusquely. "You had a speck of dirt on your cheek."

"Of course." She swallowed, wrapping her arms about her midriff as if that alone would keep her from flying apart at the seams. She had known that she had to be mistaken. Hadn't he already given her ample proof that she held no attraction for him whatsoever?

"Lord Stonehurst! What a pleasant surprise!"

At the interruption, Aimee jerked her head upward to see her sister hurrying across the garden toward them, her lips curved in a welcoming smile.

Once again the picture of casual indolence and behaving as if nothing untoward had ever occurred, Lord Stonehurst accepted Jillian's out-stretched hand as she drew near and bowed low over it. "Mrs. Monroe. I was in the area and thought I would stop in for a short visit."

"How kind. I'm certain that Connor will be— Good heavens, Aimee, what have you done to yourself?"

Jillian's exclamation had Aimee starting and reaching up to tuck the loosened strands of her light brown hair back behind her ears as adrena-line-laced panic surged through her veins. Could her sister possibly know how close she had come to losing her head and throwing herself at this man once again? Did it show on her face?

As she was desperately racking her brain for a way to explain her behavior, Lord Stonehurst came to her rescue. "Your sister was attempting to liberate a stranded kitten from a tree when I arrived, Mrs. Monroe," he said, casting Aimee an enigmatic glance. "I'm afraid she took a bit of a tumble, but I managed to break her fall."

"Well, no wonder you look as if you've been dragged through the brambles, darling." Jillian shook her head at Aimee indulgently. "Really, I can't imagine what you were thinking, climbing a tree in one of your best day gowns. Now you look a fright." She turned back to the viscount. "As I was saying, Lord Stonehurst, I'm certain Connor will be happy you stopped by, but we truly hadn't expected to see you until this evening."

"This evening?" The words echoed in Aimee's head in ominous warning. "What do you mean?"

Her sister tucked her arm through hers, clearly delighted. "That's right. I had forgotten to tell you. Lord Stonehurst will be staying with Hawksley and Maura for the next few days while he concludes his business in town, and as he has no other plans, he has kindly agreed to grace us with his presence at the dinner party tonight. Isn't that wonderful news?"

Oh yes. Wonderful news. Almost as wonderful as being informed that she was about to be dipped in a vat of boiling oil and then rolled in a pile of feathers.

Aimee wasn't sure whether to laugh or cry as she studied the viscount's unreadable expression while Jillian continued on blithely, unaware of her sister's increasing alarm. This had to be her worst nightmare come to life. Now not only would she have to put on a carefree mask and pretend that she was genuinely enjoying a party she had no desire to attend, but she would have to figure out a way to be in the same room with the one man she wanted most in the world to avoid. A man who was still far too capable of arousing emotions that she had been convinced she had rid herself of long ago.

It was definitely going to be a most trying night.

Chapter 3

With a low, irritated growl, Royce Grenville, Viscount Stonehurst, shifted his weight from one foot to the other, reaching up to give the starched linen of his cravat an impatient tug in the vain hope of easing its constriction. The air around him was growing more stifling and oppressive with every moment of this hellish torture that passed, and he found himself wishing, not for the first time this evening, that he were somewhere else.

Anywhere else but here.

His brow furrowed in a fierce glower, he watched from the shadows as the rest of the dinner party guests moved about Lord and Lady Hawksley's elegantly furnished drawing room, laughing and chatting with evident ease. A few feet away, the Duke of Maitland appeared to be involved in an intent discussion with the Baron Bedford, while the duke's stepmother, the elderly dowager duchess, was ensconced on a settee before the fireplace, conversing in a most animated manner with former stage actress Violet Lafleur.

I don't belong here, Royce thought bleakly, turning to stare out through a nearby set of French doors at the moonlit night beyond the glass. With the exception of Hawksley, Monroe, and their respective wives, he had little more than a passing acquaintance with those who were present, and he couldn't help but feel like the proverbial bull in the china shop. Awkward and out of place.

Of course, that was something he was more than used to. All his life he had been made to feel like nothing short of a pariah by a father who had hated and reviled him with a passion usually reserved for a sworn enemy. Their mutual antagonism had been the talk of the ton, and the whispered speculation had only increased with Royce's return to England's shores after the war. Wounded, battle-weary, and drowning in his guilt and grief, he had withdrawn from everything he had once known, becoming something of a recluse and a curiosity to the aristocratic members of society. As far as they were concerned, he was an oddity to be gawked at and pitied, but never to be fully welcomed back into their ranks.

In a gesture born of habit, he lifted a blunt-tipped finger to trace the ridged line that snaked along his cheekbone. His time with the British Cavalry might have left him physically scarred, but he had received his emotional scars long before he had even left home to accept his commission. And the nightmare of Waterloo had finally succeeded in destroying what remained of his soul, leaving him an empty shell of a man who was so badly damaged that it was doubtful he would ever be whole again.

Cursed. That's what he was. Forever cursed to live a life apart and alone. He had learned from bitter experience that he could never allow anyone to get too close to him, for those who made the mistake of doing so always ended up suffering for it in the end.

"Ah. Here you are, Stonehurst."

Pulled from his ruminations by the velvety drawl, he looked up to see the tall, lean figure of Gabriel Sutcliffe, Earl of Hawksley, striding toward him, cradling a snifter of brandy in each manicured hand.

"I should have known I'd find you here, lurking in the background like the brooding villain from some melodramatic novel," the earl continued, coming to a stop at Royce's side and extending one of the glasses he was holding with an expression of ill-concealed humor. "You look as if you could use this."

Royce gratefully accepted the offering and took a hefty swallow of the amber liquid, savoring the slow burn as it worked its way into his stomach. As always, the bite of the liquor braced him, restoring some small fraction of his equanimity.

With a soft chuckle, Hawksley tossed back a portion of his own drink before tilting his head to survey Royce from under arched brows. Impeccably attired in well-tailored evening clothes and with his blond curls artfully tousled, he looked every inch the wicked angel that all of London had once proclaimed him to be. "Correct me if I'm wrong, but I don't believe I've seen you move from this spot since our guests started arriving. I was beginning to think you had taken root here like some rare breed of plant."

The glare Royce sent the other man was fulminating. "I warn you that I am in no mood for a lecture. You know how much I hate assemblages of this sort, and I am sure that I made it quite clear that I had no desire to attend this one, yet you refused to take no for an answer. If I had known that you intended to plague me about my unsociable behavior once you had me under your roof, I never would have agreed to your suggestion that I stay with you and your family while in London."

The earl lifted a broad shoulder in an indolent shrug. "It would have been foolish of you to insist on taking up residence at the Arms when we have plenty of room here. And if you are expecting me to apologize for browbeating you into joining us for dinner instead of letting you spend a solitary evening in your chamber, I'm afraid you are doomed to disappointment. Since you sold your London town house, you've spent most of your time closeted away at Stonecliff, and it has been too long since we last saw each other. Surely after missing Fiona's christening, your presence at a single social gathering is the least I am owed in the name of friendship?"

Stifling a curse, Royce avoided the glittering green eyes that studied him so knowingly by whipping his head about to gaze out through the French doors once again. It was true that he owed Hawksley a great deal. The earl was one of the few people from his former circle of compatriots who had remained loyal in spite of everything, stubbornly ignoring blatant and oft repeated attempts to push him away. And even though Royce knew it would be best for all concerned if he kept his distance, he couldn't quite bring himself to permanently sever the one last tie he had to Alex. After all, it had been his deceased elder sibling's childhood bond with Hawksley that had led to his own association with the man.

As always, thoughts of his brother pierced him like a scalding hot blade, bringing back painful recollections of the tragedy that had driven him away from England all those years ago. The horrific sequence of events that he had set into motion on that fateful day were emblazoned in his mind in a fragmented jumble of impressions and images: Alex's phaeton overturning as if in slow motion, being dragged several feet by the frantic horses before slamming into the trunk of a tree with a sickening crack. The slow drip of Cordelia's blood pooling on the ground beneath her . . .

Almost immediately, that scene gave way to another. One that was just as grisly, if not even more so. The mental picture of a smoke-obscured battlefield where the fallen bodies of the dead littered the ground. Where the sound of cannon fire and the screams of the wounded filled the air.

And where Royce had knelt in the midst of the carnage, helpless to do a thing as Benton Garvey, his fellow cavalry officer, had died in his arms.

Flinching, he closed his eyes, fighting off the sudden onslaught of visions. This wasn't the time for him to get caught up in his memories of the past. Most of society already eyed him askance as it was, and he could just imagine the reaction should he lose control now, in front of a roomful of dinner guests.

With a supreme effort of will, he shoved the images away and forced himself to focus once more on Hawksley, who was still speaking as if he had been completely oblivious to Royce's distraction.

"It's not as if I am asking you to mingle with the crowd or strike up a conversation, and I know it is a bit much to actually expect you to enjoy yourself," the earl was saying, dry amusement lacing his tone. "But the other guests might not be quite so wary if you didn't look as if you were considering snapping off the arm of the first person who ventures too close."

Royce's grip tightened on his snifter until the fragile crystal threatened to crack from the pressure. "You don't understand."

"On the contrary. I *do* understand. But bloody hell, Stonehurst, don't you think it's time to stop punishing yourself? Cordelia has been dead for nine years now, and Alex for almost eight. Neither of them would want you to go on this way, wasting your life in mourning for them."

Hawksley's words lashed Royce like a whip, ripping open wounds that were still raw and painful. If only it were that simple. But it wasn't. Cordelia and Alex had been only two of the victims on a long list of casualties that could be laid at his doorstep, starting with his mother's demise giving birth to him twenty-nine years ago, and if he let down his guard for even a moment, there was no telling who would be next.

"It has nothing to do with punishing myself," he gritted out from between clenched teeth, then gestured with his free hand, indicating the guests who were milling about the drawing room. "I have no idea how to do . . . *this* anymore. How to behave normally around other people. That's something the war took away from me, and I doubt that I shall ever get it back. Sometimes I think—"

He broke off, unable to go on. For how could he tell Hawksley about the darkness that had lurked within him for as long as he could remember? The menacing, angry part of himself that had only grown stronger since Waterloo? It was as if the stain that had been left behind by his transgressions had taken on a life of its own, and now it crouched just beneath the surface of his reserved demeanor, waiting for the chance to break free.

Several seconds ticked by in silence. Then Hawksley expelled a harsh gust of air and shook his head. "Believe it or not, Stonehurst, I do realize how difficult all of this must be for you," he said quietly. "If you will recall, up until a few years ago everyone was under the impression that my father was a murderer who had killed Maura's mother before committing suicide, and they treated me accordingly."

Royce had to concede that point. It hadn't been until after the late earl had been proven innocent in the death of the notorious Lady Albright, and Hawksley had wed the Lady Maura, that the members of the ton had ultimately relented and accepted him back into the fold.

"And despite the fact that my father's name has been cleared," the earl went on, "there are still those who would prefer it if I were to fade into obscurity, though I have no intention of doing so and giving them the satisfaction." With a sardonic twist of his lips, he lifted a hand to slap Royce on the back. "And you shouldn't either. In any case, reinforcements should be arriving shortly. Lord Albright and Lady Aimee are due at any minute."

At the mere mention of her name, Royce's whole body tensed, and he sucked in his breath as if he had taken a solid blow to his midsection. Damnation, but *she* was the last person he needed to see! Their unexpected encounter earlier that afternoon had left him more than a trifle on edge, and had succeeded in unearthing all sorts of unwanted feelings within him. Feelings that he had spent the past year trying desperately to bury and forget.

Before he had even arrived in town, he had made up his mind that he was going to do his best to avoid Aimee's company, and the instant he had stepped out into Monroe's garden and found her shimmying up the trunk of that tree, he should have turned right around and gone back inside. Every instinct he possessed had screamed at him to do so, but he'd been frozen in place, riveted by the provocative wriggle of her hips and bottom beneath the material of her skirt. And when she had fallen into his arms, her familiar flowery fragrance had filled his nostrils, firing his blood and making it impossible to resist the temptation to tease her a bit, to see that rare spark of temper flare to life in her eyes.

But it had backfired in the worst possible way, and he had ended up aroused and aching, every male part of him brought to rigid attention by his proximity to her.

He barely restrained a groan. Apparently distancing himself from her for the past several months had done little to lessen her effect on him, and he was at a loss as to how to deal with it all. The only thing he knew for certain was that he was in no frame of mind for another confrontation with her. Not when the walls were already starting to close in around him.

Draining the last of his brandy, he placed the empty snifter on a nearby marble-topped table and schooled his features into what he hoped was a relatively calm expression before turning to address the earl.

"Your concern is appreciated, Hawksley," he said aloud, gratified to note that his voice remained steady despite the confused welter of emotions that boiled and seethed within him. "Truly, it is. But this is not the way to help me. I would have been much better off if I had stayed in my bedchamber. And while I hate to disappoint you and your lovely wife, I am afraid that is exactly where I intend on spending the rest of this misbegotten evening. So if you will excuse me?"

With a stiff inclination of his head, he pivoted on his heel and stalked from the room before the earl could offer a word of protest.

Once out in the hallway, where the din of conversation from the drawing room was reduced to little more than a discordant hum, he paused and braced one hand against the wood paneling, taking a second to rein in his wavering control. He knew he had been rather abrupt with his friend, but there was no help for it. If he had remained in there any longer, he would have ended up creating a spectacle, and that was something he had to avoid at all costs.

There was no time to congratulate himself on his lucky escape, however, for at that moment a familiar voice unexpectedly hailed him from the other end of the corridor.

"Stonehurst, my good man!"

He smothered an imprecation, knowing even before he straightened and looked back over his shoulder whom he would see. Sure enough, the Marquis of Albright was stepping through the archway from the entrance foyer, his spinster sister, Lady Olivia, clinging to his arm.

And Lady Aimee followed in their wake.

Clad in an unadorned, square-necked evening frock of amber silk that effectively hid the subtle curves of her small figure, she was marching along primly, her head bowed. As usual, it seemed that she had dressed for the sole purpose of blending into the plasterwork. Many another gentleman would have more than likely written her off as plain, overlooking her in favor of the more vibrantly attired and conventionally beautiful young ladies that overpopulated the ton.

But Royce wasn't one to be swayed by surface

appearances. When he looked at Aimee, he saw the gentleness and strength of character that radiated from within, lending her delicate, elfin features an understated prettiness that was just as appealing. The hair that she had pinned about her head in a tidy coronet of braids might have been a rather ordinary shade of brown, but it was thick and lustrous and shone with touches of gold in the light of the hallway lamps, and her heavily lashed eyes glowed with an inner fire.

Those eyes widened as she caught sight of him now, and he could have sworn that he detected a slight hitch in her step, a minute hesitation before she rallied and hurried to catch up with her father and aunt.

Bravo, he silently applauded, temporarily forgetting his own consternation at her show of courage. The mouse was apparently learning to assert herself, but he had always known that she possessed far more spirit than others gave her credit for.

At that moment, Lord Albright came to a stop before him, drawing his attention.

"And just where are you off to in such a hurry?" the marquis inquired in a jovial tone, reaching out to shake his hand in greeting. A tall, scholarly looking man with thick, graying hair the same shade of golden brown as his youngest daughter's, he had treated Royce with warmth and respect from the very beginning of their acquaintance, and an easy camaraderie had developed between them. "Surely you aren't retiring already? I know we are a trifle late, but dinner isn't due to be served for another hour."

Royce returned the handshake, conscious all the while of Aimee hovering at her father's elbow, her countenance unreadable as she observed their exchange. "I am afraid so, yes. It seems the coach ride from Cornwall was more taxing than I had realized, so I thought it best to go ahead and turn in for the night."

"I am sorry to hear that. I had hoped that we would have a chance to talk this evening."

Albright's crestfallen expression filled Royce with regret. Unfortunately, cutting himself from Aimee's life had more or less meant cutting himself from her father's life, and though he knew it had been the only viable solution in the circumstances, that knowledge did nothing to alleviate his guilt.

"I had hoped so as well, and I offer my most abject apologies," he said smoothly. "Perhaps I could set aside some time to stop by Belgrave Square one afternoon before I depart for Stonecliff. If I am recalling correctly, you gave me a thorough trouncing in our last chess match, and I should like the chance to redeem myself."

"Indeed, and there is no need for apologies," Albright assured him. "Though it seems a shame to miss what promises to be a most delicious dinner. Hawksley's cook makes an excellent braised duck—"

"Really, Philip, do quit badgering the poor man." This came from Lady Olivia, who interrupted her brother with a careless wave of her hand, then tilted her head to coolly peruse Royce over the top of her fluttering fan. Though she might have once been a handsome woman, her patrician features had become more sharply drawn with age, and her graying brown hair was pulled back from her face so severely that it tugged her eyebrows skyward, giving her a vaguely surprised look. "As bereft as we shall be without his company, Lord Stonehurst is clearly exhausted from his journey. We wouldn't want to overtax him on his first night in town, would we?"

Royce wasn't fooled by the deceptive civility of her words. He was well aware that the marquis's elder sister disapproved of him. But as Hawksley was fond of pointing out, the woman was a stiff-rumped harpy who didn't seem to approve of much of anything, including the nieces she had helped her brother to raise.

Most especially Aimee.

Prodded by the thought of her, he sent a veiled glance in her direction. She stood with her hands clasped before her, her visage blank and utterly remote. It was as if she were completely removed from the discussion taking place before her. As if she had not the slightest interest in whether he chose to be present that evening.

For some reason, her air of detachment grated on him. A show of anger or hurt pride he would have understood and could have tolerated. But her apparent indifference rankled. Suddenly, the devil on his shoulder took control, and all he could think about was finding some way to shatter her veneer of aloofness.

So, instead of excusing himself and continuing on to his chamber as he knew he should, he captured Lady Olivia's hand in his and bowed low over it in a great show of solicitude. "Bereft, you say? Why, my lady, I had no idea that my absence would cause you such distress. In that case, I wouldn't dream of depriving you of my presence. In fact, I can't think of anything that would give me more pleasure than to join you for dinner."

Even though quite a bit of distance separated them, Royce still heard Aimee's soft gasp, and his mouth curved in a grin of predatory satisfaction. So she wasn't quite so detached after all. As much as he would have liked to see her expression, however, he managed to stay focused on Lady Olivia, who had wrinkled her nose and was peering down at him as if she had smelled something foul.

"How . . . lovely," she drew out, her thin lips

compressing into a tight line as she freed her hand from his grip. "I'm sure that everyone shall be delighted to hear that you have changed your mind."

That was highly doubtful. As it was, he was convinced that his wits must have gone begging. After spending most of the evening trying desperately to extricate himself from the proceedings, he had now volunteered to go right back into the lion's den.

The marquis chuckled and clapped him on the shoulder. "Splendid, Stonehurst. Though 'bereft' might have been a bit of an overstatement on my sister's part, I'm sure the evening would have been much less enjoyable without you."

Royce slowly turned his head to meet Aimee's eyes. She was gaping at him as if stunned, and it was plain from her look of appalled dismay that she didn't share her father's sentiments. For what felt like an inordinate amount of time, their gazes locked and held. Then a mutinous light entered those amber depths, and she lifted her chin.

So much for his determination to avoid her. It now seemed they would be forced to deal with each other for the rest of the evening, thanks to his all-consuming need to goad her into a reaction. But he shouldn't have expected anything less. He had all but thrown down a gauntlet, and she wasn't the sort to balk at a challenge, no matter what others thought.

Now there could be no backing out for either of them, and all he could do was pray he wouldn't regret his reckless impulse.

Chapter 4

"Really, Aimee, must you fidget so? It is most irritating and very unladylike."

Lady Olivia's less than gentle rebuke jolted Aimee from the depths of her reverie, and she jerked her head up with a start, meeting her aunt's reproving gaze as her fingers froze mid-pleat in the folds of her skirt. Drat and blast, but she had lost track of the number of times her father's sister had caught her woolgathering this evening. With everything she had to contend with, she couldn't afford to let her wits go wandering, but keeping herself from drifting off when so much was weighing on her mind was proving to be an almost impossible task.

Taking a deep breath, she gathered the frayed threads of her composure and clasped her hands together tightly in her lap before attempting to speak.

"I'm sorry, Aunt Olivia," she murmured, doing her best to inject a note of contrition into her voice that she was far from feeling. "I suppose I'm a bit restless."

Her aunt, who was seated on the plump-cushioned settee next to her, gave a haughty sniff. "That much is obvious," she snapped, her words holding an edge of frosty disapproval. "Those ill-mannered twin vagabonds of Jillian's do less squirming and wriggling about than you have since we arrived here this evening. What on earth is the matter with you?"

Now there was a question, Aimee thought ruefully, and she doubted Olivia would appreciate hearing the answer.

She cast a veiled glance toward the other end of the drawing room, where her father was busy conversing with Violet Lafleur, Maura, Lord Hawksley, and the very man who was causing Aimee such discomfort.

Lord Stonehurst stood at indolent ease, one elbow propped on the fireplace mantel and head tilted forward as he listened to whatever it was Lord Albright was saying. With his overlong dark hair hanging loosely to frame his saturnine features, and his muscular frame garbed in dark evening clothes that had been expensively tailored to fit him to perfection, he looked even more intimidating—and dangerously attractive—than usual.

Aimee's heart gave a lurch, slamming against her rib cage as if trying to escape. She had truly believed that she was prepared to see him again.

That she was capable of coping with the maelstrom of emotions that his presence stirred to life within her. But it had taken very little time for her to realize that she had been fooling herself.

All through dinner, she had felt his eyes upon her, burning into her like a brand, following her every move. It had been disconcerting, to say the least. While everyone else had been chatting and laughing, she'd been unable to relax enough to join in, and the only saving grace had been the fact that none of the others seated around the table had appeared to notice her subdued mien.

The man was trying to drive her mad, she fumed. And he evidently enjoyed watching her squirm as well. Why else would he seem so set on provoking her?

At that moment, a comment from buxom, red-haired Violet made Stonehurst laugh, and Aimee found herself curiously arrested by the all too rare sound of his deep, rumbling chuckle. That wide, mobile mouth curved in a genuine smile, and for a brief instant she caught a glimpse of the handsome, carefree young man he must have been before the war had changed him. The transformation held her spellbound, setting her to tingling all over and filling her with the unexpected urge to rise and go to him, to draw his head down to hers so that she could trace those firm lips with the tip of her finger, then the tip of her tongue . . .

Dear heaven, but where had that come from?

She had to get hold of her wayward thoughts before she ended up doing something she would regret.

Tearing her gaze away from him, she forced herself to turn and face her aunt once again. "Nothing is the matter with me, Aunt Olivia," she said aloud, ignoring the swarm of butterflies that seemed to have taken up residence in her stomach. "Nothing at all."

"Then I suggest you take your head out of the clouds and use this opportunity to your advantage," Olivia clipped out, nodding in the direction of a tall, barrel-chested man with thinning blond hair who was leaning against the far wall. "It would behoove you to ingratiate yourself with the Duke of Maitland. His wife passed away well over a year ago, and I imagine that he shall be turning his attentions to finding a new duchess before too much longer."

Aimee surreptitiously studied the duke through a screen of lashes. He was a nice enough gentleman, if a bit blustery, and closer to her father's age than her own. The stepson of their mother's old friend, the Dowager Duchess of Maitland, he had lost his wife the previous spring to a bout of pneumonia, but not even Aimee's sympathy at his loss could have induced her to entertain the possibility of wedding him. The very idea left her cold.

"I have no interest in marriage right now," she stated firmly, brushing aside the mental picture

of a certain infuriating viscount that flashed un-
bidden across her inner vision. "And I am most
certainly not interested in marrying the Duke of
Maitland."

Olivia's forehead creased in a displeased frown.
"Apparently you have very little interest in anything, aside from your books and idle daydreams."
Narrowing her icy blue eyes, she subjected Aimee
to a head-to-toe inspection that was rife with disdain. "It is really rather pitiful. Of course, perhaps
I am expecting a bit much, especially when it is
quite obvious that you are severely lacking in all
of the traits that most gentlemen look for in a pro-
spective bride. But the duke is of an age where
such qualities as beauty, poise, and charm aren't
nearly as important as a young lady's ability to
provide him with an heir. As that is a requirement
that even you are capable of fulfilling, it occurred
to me that he might be willing to overlook your
more glaring deficiencies."

The scathing evaluation of her inadequacies
hurt, though it wasn't anything Aimee hadn't
heard before. For some reason, Lady Olivia had
made it her self-imposed mission to find fault with
everything her youngest niece said or did from
the moment she had come to live with the family
after Lady Albright's death. Over the years, Lord
Albright had often counseled his daughters to try
and be more patient when it came to their aunt's
bitter disposition, but he would have been furious

had he known just how cruel the woman could be. Olivia tended to blunt her criticisms whenever they were within his hearing, and Aimee couldn't bring herself to be the one to disillusion her father as to his elder sister's character.

That didn't mean that she wouldn't defend herself, however. Lately she had grown tired of the endless barrage of censure and disparagement, and tonight she was just in the mood to return the slings and arrows in equal measure.

So, lifting her chin, she did just that.

"I refuse to be reduced to the level of a broodmare," she informed her aunt unequivocally. "And I won't be pushed into pursuing a match I do not want. I'm happy as I am."

The woman gave a scornful laugh. "Come now, do you truly wish to live under your father's roof for the rest of your life? To be both a physical and financial burden on him in his advancing years? Surely you are not so selfish?"

Selfish? The accusation was grossly unfair and struck Aimee on the raw, causing her to lash out before she could call back the words. "*You* certainly seem to be content enough with such an existence."

Olivia blinked, obviously startled by her niece's uncustomary show of vitriol. "How dare you—" she began, her tone one of outraged affront, but an imperious voice suddenly rang out, cutting her off mid-sputter.

"What are you haranguing the gel about now, Olivia?"

Aimee glanced up and breathed an inner sigh of relief to see Theodosia Rosemont, Dowager Duchess of Maitland, shuffling toward them from across the drawing room with the aid of her ivory-handled cane.

Lady Olivia drew herself up and addressed the elderly lady with some asperity as she came to a stop before them. "I was merely pointing out that the time has come for her to start thinking about her future. The foolish child believes that things can go on as they are indefinitely, but you and I both know that they cannot. What prospects are there for a female of her breeding and station other than marriage? There are worse things than to wed a man for convenience's sake, and it would make Philip most happy to see his youngest daughter finally settled with a husband to care for her and a home of her own."

Theodosia pursed her lips and considered first Olivia, then Aimee for several long seconds before shaking her snow-white head. "True," she conceded. "But I doubt that he would want her to tie herself to someone in the bonds of matrimony, simply to put his mind at ease."

"But I was only suggesting that an arrangement with your stepson might be of—"

"Maitland? He is a buffoon and not at all the right match for Aimee. In any case, now is not the time or place for this sort of discussion." The duchess lowered her plump form into a brocade-padded armchair across from the settee, then reached out a wrinkled hand to pat Aimee on the knee, her brown eyes brimming with kindness. "When the gel is ready to make a decision about her future, she will make it without any help from you."

Olivia made a sound of annoyance and subsided back into her seat with a sour expression. "I only want what is best for this family."

"No, you want what is best for you," the dowager said sharply. "You would sell her off to the highest bidder without a thought to her wishes, simply to get her out from underfoot. But marriage is not a means to an end. It is a union that should never be entered into for any reason other than love."

She paused, a sad, faraway look passing over her features, and Aimee couldn't help but think that the woman must be remembering her own beloved husband, gone now for many years. "Marriage is about making a commitment to stand together and share everything, the good and the bad. It is about trust and fidelity and a willingness to do anything for each other."

"Hear, hear!"

The resounding exclamation came from the Baron Bedford, who suddenly materialized at the dowager's side, a snifter of after-dinner port cradled in one elegant hand. "I couldn't have said it better myself, Your Grace," he concluded approvingly, his eyes never wavering from Lady Olivia's face.

Aimee had to stifle a laugh as her aunt's cheeks flushed a dull red. A former suitor of the late Lady Albright during her days with the theater, the baron was a handsome gent of middle years and dwindling fortunes who had gained a reputation in his youth as a scapegrace and notorious skirt chaser. He had also been paying court to the Lady Olivia in a rather sporadic fashion for some time. While his attentions clearly flustered her, however, she appeared to be determined not to fall prey to the charms of a man who had once nursed an unrequited affection for the sister-in-law she had despised.

"Do be quiet, Bedford," Olivia hissed now, straightening her shoulders and glaring up at him in indignation. "What could you possibly know about trust or fidelity? Or love, for that matter? You cast off women as easily as an old suit of clothes, going from one to another like a bee flits from flower to flower."

The corner of his mouth quirking wryly, the baron laid his free hand over his heart as if he had been struck a mortal blow. "My darling, you wound me to the quick. I do not *flit*. And haven't I said over and over that I would become the most faithful of husbands if you would but do me the honor of accepting my proposal?"

"I would have to be addled to take your word for that, wouldn't I? Unfortunately, I have learned to my detriment that most men—especially men of your ilk—have a tendency to be fickle."

"Fickle? I say, that's a trifle harsh!"

"It is the truth, nonetheless. And you have given me little reason to change my opinion."

As the twosome continued to argue in hushed whispers, the dowager duchess leaned forward, drawing Aimee's attention away from them. "Are you all right, dear?" she asked, her gaze sympathetic.

Aimee nodded and offered her a reassuring smile. While she wasn't quite as close to Theodosia as her sisters, she liked the elderly lady a great deal and was grateful for her intervention. "Yes. Thank you, Your Grace."

"Olivia will try to bully you, but you mustn't let her. You are young yet, and after everything you've been through, it is perfectly understandable if you are not quite ready to think about falling in love or sharing your life with a husband. Sometimes we must make peace with the demons of our past, find out who we really are and whether we can stand on our own two feet, before we are strong enough to give a piece of ourselves to someone else."

The dowager's words reminded Aimee of the nightmares that had been tormenting her for weeks, and the dark images came clawing their way out from the farthest recesses of her consciousness as if in answer to a summons. Once more, she saw Lord Stratton's maniacal face, saw her mother's accusing eyes, as it all played out in her head in terrifying detail.

Shuddering, she glanced over at her father, who was now standing a few feet away with Violet still at his side. He was smiling and looked more at ease than he had in quite some time.

For years, the Marquis of Albright had been a very sad and melancholy man. Though he had truly loved his late wife, it was no secret that the two of them had caused each other a great deal of pain during their marriage. The vast difference in their backgrounds, Lady Albright's flirtatious nature, and the wagging tongues of the gossip-mongers had eventually led to an estrangement that had lasted right up until the marchioness's death. Devastated by her loss, Lord Albright had withdrawn into himself, becoming a rather tragic figure who rarely smiled or laughed or took joy in much of anything.

Recently, however, the marquis had begun to emerge from his despondency, to show more of an interest in life again. An expert in the field of criminology, he had taken up where he had left off with his research on the subject, often serving as a consultant of sorts for the private investigative agency owned by his friend, former Bow Street Runner Morton Tolliver. The darkness had faded from his eyes once and for all, and he finally seemed content.

She had made the right decision in keeping the details of her dreams to herself, Aimee thought now, her eyes blurring with tears. Telling her father about her nightmares would do nothing but bring back painful memories for him, and she refused to be the one to ruin his newfound happiness.

"Are you sure that nothing else is wrong, child? You look very pale of a sudden."

At Theodosia's concerned query, Aimee swallowed back the lump that clogged her throat and tried to keep her voice from shaking when she replied. "I'm fine, though it is frightfully warm in here. I believe I could do with some fresh air. If you will excuse me?"

Desperate to escape the dowager's perceptive stare, she rose to her feet, made a hasty curtsy, and hurried toward the far side of the room, where the louvered panels of the French doors stood open to the night. She sent a prayer of thanksgiving skyward when no one attempted to stop her as she slipped out onto the terrace and made her way down the curving set of stairs to the walled-in garden.

Here, all was dark and still, the flowers and tall hedges illuminated only by the light of the moon as Aimee sank down on one of the stone benches that lined the winding pathway. Savoring the slight breeze against her heated skin, she closed her eyes for a fleeting instant and let the peacefulness settle over her. Slowly but surely, bit by bit, the weight of her troubles lifted off her shoulders.

She had barely begun to relax her guard, however, when a faint rustling sound drifted to her on the evening air. Startled by it, she jerked her head up and glanced back over her shoulder toward the terrace, her heart pounding in her throat.

Just in time to see Lord Stonehurst step out of the shadows.

Chapter 5

At first, neither of them said a word. They simply stared at each other, the tension-fraught silence stretching out between them like an invisible cord that was in danger of snapping.

Taking advantage of Aimee's temporary state of shock, Royce studied her as she sat huddled on the garden bench. Moonlight spilled over her in a swath of silvery radiance, limning the delicate oval of her face and revealing the heartbreaking vulnerability of her expression. Her obvious melancholy roused his long-dormant protective instincts, filling him with an unexpected and inexplicable urge to wrap her in his arms and comfort her.

It was an urge that he was well aware he could not afford to give in to.

Damnation! He had known this was a mistake the instant he had followed her onto the terrace, but no matter how many times he had tried to tell himself that it would be better for both of them if he left her alone, he couldn't seem to resist the need to seek her out. It was as if she had cast some sort of spell over him, and he was powerless against her siren's call.

Finally growing impatient at the continuing silence and in need of a distraction from his straying thoughts, he folded his arms and propped one shoulder against a nearby stone column, before addressing her in a deliberately provoking manner. "And here I was under the impression that it was only me you were attempting to avoid."

Aimee visibly stiffened at his mocking tone. Her lips tightening into an angry line, she lunged to her feet and closed the distance between them at a rapid march, her full skirts billowing about her ankles with each step. "What are you doing out here?" she hissed furiously as she drew up before him. Her gaze traveled in the direction of the house as if to ascertain that no one else was about before settling on him once more. "Have you taken leave of your senses?"

The question struck him as rather amusing, given that he'd just been wondering the same thing himself, and the unscarred corner of his mouth took on a self-deprecatory slant. "Yes, I believe so," he conceded. "Either that, or I am severely lacking in willpower when it comes to you."

"And what on earth does that mean?"

"It means that I was worried about you, and I wanted to make sure that you were all right."

His confession seemed to catch her off balance, and she subsided, blinking up at him in confusion as her ire slowly drained away. "What?"

"I saw you talking to your aunt, and I could tell that she had upset you." Tilting his head, Royce searched her wan countenance. Here in the dimness, it was harder to make out her waiflike features, but the anxiety that held her in its grip was almost palpable. "What did she say to you?"

A hint of color crept into her cheeks, and she glanced away. "Nothing. Nothing worth repeating, at any rate. She was just taking the opportunity to once again point out all of my inherent shortcomings. As if I'm not already fully aware of each and every one."

Royce felt his whole body go rigid in seething resentment. He couldn't help but be incensed on her behalf. The Lady Olivia's contemptuous attitude often reminded him of the disparaging remarks his father had doled out to him on a daily basis, and it rubbed him on the raw to witness Aimee being subjected to the same sort of treatment. "The woman is a harridan," he growled. "I've never been able to understand why your father puts up with her."

"She is his sister. And he feels sorry for her."

"But why?"

Aimee lifted her shoulder in a slight shrug. "I'm not entirely certain. Many years ago, there was a man she loved and planned to wed, but he jilted her when his family did not approve of my father's marriage to my mother. No one seems to know who he was. It happened while Papa was estranged from Grandfather and living with us in Dorset, and the betrothal was never officially announced." She turned and moved back along the path toward the bench she had occupied before, her voice drifting faintly to Royce on the breeze. "She has been bitter ever since, and I think Papa has always felt responsible."

"Surely that doesn't give her leave to be so vindictive with you," he insisted, pushing away from the column and striding after her. "None of it was your fault, and your father should have put a stop to her behavior long ago."

Coming to a halt next to a small fountain, she peered down into the sparkling water, as if looking for answers in its crystalline depths. "He doesn't know. She is very careful to guard her words in front of him, and I haven't told him about it."

"Why the bloody hell not?"

"It would hurt him too much."

"So you are content to let her keep on hurting *you* instead?"

Suddenly, without warning, Aimee astonished Royce by whirling on him, her eyes blazing with a wounded hostility that was undeniable. "I cannot imagine why any of this should matter to you. I thought you had no interest in timid little mice who flinch from the sight of their own shadow."

The stunning outburst was followed by another lengthy span of silence, and several seconds ticked by before the paralysis that had seized them both finally loosened its numbing tentacles enough for them to react.

Aimee was clearly appalled by her loss of control, and she shook her head in distress, one hand flying to her throat. "I'm sorry," she whispered, her apology sounding thin and broken. "I should go back inside now."

She lifted her skirts and started to duck around him, apparently intending to escape back into the house. But he reached out and caught her by the wrist before she could get too far, determined not to let her run away. "Wait."

Jerking up short, she gasped and stared down at his fingers wrapped about her wrist just above her white kid glove, then regarded him uncertainly. The apprehensive way she nibbled at her lower lip told him that she had felt it too. That flickering flame of awareness that had turned his blood to fire the second he had touched her. Even through the material of his own glove, she singed him as if there were no barrier at all between his palm and the silkiness of her skin.

The contact was dangerous for both of them, but he didn't let her go. He ignored his body's response to her nearness and concentrated on the matter at hand. "I don't understand," he said softly. "Why would you say something like that?"

A shadow flitted across her features before she averted her gaze. "Don't you remember? It is what you said to me that day. The day that we—"

She broke off, but there was no need for her to go on. He mentally finished the sentence for her.

The day that they had accidentally collided in the hallway of the Albright town house and everything between the two of them had changed forever.

Even after the year that had passed since then, Royce could still recall the jolt of awareness that had sizzled along his nerve-endings at the feel of Aimee's delicate curves pressed along the length of him. Could still picture the slight parting of her rosy lips as she had stared into his eyes, her heart-shaped face scant inches from his own. In that instant, his blinders had been torn away and there had been no more ignoring the fact that she was no longer the solemn child of fourteen he had once taken under his wing and who had been so in need of his friendship.

Suddenly, all he had wanted to do was seize that sweet mouth with his own, to peel away the layers of her modest gown so that he could explore every newly ripened curve, and he had been left stunned by the force of his passion for a girl who had long been like a younger sister to him. But what had terrified him even more than his own feelings of attraction had been the hope in her expression and the utter devotion in her voice as she had whispered in his ear.

I love you, Royce.

That had been the day that he had made the decision to slice the fragile thread that linked them and exit her life. It had been a mistake to allow such a close bond to develop between them in the first place, no matter how innocent, and while he had known that his defection would hurt her, he had been convinced that it was the only way to rectify the situation. Even if his longing for her hadn't been a betrayal of the trust her family had placed in him, he couldn't let himself forget the unfortunate fate that awaited those he was foolish enough to care for.

Looking down into her heart-shaped face now, however, he could clearly see the anguish she tried so hard to hide, and he realized that he had hurt her far more than he had ever imagined. Though he had no memory of exactly what he had said in response to her shy declaration of love, he hated to believe that he could have been so cruel. But in his desperation to push her away, to slam his defenses back into place, he hadn't given much thought to the words he had used to accomplish that goal.

"Aimee," he began, doing his best to keep his tone low and placating, "whatever I said then, you must know that I didn't mean it. You caught me off guard and I didn't handle it very well, I'm afraid. But—"

"Please." She cut him off with a glare. "I am not interested in hearing any explanations. Just as you weren't interested in offering any before you chose to turn your back on me a year ago without a by-your-leave. In any case, none of it is of any consequence now."

Her assertion pricked at his temper, and he tugged her closer to him, easily overcoming her initial resistance when she balked. His grasp on her arm was firm, yet gentle. "It's of consequence to me."

"Is it?" She didn't sound convinced, and when she looked up at him once again, he could see the doubt that was reflected in the amber pools of her eyes. "Your actions prove you false, so you will have to forgive me if I find that difficult to credit. And I can't imagine that there is anything you could possibly tell me that would make me believe otherwise."

She was right, Royce acknowledged to himself grimly as he scrutinized her mutinous expression, a muscle flexing in his jaw. Even if he could make her understand that he'd had a good reason for his actions, it wouldn't change anything in the end. She would still be hurt by his decision, and he would still have to stay away from her. There was simply no other option. He would rather slit his own wrists than see her end up like everyone else who had ever been close to him.

So he held his tongue. And just as he had known it would, his failure to defend himself damned him even further in Aimee's estimation. Breaking free from his hold, she rubbed her wrist as if trying to erase all traces of his touch before lifting her chin at a defiant angle.

"Then there is nothing more to discuss, is there?" she said coolly, her voice wavering a bit despite her haughty demeanor. "And as our conversation is now at an end, I would be most appreciative if you would find someone else to torment with your presence and leave me in peace."

She backed away from him, taking an unsteady step or two that brought her right into a stray patch of moonlight. It bathed her in its brilliant glow, turning the gold strands in her hair into a halo about her head and illuminating her troubled visage.

Royce couldn't help but notice how very small and fragile she looked. And to his swiftly mounting alarm, she also looked as if she were on the verge of collapsing at any moment. By God, how had he missed those dark circles under her eyes and the lines of strain around her mouth? It was as if the slightest puff of air would shatter her into a million pieces, and he would never be able to put her back together.

Surely this latest confrontation wasn't responsible for this? There had to be something more troubling her. But what?

Quickly, he sifted through his options. Aimee had asked him to leave her alone, and perhaps he should. All he had to do was go back inside and send one of her sisters or her father out to aid her. It would be a quick, clean break, and he could wash his hands of it all and start trying to put his maddening fascination with the girl behind him. But he couldn't quite bring himself to just abandon her like that.

He had to know what was wrong.

"Aimee," he ventured cautiously, feeling his way with great care. "Is there something else upsetting you? Something besides your aunt's tirade and your anger with me?"

She froze, going as still as a fawn in a hunter's sights. "What do you mean?"

"I would have to be blind not to notice how on edge you are." He lifted a hand, cutting her off when she would have spoken. "Before you say it, I know that my return to town has caused you a fair share of turmoil, but there is more to it than that. You are pale and drawn and obviously exhausted, as if you haven't been sleeping well of late. And since I am only newly arrived in London as of this morning, that is something that not even I can be held accountable for."

Whatever color had still tinged Aimee's cheeks drained away, leaving her complexion positively ashen, but she straightened her shoulders, managing to maintain an air of composure despite her obvious disconcertment. "I thank you for your concern, my lord," she responded aloofly. "But I can assure you that I am just fine."

Her assurances did not deceive Royce, however. "Don't lie to me, Kitten."

"Don't call me Kitten. And I'm not lying."

"You are. I've always been able to tell. I know you too well, and you're a terrible liar."

Flinching at this observation, Aimee wrapped her arms about her waist in a defensive posture. "It's nothing. Really. I've . . . I've just . . ." She hesitated, letting her eyes drift closed for a second as if mentally debating something, then continued in an almost offhand tone, "I've been having some bad dreams lately. That's all."

Royce frowned. "What sort of dreams?"

"Does it matter?"

"Of course it matters. Especially if they are bad enough that they are keeping you from sleeping."

"Dreams can't hurt you. And they will go away eventually. They always do."

Something about Aimee's resigned tone struck a chord with Royce, and he turned it all over in his mind, trying to fit the pieces together. In the past, both she and her father had confided in him about the terrible dreams she had suffered after witnessing her mother's murder as a child, and he knew what a debilitating effect they'd had on her. It had taken her years to get over them, and in many ways they had left her almost as traumatized as the actual incident itself.

Was it possible . . . ?

"These dreams," he drew out slowly, as he

shifted closer to her. "Are they like the nightmares you used to have as a little girl? About your mother's death?"

Aimee didn't bother to reply. She simply bowed her head, focusing her attention on the ground.

That was answer enough for Royce, and his concern for her grew apace with his sense of foreboding. "I thought you told me that they went away a long time ago."

"They did. But in the past few weeks, they've come back."

"Why now? After all these years?"

"I don't know. But they're different somehow. More vivid. I'm beginning to wonder—" Aimee stumbled to a halt and glanced up at him through a screen of lashes, licking her lips nervously before blurting out the rest in a rush. "I think my memories of that evening are returning."

"Have you told your father?"

At Royce's question, she gave a vehement shake of her head, and her eyes widened in sudden panic. "No! And I have no intention of doing so."

Her fearful reaction stumped him. What possible reason could she have for wanting to keep something of such importance from the people who loved her? "Why not?"

"Because all of that is supposed to be in the past. It's over and done with. Stratton confessed and he is dead, so what good would it do to upset my father and sisters by dredging it all up again."

Royce took a deep breath. He would have to try to reason with her, for this was not a trifling matter to be brushed under the rug. These nightmares had put her through a living hell before, and he would not stand by and let her suffer through such an experience alone. Never mind his resolve to stay uninvolved.

"We both know these are no ordinary dreams, Aimee," he reminded her gently. "You must be having them again for a reason. And if your memories of that time are returning, your family has a right to know. You *have* to tell them. There is no other choice."

"Yes, there is. I can choose to keep it to myself. And you must promise me that you won't mention it to them either."

"Aimee, you can't ask that of me. Your father—"

"Promise me!"

When he firmed his lips and refused to answer, she flew at him in an unexpected frenzy.

"You blackguard! I don't even know why I entrusted you with this, but now that I have, you cannot tell anyone! You cannot!"

Royce seized her by the wrists, holding her so that her flailing fists were rendered all but ineffectual. This close, he could see the weariness carved into her delicate features, and he felt her sway against him, as if she were having trouble remaining upright.

"Damn it, will you stop it!" he snapped. "Look at you. You can barely stand. Can't you see—"

"Do stop pretending as if my welfare is of the slightest consequence to you. I used to think we were friends, but I've never really meant anything to you, and you know it. You just as good as confirmed it a few minutes ago, so I don't know why you insist on playing out this charade."

His jaw tautened at her accusations. By God, the only reason he had insisted on ending their friendship was that he *did* care. Too much. Her infuriating obduracy had his blood boiling, and he didn't know whether to yell at her, shake her, or kiss her.

He chose the last.

Yanking her against him, her drew her up onto her toes, bent his head, and brought his mouth down on hers.

Chapter 6

The kiss was so utterly unexpected that it shocked Aimee into a momentary state of incredulity. She could hardly believe it was happening. One second she had been shouting at the man like some irate fishwife, and the next his mouth was on hers, stealing her voice, her breath, and her ability to think rationally.

Her head reeling, she clutched at Stonehurst's muscled biceps, her fingers twining in the expensive material of his frock coat. Whether to push him away or draw him closer, she was not certain. Locked in his strong arms with her small breasts pressed against his broad chest, she could feel the pounding of his heart, hear his muffled groan as his lips moved on hers, bold and demanding.

Heavens, she thought dimly. This was not at all the way she had imagined her first kiss would be! Not that she had ever expected it to actually happen. Plain little mice who were destined to remain forever on the shelf were not likely to be

kissed in any fashion. But she had often fantasized about what it might be like. And she would
be less than truthful if she didn't acknowledge
to herself that Lord Stonehurst had usually been
the one doing the kissing in most of her romantic
scenarios. Those exchanges, however, had always
been courtly and tender. The sort of pure and
sweetly innocent embrace that the lovers in her
favorite novels indulged in.

This was a ravishment. There was no other way
to describe it. The viscount plundered and devoured her with a bold thoroughness that put her
daydreams to shame. Over and over, his tongue
darted forth to trace the outline of her lips, skimming their moist surfaces before slipping between
her teeth to plunge deep into the warm cavern of
her mouth. It was a strange yet heady sensation
that sent heat coursing through her veins. All the
while, his restless hands roamed up and down
the length of her spine, the smooth stroke of his
palms through the material of her gown wringing
a shiver from her.

Falling further and further under the erotic
spell he was weaving around her with every
second that passed, Aimee responded to his ardor
by molding herself against him and winding her
arms tightly around his neck, her hurt and anger
all but forgotten. Suddenly she could picture him
lying down with her in the soft grass next to the
fountain, slowly peeling away her clothing so

that he could explore her body with his hands and mouth and that agile tongue. She envisioned the look of fierce hunger that would suffuse his darkly handsome visage as he reared up over her and . . . and . . .

And she had to end this now!

With a smothered cry, she tore her lips away from his, shoving at his chest in a desperate attempt to free herself. It didn't take much of a struggle on her part, for she was released almost immediately. She staggered backward, dazed and disoriented, barely managing to stay upright as the world spun around her.

Her pulse pounding in her ears, she lifted a trembling hand to tuck a few loosened strands of her light brown hair back behind her ear, giving herself an opportunity to regain control of her teetering emotions before looking up to meet Stonehurst's gaze. He was staring at her, his chest heaving and his high cheekbones stained with a hectic flush, though he said not a word. He just stood there, gloved hands fisted at his sides, almost as if he were battling the urge to reach for her again.

That's a ridiculous notion, a patronizing little voice hissed in the far corner of her mind. He didn't want her. Not as a friend, and certainly not as anything more. His abandonment last year had made that more than clear, and their conversation this evening had only borne that out.

But then why had he kissed her?

He'd been furious with her. Perhaps it had been some form of punishment. It seemed rather extraordinary lengths to go to, and not at all like the viscount, who was normally a very dispassionate and reserved person. But what other reasonable explanation could there be?

He couldn't possibly have wanted *to kiss you,* the little voice piped up again in a particularly vicious manner. *What man would? You have nothing to offer. You are not pretty enough or charming enough or interesting enough to inspire such desire in anyone. You are simply not enough of anything, and he deserves much more than you could ever give him.*

Not enough . . .

The taunting words reverberated in her skull, and a strangled sob escaped her, jolting Stonehurst from his stupor. His gray eyes narrowing, he took a tentative step toward her, a muscle leaping in his taut jaw.

"Aimee," he began, but she held out a hand to ward him off. She couldn't handle it if he touched her. Not now. If he did, she would fly apart at the seams.

She had to get away!

Her vision blurred by tears, she whirled about, prepared to make her escape before he took it into his head to try and prevent it—only to choke back a startled cry when she almost collided with someone coming from the other direction.

Lady Olivia.

Panic washed over Aimee in waves. Dear God, but how long had her aunt been out here? she wondered wildly. How much had she seen and heard?

Blue eyes glittering with suspicion, Olivia frowned in Lord Stonehurst's direction before settling her penetrating gaze on Aimee in obvious disapproval.

"The two of you should not be out here alone," she snapped. "Just what is going on?"

Aimee swallowed back the lump in her throat and cast a swift glance over her shoulder at Stonehurst, who was watching her with an unreadable expression. Not by the flicker of an eyelash or the twitch of a nerve did he betray a hint of what had just occurred.

"Nothing," she told her aunt in a husky whisper, strangely wounded by his remoteness. "Nothing at all."

With that, she lifted the hem of her skirt and pushed past Olivia, racing toward the house as fast as her legs would carry her. It was a headlong flight, and she had no idea where she was going. She only knew she had to take her leave before she gave too much away.

Along the winding path and up the steps to the terrace she ran, passing the Duke of Maitland and the Baron Bedford, who were nursing cheroots and lounging against the stone balustrade as she rushed by. The speculative gleam in their eyes made her wonder just exactly how much they had overheard as well, and she deliberately slowed her pace, managing a polite nod in their direction before hurrying on.

In no frame of mind to face everyone in the drawing room with her emotions in such high dudgeon, she entered the town house through a set of French doors that led directly into the main corridor. There she searched until she found a small, curtained alcove just off the hallway where she could have a bit of privacy to clear her head and compose herself.

She slumped against the wall, finally giving in to her misery and letting the tears flow. Why? Why did she seem to have no instinct for self-preservation when it came to Lord Stonehurst? She had made such a fool of herself, berating him like some petulant child one instant, only to respond to his kiss with utter wantonness the next. And why had she told him the truth about her dreams? The blasted man had never promised her that he wouldn't mention the nightmares to her father, so now she was faced with a quandary she had no idea how to deal with.

All she knew for certain was that she no longer had the strength to carry on as if the evening were nothing out of the ordinary. She wanted to go home, where she could lock herself in her room and shut out the world. Perhaps if she sought out her father, she could plead a headache and persuade him to depart despite the earliness of the hour. Then no one need ever know just what sort of coward she was.

Taking a deep breath and brushing away the last vestiges of her tears, she left the alcove and made her way back to the drawing room, where one quick glance revealed that Lord Albright was nowhere to be seen. However, she caught sight of Violet on the far side of the room and went to join her, hoping to ascertain the marquis's whereabouts.

"Hello, darling," the red-haired woman greeted her, her heavily rouged face wreathed in a welcoming smile as Aimee drew near. A good friend of the family who had once shared the stage with the deceased marchioness, she now owned a costume shop on Bond Street and was a frequent visitor to the Daventry household. Aimee also often suspected that the former actress had developed more than a passing fondness for the marquis. "How lovely to see you. We haven't had a chance to talk all evening."

Aimee summoned up a smile for her. She genuinely liked Violet and would have enjoyed catching up, but she was in no mood for idle conversation right now. "I know. I apologize, Vi, but I'm afraid I'm feeling unwell and was hoping that Papa would agree to bow out a bit early. Have you seen him?"

"I believe that Maura took him up to the nursery along with Jillian to visit with the baby for a short time." Violet pursed her lips and surveyed Aimee, her hazel eyes full of concern. "You know, you do look a trifle peaked. Do you need me to come with you to look for your father?"

"Please don't trouble yourself. I'm sure I'll be fine. I'm just in need of a good night's sleep, that's all."

Giving the woman's hand a warm squeeze, Aimee politely excused herself and left the room once more.

Out in the dimly lit corridor, all was quiet, and she encountered no one as she hurried along the hallway, not even a servant. The main staircase spiraled upward from the entrance foyer, steep and winding, and as she was already feeling a touch light-headed, she held tight to the banister as she started to climb. Halfway up, however, an unexpected noise arrested her attention, bringing her to an abrupt halt.

It was a stealthy rustling, like the muffled tread of a footstep, and it came from out of the darkness at the top of the stairs. For some reason, it sent a chill inching its way up her spine.

"Hello?" she called out, restraining a wince at the nervous squeak of her voice. "Is anyone there?"

There was no reply, and though she strained her eyes, it was impossible to make out anything in the inky blackness. Not knowing what else to do, she waited in tense silence, her sense of dread settling over her like a shroud as she tried to tell herself that she was just being silly, that she was safe in her sister's home and there was nothing here to hurt her. It had to be her imagination playing tricks on her. But somehow she couldn't escape the feeling that someone was up there waiting. Someone who meant her harm.

It will never be over until you remember it all . . .

The ominous whisper rose up, repeating itself over and over, increasing in volume until it became a roar in her head, and she was thrown back in time to the night her mother had been killed. To the darkened library where Lord Stratton had stolen away everything that had been good in her life with a single shot.

Threatening images flashed before her eyes, blurry and indistinct, and she blinked in an effort to clear away the mist. If she could just bring it all into focus, she was convinced she would finally be able to see what had really happened . . .

At that moment, the shadows on the landing above Aimee shifted and moved, and a dark shape flung itself forward, straight at her. With a terrified scream, she lost her grip on the banister, and suddenly she was falling backward. Falling . . . falling . . .

Falling into nothingness.

She hit the ground with a jarring thud, her head making brutal contact with the marble floor of the entrance foyer.

And she knew no more.

Damn it all to everlasting hell!

His blood simmering in his veins, Royce made his way back to the town house, thoroughly disgusted with himself, Lady Olivia Daventry, and the evening in general.

He had temporarily lost his sanity, he decided. There was no other possible explanation for what he had done. He had promised himself that he would leave Aimee alone. That he would never betray by word or by deed that he wanted her with a fierceness that bordered on obsession. Yet he had taken her in his arms and kissed her as if he had every right to. As if she belonged to him.

What had he been thinking?

Ah, but there was the rub. He *hadn't* been thinking. Or, rather, he'd been thinking with his cock instead of his head. He had let his temper and his desire for her get the better of him, and the result had been an explosive kiss that had left him reeling.

He winced, recalling the myriad of expressions that had crossed Aimee's face in the aftermath of their embrace. Embarrassment, confusion, and hurt had all passed over her piquant features, and there had been nothing he could do to help her. Christ, but how could he make her understand when he barely understood himself?

And to top it all off, Aimee's shrew of an aunt had seen fit to take him to task.

You are to stay away from my niece, Lord Stonehurst, the woman had warned him bluntly the moment Aimee had disappeared up the garden path and they had been left alone. *You are not at all an appropriate companion for an impressionable young girl, and now that she is of age, your continued association would be completely unacceptable. It is bad enough that my two eldest nieces have ended up wed to men who are frowned upon by the ton, but I will not stand by and let Aimee bring even more disgrace upon this family by linking herself with someone who is little better than an outcast in the eyes of society.*

The only thing that had kept him from throttling the witch had been the fact that most of what she'd said about him had been nothing but the truth. He had made up his mind that it would be best if he stayed away from Aimee, and tonight he had only proven just how right he'd been to make that decision.

Yet there were her nightmares to consider. There was no telling what the return of her memories could mean, and regardless of her wishes, keeping a secret of this magnitude from her father and the rest of her family did not sit well with him.

It was quite a tangle, and he had no idea what

he was going to do. He knew what he *wasn't* going to do, however, and that was return to the party. It had been a mistake to join in the proceedings from the very beginning, and it was one he was going to rectify right now.

Striding through the French doors into the drawing room, he noticed with some surprise that the chamber was fairly deserted. The only people present were Miss Lafleur, the Dowager Duchess of Maitland, and Connor Monroe, who were seated before the fireplace, chatting comfortably. He nodded to them, but didn't stop to speak. Instead he exited into the hallway, intending to locate Hawksley so that he could wish his friend a good night before heading for his bedchamber.

Deep in thought, he had just stepped through the archway into the foyer when a shrill scream rang out, echoing off the walls around him. It brought his head up with a jerk to meet the wide-eyed stare of a terrified young maid who stood at the opposite end of the entrance hall, one hand covering her mouth, the basket of linens she had been carrying lying on its side at her feet. She was pointing a trembling finger in the direction of the staircase.

Royce's gaze came to rest on what at first appeared to be a heap of clothing at the bottom of the steps. But as he peered at it more closely, he realized that it wasn't clothing. It was a body. A small, female body clad in a gown of amber silk.

Aimee!

His heart seemed to cease beating for one awful moment, then started up again at an adrenaline-fueled gallop as he rushed to her side and knelt next to her. The deathly pallor of her face had his lungs seizing in his chest, and he couldn't tell whether she was breathing. Reaching out, he brushed aside her tumbled hair so that he could check her pulse. It was so weak and thready that he could barely detect it, and his mouth tightened into a grim line when he noticed the spattering of blood on the floor beneath her head, oozing from an angry-looking gash just behind and a little above her left ear.

But what frightened him more than anything was her absolute stillness. Not once during his inspection had she stirred even the slightest bit.

"My God, what's happened?"

The worried exclamation came from Lord Albright, who was descending the stairs as rapidly as a man of his advancing years could manage, his two elder daughters and Hawksley following in his wake.

Sweeping Aimee into his arms, Royce rose to his feet, only barely hearing Lady Hawksley's frantic instructions to the hovering maid to send a footman for the physician at once. He was far too preoccupied with the way Aimee's head lolled limply against his shoulder to register much of anything else.

Behind his eyes, he saw once again a fleeting image of Cordelia's body lying crushed beneath the wheels of Alex's phaeton, and heard his father's voice as if from a great distance, scathing and hate-filled.

From the moment you ended your mother's life with your birth, you've done nothing but wreak destruction upon this family. And anyone who is ever foolish enough to care for you in the future will only end up suffering for it in the end.

He shook off the condemnation with an effort. Aimee had to be all right. She simply had to. He refused to believe that his damnable curse had stolen her away. The mere possibility was far too painful to even consider.

"I don't know what happened," he finally said aloud, looking up to meet the marquis's anxious gaze. "But I can assure you that I have every intention of finding out."

Chapter 7

The first thing Aimee became aware of was the murmur of voices.

Hushed, indistinct, and laced with varying degrees of concern, they blended together in an annoying hum at the very edges of her consciousness. Through the fog that clouded her senses, she struggled to make out what they were saying, desperate to know why they sounded so worried. But try though she might, she couldn't understand any of the words. They were far too low and garbled.

The next thing she became aware of was a throbbing ache in her temples that seemed to grow worse with each passing minute. And when she tried to shift her body to test its condition, she realized that the rest of her wasn't in much better shape. She felt as if she were a mass of bumps and bruises all over, and if she didn't know any better, she would think she'd been run over by a carriage.

Slitting her eyes, she peered up through a screen of lashes, trying to determine her whereabouts. She appeared to be lying on one of the sofas in Maura and Hawksley's front parlor, and she could just make out the vague shadows of people gathered around her. As she strained to hear over the buzzing in her ears, bits and pieces of their conversation finally began to jump out at her with startling clarity.

"She looks so pale . . ."

"I never should have prodded her into coming this evening, but I thought it would be good for her . . ."

"I don't understand why she didn't tell us sooner . . ."

It was this last comment that had her gasping and pushing herself upright in alarm, but the moment she did, the pain in her head exploded into a fireball of agony, and she cried out.

"Don't try to move too quickly, my dear."

The kind male voice was accompanied by a gentle hand that pressed her back against the propped-up cushions on the sofa, and she didn't try to resist. Instead she reached up to explore the tenderness at the back of her head with the tips of her fingers and encountered the thick folds of a bandage.

"I suppose it's a good thing your head is so hard."

She knew instantly who had spoken, and she glared up accusingly at her tormentor.

Stonehurst.

He was leaning against the back of the sofa, his brow furrowed as he stared down at her inscrutably. It was impossible to discern from his dispassionate expression what he was thinking, if anything.

Drat the man! Aimee fumed. If he had betrayed her confidence and told them about her dreams, she would never forgive him!

Fighting to keep her uneasiness from showing, she glanced around at the rest of her family members, who had all assembled in the room as well. Her father and an older gentleman she recognized as Dr. Merriman, the family physician, were both bending over her, their faces grave.

"What happened?" she whispered, barely able to force the question out through parched lips.

"We were hoping you could tell us." This came from Lord Hawksley, who stood behind the doctor and the marquis, one arm wrapped about the waist of an obviously distressed Maura.

"What do you mean?"

"We found you lying at the foot of the stairs, darling." Jillian was perched at the other end of the sofa, her eyes wide and troubled behind the lenses of her spectacles. "We're not sure how you came to be there, but you must have fallen and hit your head."

Fallen. Yes, she could remember now. She had been climbing the stairs to the second floor when someone had swooped out of the shadows and pushed her—

No, wait. *Had* someone pushed her? Now that she thought back on it, she realized that she hadn't felt anyone actually touch her. She had been so frightened, so confused, and so overwhelmed by the nightmare images from her past that she couldn't be sure what had actually occurred. And it didn't make sense. What reason could anyone possibly have for wanting to harm her? Regardless of the dread that had taken control of her, the certainty that someone had been lurking in the darkness, it was likely that no one had been there at all. She had imagined it all.

But she couldn't possibly tell anyone that. Her family would be sure to think her a madwoman.

So she deliberately brushed aside her recollection of the incident and forced herself to address her father in a calm and even tone. "I was looking for you, Papa. I've been feeling unwell for most of the evening and was hoping that you would agree to take me home."

Lord Albright frowned, examining her with anxious eyes. "So Violet informed us. Is that why you fell, Mouse? Did you have some sort of dizzy spell?"

"Yes, I think so." She nibbled at her lower lip, ignoring the burn of Stonehurst's gaze as it scorched the back of her neck. She absolutely refused to let him make her feel guilty for trying to protect those she loved from further pain. "I had a bit of a headache, and I suppose I must have grown light-headed and lost my balance."

Dr. Merriman, who had clasped her wrist and was busy monitoring her pulse, offered her a sympathetic smile. A portly, balding man of middle years, he had been Aimee's childhood physician, and she had always been fond of him.

"You'll have to take it easy for a few days, my girl," he advised her, patting her hand before releasing her. "Plenty of bed rest. And we'll need to keep an eye on that swelling. A concussion is nothing to be taken lightly." His smile suddenly faded, and a stern light entered his eyes. "Of course, it doesn't help that you were apparently already exhausted and in a fairly weakened state before this even happened. Exactly how long have you been ill?"

Aimee flushed and focused on her fingers twined together in her lap. "I wouldn't say I've been ill, precisely. I've been nursing a headache, that's all. And—"

"Oh, Aimee," Maura interrupted her, her own complexion whitening. "You told me this afternoon that you were feeling unwell and I didn't believe you. I thought it was just an excuse."

"I'm fine, Maura."

"That remains to be seen, young lady." The doctor straightened and moved to retrieve his medical bag. "In any case, some rest will do you good. You are not to exert yourself, and if the headaches continue, I expect you to inform me at once." He looked back at her over his shoulder. "Is that understood?"

Aimee nodded, too weary and in too much pain to think about anything else except returning to the Albright town house and clambering into her big, soft bed. Perhaps after the excitement of this evening, she would be so tired for once that she would be able to sleep through the night without her nightmares troubling her. "Papa, do you think that Connor or Hawksley could help me out to the carriage?" she asked the marquis. "I am more than ready to depart for home, but I am afraid I would prove to be rather unsteady on my feet right now."

"Is that wise?"

The question came from Stonehurst, and it brought her eyes snapping in his direction in wrathful indignation. He hadn't contributed to the discussion since his initial comment about the hardness of her head, and his interference now was provoking in the extreme.

"If you aren't to exert yourself," he continued, not affected in the slightest by her fierce scowl, "I doubt that being jostled about in a coach all the way to Belgrave Square is a good idea."

"I say, Stonehurst, that hadn't even occurred to me," Lord Albright exclaimed. He turned and lifted an inquiring brow at the doctor. "Merriman?"

The physician contemplated Aimee for a moment in silence before replying. "Lord Stonehurst is correct," he finally concurred. "It would probably be best if she isn't moved for a little while. Even without a concussion to contend with, her tumble down the stairs will probably leave her sore for a week or two."

Maura stepped forward and drew the marquis's attention by placing a hand on his arm. "She can stay here with us for a few days, Papa. We have plenty of room. You're welcome to stay as well, if you wish."

A look of relief suffused Lord Albright's features. "A capital idea, dear."

Aimee felt a sudden surge of nausea and couldn't decide whether it was because of the bump on her head or her swiftly growing apprehension. She couldn't stay here. *He* was staying here.

Lifting her chin and praying that her voice wouldn't give away her agitation, she swallowed back the bile rising in her throat and tried to protest. "Maura, please. I wouldn't want to impose."

"You're not imposing. I insist."

"But this is completely unnecessary. I'm fine. See?"

Aimee started to sit up, intent on proving her claim, but had to stifle a groan when the room began to swim around her and her stomach heaved.

Hurrying to her side, Maura helped ease her to

a lying position once again. "You are *not* fine, little sister. And if Dr. Merriman believes it is necessary, then it must be. So I'll thank you not to argue with me about it."

It seemed that the choice had been taken out of her hands. Before she could utter another word of protest, there was a mass exodus from the parlor. Maura scurried off to have one of the guest rooms readied for Aimee's use while Lord Albright, Jillian, and Hawksley followed the doctor as he stepped out into the hallway, still issuing instructions for her care.

"She'll need to be looked in on throughout the night," he was saying. "I'm going to leave a bit of headache powder and some laudanum for the pain. Of course, if you should have need of me, I . . ."

His sentence trailed off into an indecipherable mutter, and Aimee was left alone in the abrupt quiet with the aggravating Lord Stonehurst.

"Do you realize what you've done?" she hissed at him, pounding her fist impotently against the cushions next to her. "You've trapped us both in the same house for who knows how long. Or have you forgotten that you are staying here as well?"

Strolling casually around the end of the sofa, he took up a position a few feet away and returned her venom-laced stare with a probing gaze that was unnerving. "I haven't forgotten."

"Then what were you thinking?"

"I was thinking that you need someone to keep an eye on you. You and I both know that your fall down the stairs was a direct result of those blasted nightmares of yours. You're not sleeping and barely eating and it's made you ill. How else do you explain your sudden dizzy spell?"

Aimee cast a quick glance out into the corridor, where her family members were still conversing with Dr. Merriman in muffled voices. Assured that they were well out of earshot, she responded to the viscount's observations with feigned incomprehension. "I'm sure I don't know what you are talking about."

"And I'm sure you do." Stonehurst's face suddenly hardened, and for the first time since she had regained consciousness, she glimpsed a spark of real emotion in his gray eyes. "Damn it, you could have been killed. Do you have any idea how I felt when I found you lying there in the entrance hall? You were so still, and the blood—" His words ground to a halt and his jaw visibly tensed, his scar standing out like a vivid brand against the waxen pallor of his visage. After a second or two, however, a blank curtain descended over his features, and he went on in a much more controlled tone. "I don't like it any more than you do. But if you are not going to be honest with your father about all of this, then I suppose I must appoint myself your guardian angel."

Aimee was shaken by the brief crack in his

formerly impenetrable armor, but she disguised her bemusement by giving a less than delicate sniff. "Perhaps what passed between us out in the garden has slipped your mind, but at this point I can't help but think that you are the last person who should be watching over me."

He shrugged. "I suggest that we both do our best to pretend that never happened. It was a kiss. Nothing more. And I'm willing to put whatever differences we may have aside if it means making sure you stay out of trouble. I happen to think a great deal of your father, and I would be remiss indeed should I allow anything to happen to his beloved daughter because of her obstinacy."

"Obstinacy? How dare you?"

His brows arched skyward at her outraged gasp. "What's wrong, my lady?" he queried mockingly. "Surely if I can survive for a few days under the same roof with you, you can tolerate my company for a short while as well. Unless there is some reason you think you might have a difficult time. Perhaps that kiss meant more to you than you pretend."

"You—you arrogant—"

"You there, Stonehurst. I saw the physician depart. Tell me how the gel is."

The peremptory command cut Aimee off mid-sputter, and she looked up to see the Dowager Duchess of Maitland entering the room.

Quickly smoothing her features into the most

pleasant expression she could manage in the circumstances, she gave the elderly woman a wan smile. "You can ask me yourself, Your Grace."

"Ah. So you're awake." Leaning heavily on her cane, Theodosia seated herself in the armchair directly across from the sofa, her lined face bespeaking her concern. "Glad to see it. We were quite beside ourselves, you know. You took a nasty tumble."

A flash of movement from beyond the dowager's shoulder drew Aimee's attention to the hallway outside the door. Her father, Jillian, and Hawksley had disappeared from view, but her aunt, Lord Bedford, and the Duke of Maitland had taken their place. The three of them were clustered together in a tight little knot, murmuring to one another as the two gentlemen cast furtive looks into the room.

There was nothing furtive about Olivia's intent regard, however. The woman's glacial stare would have been enough to induce a shiver from the most stalwart of individuals.

"My dear?"

Theodosia's prompting brought an end to Aimee's distraction, and she tore her gaze away from her aunt to face the dowager once again. "Yes, Your Grace, it was a bit of an ordeal," she agreed. "But as you can see, I'm fine."

"You are *not* fine."

Not surprisingly, this contradictory assessment

came from Stonehurst, and Aimee bristled with resentment at his temerity. "I'm fine if I say I'm fine."

"You will have to forgive me if I advise Her Grace not to put much store in your opinion, as you are the only one who seems to think so."

"You know, you never used to be such a dictatorial tyrant, my lord. I liked it better when you were withdrawn and taciturn."

"And I preferred it when you weren't so ill-tempered and waspish."

"If I am waspish, it is only because—"

Theodosia, who had been observing their antagonistic exchange with mouth agape, struck the floor with her cane, effectively bringing a halt to their dispute. "Here now," she barked, her too perceptive brown eyes jumping back and forth between them. "What's the meaning of all this? Have I missed something?"

Aimee took a deep breath, attempting to rein in her escalating temper. It was mortifying to realize that she had let herself be drawn into another war of words with him, especially in front of the dowager. She was supposed to be the timid Daventry sister. The one who never got angry or spoke crossly to anyone. But ever since she had discovered that Stonehurst had returned to town, her emotions had become extremely volatile, and her lack of control over them was disconcerting to say the least.

"I apologize, Your Grace," she said stiffly. "Apparently Lord Stonehurst is under the mistaken impression that I am incapable of looking after myself."

"Surely I can hardly be blamed for having formed that impression?" he countered. "I should think that after the events of this evening, any reasonably intelligent human being would be forced to agree that your judgment when it comes to your own well-being leaves much to be desired. But I am in no mood to argue the point any further." His gray eyes as hard as granite, he inclined his head to the dowager duchess in a stilted bow. "If you will excuse me, Your Grace?"

Livid, Aimee glared after him as he stalked from the room, then turned back to Theodosia with arms crossed in an indignant pose. "Do you see how he insults me? Now he is questioning my intelligence. And to think, I shall have to endure his insufferable presence for the next several days. Thanks to his machinations, Maura has insisted that I stay on here where she can keep an eye on me while I recover from my fall. The loathsome cad will drive me to murder before it is all over."

The dowager blinked at her, clearly shocked by her hostility. "I vow, I am astounded. I have never seen you like this before. I had always believed that the two of you got along fairly well. And now here you are, bickering like . . . like—"

She broke off abruptly and her eyes narrowed,

taking on a speculative gleam that did not bode well. Her expression was that of someone who had stumbled upon something of supreme interest and was now trying to decide what to do about it.

It was enough to make Aimee extremely nervous.

"Your Grace?" she ventured when it became obvious that the duchess wasn't going to continue. "What were you about to say?"

"Hmmm?" Theodosia blinked again and came out of her trance with a visible start. "Was I going to say something? I'm sorry, my dear. I'm afraid the memory is the first to go at my advanced age. What were we discussing?"

"We were discussing my impending stay under the same roof as Lord Stonehurst."

"Yes, that should prove to be interesting," the duchess mused, a sly smile curving her lips. "Most interesting, indeed."

The woman's knowing words filled Aimee with a distinct sense of uneasiness, and she suddenly had the very bad feeling that things were about to get far more interesting than even the dowager suspected.

Chapter 8

Royce was striding along the upstairs hallway early the next morning on his way down to breakfast when he ran into Lady Hawksley, who was just exiting one of the other bedchambers that lined the corridor.

With her ebony tresses coming loose from her elegant chignon and her brilliant blue eyes drooping with exhaustion, the countess looked harried and a bit worse for wear. Nonetheless, she mustered a smile of genuine warmth the moment she caught sight of Royce.

"Good morning, Lord Stonehurst," she greeted him. "I trust that you slept well?"

He thought back on the last several hours spent tossing and turning in his bed with an inward grimace. No matter how hard he had tried to block it all out, he had been plagued by images of Aimee lying at the bottom of the stairs. Finding her like that, so very pale and motionless, had left him reeling, numbing his mind and body with shock.

Perhaps because of that, he hadn't handled his confrontation with her afterward in the most tactful manner. Not that he had ever been known for his tact, but he had been even more high-handed than usual. He couldn't be displeased with the results, however. While he hadn't set out with the intention of maneuvering things so that she would be forced to stay under the same roof with him, it had worked out for the best. Now all he had to do was figure out a way to keep an eye on her and avoid any further direct contact at the same time.

A rather monumental task, indeed. And not one he could confide in anyone about. Including Lady Hawksley.

So, schooling his features into a bland mask, he replied to her query in a politely offhand tone that gave away not a hint of his inner turmoil. "I suppose I slept as well as can be expected in the circumstances."

The countess sighed. "Yes, last night was rather eventful, wasn't it?"

That was certainly an understatement, but Royce didn't bother to point that out. Instead he nodded toward the door she had closed behind her. "How is she?"

"She seems to be suffering no ill effects, thank goodness. Though I must say, I never realized just what a troublesome patient she can be. She is already complaining about being cooped up, and she insisted on rising and dressing this morning, even though I have drawn the line at allowing her to come downstairs. I'm afraid she is not very happy with me at present, but I am determined that she will adhere to the physician's instructions in that regard."

"Quite admirable of you. Once she is fully recovered, I'm sure she will appreciate the fact that you only had her best interests at heart."

Lady Hawksley's expression sobered. "I feel responsible in a way," she admitted softly. "I was the one who pushed her into coming last night, but I had no idea that she had been feeling poorly."

"I expect she didn't want you to know," Royce pointed out, attempting to alleviate some small portion of the woman's self-blame. "Your sister doesn't like to be a burden on those she loves, and she is very good at keeping things to herself when she wants to."

"Yes, she is." She tilted her head, studying him with keen interest. "You appear to know her exceptionally well."

And here was where he would have to tread carefully. He had learned that the Lady Hawksley was a most astute female, and it wouldn't do at all to arouse her curiosity where his feelings for Aimee were concerned. "I know her well enough to be aware that she is far more strong-willed than her timid exterior might at first suggest."

A rueful laugh escaped the countess at his observation. "That is certainly true," she agreed.

"She tends to get annoyed with me because I badger her incessantly, but she has been through so much since Mama died. She would close herself off from everyone if she could, so I try to help by prodding her into attending the occasional social event and by introducing her to some of the more eligible gentlemen in our circle. The sort of good-natured young men who might pique her interest without making her feel threatened."

In other words, the sort of young men that Aimee would find far too vacuous and callow, Royce concluded with more than a trace of derision. Young men who could never identify with the pain she had suffered or the trauma left behind by the experience. Such empty-headed fools weren't for her. She needed someone who could understand and empathize with the fact that she had been scarred by the tragedy that still haunted her. Someone like—

But he refused to finish the rest of the sentence, even in his own mind. Or to contemplate the tiny sliver of jealous fury that pierced him at the thought of her with another man. That way lay nothing but madness.

Oblivious to Royce's brooding ruminations, the countess was still speaking, unable to hide the edge of frustration that had crept into her voice. "Unfortunately, my sister is most resistant to my matchmaking efforts. Why, when Gabriel first brought up the idea of planning a dinner party to coincide with your arrival in town, I thought it was a perfect opportunity to invite a few of our male acquaintances, but Aimee . . ." She trailed off, her cheeks reddening as she noticed the narrowing of his eyes and realized that she had blundered. "Oh dear."

"It's quite all right, my lady," he assured her, one corner of his mouth quirking wryly. "I had already surmised that last night's gathering was more or less for my benefit. Hawksley's attempt to try and drag me out of my self-imposed exile, I assume?"

"He only wants to see you happy, my lord. The same way I want to see Aimee happy."

Royce could have told the countess that some people didn't deserve happiness and only reaped what they sowed, but he held his tongue. He somehow doubted that the woman would see things from his point of view.

At that moment, the door to Aimee's room opened and a thin, freckle-faced maid ducked out into the hallway, bearing a tray of tea and toast. "My lady, she refuses to touch even a bite of her breakfast," the servant reported, sounding more than a trifle harassed. "She says that she will eat when she is hungry and not a moment before."

Lady Hawksley's hands went to her hips as she frowned at the wooden panel in a disgruntled fashion. "Heavens! I'm sure I don't know what has come over her. It isn't at all like her to be so difficult."

There was little doubt in Royce's mind as to what was driving Aimee's obduracy. She was angry with him, and apparently she planned to spend the duration of her convalescence taking it out on everyone else.

The countess had begun to pace back and forth in front of him, her steps agitated. "Aimee simply must eat something," she fretted. "Dr. Merriman was most adamant about that, but she seems set against listening to a word I have to say, and I don't have time to argue with her. It is long past Fiona's feeding time, and I'm sure she must be putting up a fuss by now."

Royce stared at the door, then contemplated the tray in the maid's hands from under lowered brows as he mulled things over. He should stay out of it. He knew that. Hadn't he just finished telling himself that he had to avoid any direct contact if he wanted to get through the next few days with his sanity intact? But his conscience wouldn't let him disassociate himself from a situation that was partly of his making, and he spoke before he could call the words back. "Give me her tray. I'll see that she eats."

Lady Hawksley came to an abrupt halt and blinked up at him in astonishment. "Lord Stonehurst," she drew out slowly, "I wouldn't precisely be the most conscientious of chaperones if I gave you my permission to do such a thing. You are not a servant or nurse to handle such a task, and

I'm sure I needn't remind you that it is not at all proper for a gentleman who is not a relative to be alone with a young lady in her bedchamber."

"Ah, but I am practically a member of the family," he drawled in a nonchalant tone. "Or so your husband has claimed often enough. And when weighed against Lady Aimee's speedy recovery, the rules of propriety seem rather inconsequential. Wouldn't you agree?"

The countess crossed her arms and scrutinized him with an intensity that was unsettling, almost as if she were trying to read his very thoughts. After a lengthy span of silence, however, her countenance finally lightened and a glint of humor sparked in her eyes. "And you are so certain you can accomplish this feat, my lord? My sister has already chased off the most stalwart members of my staff. And after sitting up with her for most of the night, even Papa was cross by the time he departed for home this morning. I believe he was muttering something about the hangman's noose and charges of murder."

Royce cocked an eyebrow at her. "I have faced the worst that Boney's army had to offer, Lady Hawksley," he said dryly. "I think I can handle one slip of a girl."

"Very well. But should you need reinforcements, Hawksley and I will be downstairs."

"Are you trying to frighten me, my lady?"

"Is it working?"

"I suppose that remains to be seen."

The countess laughed, then inclined her head in approval before gesturing to the maid. "Hannah, give Lord Stonehurst the tray."

The maid handed over her burden without question, then dipped a quick curtsy before scurrying off down the corridor, as if afraid he would change his mind. Lady Hawksley followed her more sedately, after sending one last amused glance back at Royce over her shoulder.

And with a deep breath and a prayer for patience, he girded his loins and ventured forth to beard the lion in its den.

Clad in a high-necked morning gown of pale blue muslin that appeared to be a bit too large for her small frame, Aimee was seated on the four-poster bed, propped up against a mound of pillows. And as Royce had halfway expected, her nose was buried in the pages of a thick, dusty volume of poetry.

Pausing just inside the doorway, he watched her as she read, and a patch of sunlight from a nearby window spilled across her piquant face, lending her an almost ethereal quality. With the white bandage marring her temple and her light brown hair more loosely styled than usual, she looked soft and delicate and so very fragile . . .

"You know," she spoke up suddenly, startling him, "it's quite rude to enter someone's room without knocking." She peered over the top of her book, and he realized that she had been aware of his presence the whole time he'd been studying her. "It's also rude to stare."

So much for his fanciful musings. Caught off guard, he covered his disconcertment by returning her salvo. "And while we are on the subject of rudeness, I do believe that treating your family as if they were your own personal whipping boys would fall under that category as well."

When she flushed slightly and avoided his eyes, he knew his barb had struck its mark.

Leaving the door ajar behind him, he strode farther into the room and placed the tray he carried on the table next to the bed, then crossed his arms in a deliberately indolent pose. "Far be it from me to offer you advice, but you would make it much easier on yourself, not to mention everyone who is trying to help you recover, if you would simply cooperate."

"That is a matter of opinion," she sniffed as she cast him a wary glance. "What are you doing in here?"

"I told your sister that I would make sure that you ate your breakfast." Locking gazes with her, he leaned forward, injecting every ounce of his determination into his voice. "And you *will* eat, my girl, if I have to feed you myself."

"You wouldn't dare," she gasped, lowering her book and drawing herself up in haughty affront.

He braced both palms on the mattress and

closed the remaining distance between them, until his face was only inches away from hers. "Oh, I can assure you that I would dare almost anything. So I suggest that you take a moment to consider before you continue to argue with me."

The words were followed by a charged hush, and Royce felt a powerful surge of heat shoot through him when he became aware of just how close he was to her. Once again, he had put himself in a precarious position, for her nearness was wreaking havoc on his senses and bringing his body to pulsating life. Everything else slipped away, and all he could think about was tilting his head and capturing those tempting silken lips that were now on a level with his own, just as he had last night . . .

The memory of that kiss was a tangible entity, stirring the air around them. And there could be no denying that it was affecting Aimee as well. Royce could see it in the melting amber depths of her eyes.

Jerking away from her, he retreated to the foot of the bed and struggled to get himself back under control before he turned to address her again. "So, what is it to be, my lady?" he prompted gruffly.

Her lips tightened into a thin, bloodless line, and she made no reply. Just when he was beginning to think that he was going to have to follow through on his threat to feed her himself, however, she reached out, broke off a piece of toast, and shoved it in her mouth with very little finesse. Then she flounced back against her pillows, where she proceeded to chew while glaring at him.

With his stoic mask firmly in place, he sank into a nearby armchair and propped his elbows on his knees, regarding her over his steepled fingers as he contemplated how to phrase what he wanted to say next without antagonizing her even further.

"You know," he began, "I understand that you are angry with me and that you would like nothing better than to go home and forget that I exist. But is it fair to punish your family for things they are not responsible for? All they want is to make sure that you get better as quickly as possible, and your belligerent attitude is making them as miserable as you are."

There was a long pause as she stared down at her hands folded in her lap. "You are right, my lord," she finally acknowledged, her mutinous expression fading away, to be replaced by one of sincere contrition. "And I shall apologize to them the next time I see them."

Her immediate about-face flabbergasted Royce, but she didn't seem to notice his lack of response. She kept talking, as if now that the dam had broken, she couldn't stop the flow of words. "I do not mean to snap at them. I know they are only worried about me, and I know there is no excuse for my behavior. It's not at all like me to be so very disagreeable, but I—"

Breaking off, she bit her lip, obviously unable to go on. But there was no need for her to elaborate. He knew exactly what she had been going to say and finished for her. "You are overwhelmed by it all."

She nodded. "The nightmares. The accident last night. You. It's too much for me to cope with at once. It has turned me into some bad-tempered shrew that I don't even recognize, and I hate it."

"Which is why you should share your burdens, Aimee. With your sisters. Your father. The sooner you do, the sooner you can start putting all of this behind you."

"No. I can't do that, and you know why. I will get past this on my own. I must."

Royce stifled an aggravated oath at her fierce declaration. It appeared that there would be no swaying her from her resolve to handle everything herself. Her sheer stubbornness only made him even more grateful that she was here in her sister's house, where at least she would no longer be able to neglect her health. She needed someone to look after her, whether she wanted to admit it or not. And until she could be convinced to confide in someone else, it seemed he was the only person available to stand sentinel.

In any case, it was clear that any more prodding on his part would meet with little success, so he changed the subject. "How are you feeling this morning?"

"Sore, and I have a bit of a headache." She gingerly fingered her bandage. "Other than that, I am well enough."

"In your rather questionable opinion, you mean." When she stiffened at his comment, he held up a staying hand. "Wait. Believe it or not, I don't want to fight with you anymore. I know this is not the best of situations, but do you think for the sake of your family we could try to arrange some sort of truce? Just until you are well enough to go home? We are both adults, after all, and if we do our best to stay out of each other's way, surely we can manage for a few days."

After a surprisingly brief hesitation, she relented. "I suppose we could try. As you said, it is only for a few days. And it is not as if we—"

"Aunt Mee!"

It was a child's joyous greeting, and both Aimee and Royce whipped their heads in the direction of the door as Connor and Jillian Monroe's twin boys came bounding into the room.

Their mother was at their heels, pink-cheeked and breathless. "I tried to stop the little scamps from just bursting in," she told Aimee, sending Royce a quizzical glance before moving to stand next to the bed. "But they were very anxious to see their aunt after hearing about her ordeal. I had to promise to bring them over for a short visit first thing this morning so they could see for themselves that you were fine."

Royce watched as one of the boys clambered up beside Aimee and threw his arms around her neck in a tight hug. Whether it was Thane or Roderick, he couldn't be certain, as he had yet to figure out a way to distinguish one of the twins from the other.

"You fallded?" the little boy inquired, sounding horrified by the notion.

Aimee hugged him back, her countenance softening with affection. "Yes, I did, Thane. But I shall be right as rain before you know it. I only have a bit of a bump, that's all."

So that meant the twin standing next to Royce's chair and staring up at him with solemn eyes was Roderick. Or Roddy, as his family called him. "You were s'posed to catch her," the child informed him gravely. "Like before."

Royce felt his heart give a tug. "I know," he told the boy in an equally somber tone. "I'm afraid I was a little late this time. But I promise you, I won't be again."

His eyes met Aimee's over Roddy's head, rife with the vow he had just made, and the two of them were instantly swept up once again in the powerful undercurrent that arced between them.

After a few seconds, however, Jillian cleared her throat, breaking the spell.

"I see that you have been forced to borrow from Maura's wardrobe," she observed, indicating Aimee's gown as she perched on the edge of the mattress.

Aimee released her hold on her nephew and gave the ice-blue material of the ill-fitting dress a rueful grimace. "Yes, but Papa has promised to bring a few things from home later this afternoon. My gowns and some of my books and personal items. I will be glad when he does, for I dislike not having my things around me."

"Well . . ." Her sister looked back over her shoulder to crook her index finger at Roddy. "The boys have brought you something that I think will help with that a bit."

Roderick approached the bed, a smile wreathing his freckled face. Royce, who was still observing the proceedings, noticed for the first time that the child's arms were wrapped around a wriggling bundle that had been secreted within the folds of his shirt.

"We brought you a present, Aunt Mee," he announced, then deposited a ball of black and white fur on her lap.

"Your kitten!" Aimee cried, picking the creature up right away and cuddling it under her chin. She crooned to it as she ran her fingers over its small body in a soothing motion before giving a rueful quirk of her lips. "And none the worse for wear after yesterday's adventure, I see."

"His name is Mr. Tiddles now," Roddy informed her, scrambling up onto the bed to sit next to his brother.

"Why Mr. Tiddles?"

It was Thane who leaned in close to her and replied in a stage whisper, "'Cause he tiddled in Papa's best shoes this morning."

Aimee laughed, the musical sound arresting Royce with its note of pure joy. With her face lit up from within, no one watching her now would have ever described her as plain.

"So you decided it was best to remove him from Papa's vicinity, I take it?" She was ruffling the hair on each boy's head in turn, oblivious to his intent regard. "It is a lovely gesture, darlings, but I'm not sure your aunt Maura will want a kitten in the house."

"We checked with her first," Jillian assured her. "But the boys wanted to make sure that you had a friend to keep you company while you recover."

"You saved his life, Aunt Mee," the twins chorused together, their expressions earnest.

"That's rather overstating the case, I think. He saved his own life really. I was the one who made a fool of myself by falling out of the tree."

"Oh, I don't know about that," Royce interjected with a hint of humor. "If you hadn't climbed up after him, poor Mr. Tiddles might have never found the courage to get down. Why, he might have even been in that tree still."

Rising, he moved to the bed and lifted a hand to rub the kitten's pointed ear. Since its small head was cuddled to her chin, the edge of his thumb just brushed Aimee's cheek in a subtle caress.

Once, twice. She went utterly still, and he could feel her quivering as she peered up at him through a screen of lashes.

"You know," he went on, his voice low and velvet smooth, "in some cultures it is believed that when you save a life, it belongs to you."

Her mouth fell open, but no sound emerged. She simply stared at him, apparently as enraptured by the spell he wove with his words as he was by the feel of her smooth skin.

It took Jillian clearing her throat again to tear them both from their stupors, and Royce immediately stepped back from the bed, wondering what on earth had come over him. Every time he was around her, he found it harder to remember that he had to keep his hands off her. That there were reasons he couldn't touch her, hold her, kiss her . . .

He had to get out of here.

"Well, I suppose it is time for me to take my leave," he said gruffly, backing toward the door. "I have an appointment with my solicitor this morning, and several other errands to take care of before I depart for Stonecliff at the end of the week. If you will excuse me, ladies?"

And with that, he sketched a brief bow and departed the room as if the hounds of hell pursued him, counting himself lucky at his escape.

Chapter 9

"**W**ill that be all, my lady?"

At the diffident query, Aimee looked up from her quiet contemplation of her reflection in the vanity mirror to find the maid, Hannah, hovering at her elbow.

"Yes, thank you, Hannah," she said gently, offering the girl a kind smile. "You may go."

The servant didn't say anything further or even bid her good night, but simply bobbed a curtsy before hurrying from the bedchamber.

Obviously, poor Hannah hadn't quite recovered from their first encounter, Aimee mused with a rueful grimace as she turned back to the mirror and continued to absently plait her hair. Though she had tried to make up for her previous surliness, the maid still seemed inclined to walk on eggshells around her, and she supposed she couldn't blame the girl. Her behavior had been inexcusable. Never before had she let anger and frustration affect the way she treated those around her, and the fact that she had done so this time made her most wroth with herself.

A wave of guilt washing over her, she gave a long strand of hair a particularly vicious yank, then winced at the resulting twinge of soreness in her scalp. While still tender, the bump on her head appeared to be healing nicely, and just the day before, Dr. Merriman had declared her well on her way to recovery.

It had been nearly a week now since her fall down the stairs. In that time, the healthy color had returned to her cheeks and she had regained some of the weight she had lost in the weeks before her accident. She had also managed to get a few nights of dreamless sleep under Maura's watchful eye.

And of Stonehurst, she had seen very little.

Not that she had been watching for him, of course, she hastily assured herself. She couldn't help but notice his absence, however. The viscount had been out of the house by the time she rose each morning, ostensibly tending to his business affairs and meeting with his solicitor. Aside from passing her in the hallway once or twice and greeting her coolly at the few family dinners they had both attended, he had kept to his promise to stay out of her way. And though she knew that should make her happy, she found herself strangely piqued by it.

She thought back to the morning that he had shown up in her room, spouting dire threats should she not eat her breakfast and generally behaving like an autocratic tyrant. He had infuriated her. But in the next instant, his titillating touch had made her forget all the reasons she had to be angry with him.

It seemed that no matter how furious she got with him, she couldn't control her body's response to his overwhelming magnetism.

Stifling a sigh, she finished braiding her hair and rose from the cushioned vanity stool to wander over to the bed. Her father had promised her that she could go home on the morrow, and she was most anxious to do so. Though her nightmares had not troubled her nearly as often during her stay in her sister's house, they hadn't gone away completely. And she still had no idea what they were trying to tell her. They had revealed nothing more, for all she kept seeing was the same set of garbled images over and over.

As she pulled back the covers, a plaintive meow had her stifling a laugh, and she lifted her nephews' kitten from his nest against her fluffed-up pillows to nuzzle him with her nose. "I'm sorry, Mr. Tiddles," she told him softly. "I'm afraid that's my spot. But there is plenty of room for both of us, so try not to be too cross with me."

She lifted the lacy hem of her white cambric nightgown and climbed onto the high mattress, settling down with a sound of contentment. It was a warm night, and she had left the balcony doors on the far side of the room open so that the slight breeze wafting into the room could cool her skin. The moon shone in through the sheer draperies, but its bright light didn't bother her. In fact, she had found that its illumination often helped to ease her into sleep, as it eliminated the looming shadows that usually crowded around her bed. Thus reassured, and with Mr. Tiddles curled against her side, it wasn't long before she drifted off . . .

And began to dream.

Once again, she stood in that familiar darkened hallway, her heart galloping in her chest as she peered in through the crack in the library door at the terrifying scene unfolding before her. Her mother was facing the French doors, her ashen, tearstained face rife with alarm as she attempted to hold off the man who confronted her.

"Please," Lady Albright was saying, obviously shaken despite her effort to speak in a calm, even tone. "I am sorry if I have hurt you as you say, but I didn't know—"

"You knew," the man interrupted savagely, taking a threatening step forward. "I told you of my feelings for you, and you laughed as if it were all some sort of joke."

"You were so young. I thought it was simply an infatuation and that you would soon forget all about it." The marchioness gave a helpless shake of her head. "Obviously, I was wrong. But you must see that this won't solve anything."

"It doesn't matter!" An underlying thread of torment laced the man's words, and the weapon visibly trembled in his hand, though it remained leveled on its target. "Can't you understand that I don't have a choice? It's all gone too far for me to go back now. Watching you with my father was bad enough, but seeing you with Hawksley is killing me. I have to get you out of my head. I have to make it stop."

He paused, and when he continued it was with a note of unmistakable resolve. "You have to die."

The threat was enough to jolt Aimee from her petrified stupor. Galvanized into action, she shoved aside her trepidation and threw herself into the room, teeth bared and fists clenched. "Don't you hurt my mama!"

There was an instant of stunned silence as two pairs of eyes swung in her direction.

"Aimee!" the marchioness gasped, her expression one of horrified dismay. But when she whirled about as if to go to her daughter, the man brought her to a halt with a single, sharp gesture of his free hand.

"Well, what have we here?" His laughter was loud and grating and held a vaguely maniacal edge. "It seems you have a mouse in the house, my lady. Perhaps I should dispose of it for you."

The next thing Aimee knew, she was staring down the barrel of his pistol.

"Please, don't!" Lady Albright's distraught entreaty rang out in the stillness, fraught with anguish and alarm. "Don't hurt her. She's just a little girl."

"A little girl who has seen and heard too much," the

man informed her grimly. "I can't leave any witnesses, now can I?"

The marchioness wrung her hands. The very real fear that swam in the depths of her amber eyes made a knot of dread tighten in the pit of Aimee's stomach. Never could she remember seeing her mother look so scared, and that alone was enough to increase her own terror tenfold.

After a second or two, however, Lady Albright managed to recover herself enough to send her daughter a reassuring glance. Then, pasting on a tremulous smile, she turned and addressed the man in a low, surprisingly sultry voice that was so at odds with the anxiety that had lurked in her gaze that it shocked Aimee. "If I were you, I wouldn't be so rash, my lord. There are other, far more appealing alternatives open to you. You have said that you love me. That you only ever wanted to be with me. If that's true, then I have a suggestion."

"And that would be?"

"We can go away together. Just the two of us. Begin a new life somewhere else."

He started, cocking his head. His eyes, predatory and glittering, were the only part of him that Aimee could clearly discern in the dimness. "You would do that? Leave with me and never return?"

Her manner one of deliberate carelessness, the marchioness lifted a shoulder with studied nonchalance. "Why not? After all, it is not as if the life I am living now has made me so very happy. My husband is a pontificating bore who never wants me to have any fun.

And it is beyond me what sort of woman would actually choose to be weighed down by the tiresome burden of motherhood. Such a tedious existence might be enough for someone else, but it will never be enough for me."

Lady Albright's scornful tone stabbed at Aimee like the sharpest of knives, and she gaped up at the woman who had given her life in disbelief. Why was Mama saying such awful things? She wouldn't leave them. She wouldn't!

But the conversation went on, every word that spilled from the marchioness's mouth an indictment. "We'll go now. Tonight. Then the only thing the child is a witness to is the fact that her mother chose to run away with another man. She is nothing to worry about. A mouse, as you said. No one will pay her any mind."

"What about Hawksley?"

"I tried to explain to you that Hawksley means nothing to me. Perhaps you will see now that I was telling the truth."

Once again, the pistol wavered in the man's grip. "That's not part of the plan," he insisted. But to Aimee he sounded less than sure of himself.

"Plans can change." Lady Albright sidled a bit closer to him, peering up at him from under her lashes in a coy fashion. "Come now. You can't really want to see me dead. Wouldn't you much rather have me all to yourself?"

He hesitated for what seemed like a small eternity, then slowly began to lower the pistol.

And Aimee panicked. She didn't want to believe it,

but she couldn't deny what she had just heard, and her sense of betrayal was staggering. Mama was really going to do it. She was really going to walk out that door with this man and leave everyone who loved her behind.

Tears of pain and anger misting her vision, she reacted without thinking, flying at the monster who wanted to steal her mother away from her and attacking him with flailing fists. "I won't let you take my mama!"

From that point on, everything happened as if in slow motion. There was another flare of lightning, and the man shoved her away, lifting his weapon once more. At the same time, the marchioness gave a choked cry and lunged forward, throwing herself between her daughter and the pistol.

The blast of a gunshot reverberated off the walls.

Aimee halted in her tracks, a cry of denial escaping her as she saw her mother flinch and go limp, collapsing like a puppet with its strings cut. The sight filled her with the sickening urge to retch, and the room began to spin like a top around her. But even as her mind retreated from what she had just witnessed and everything started to go black, she caught a brief glimpse of something over the man's shoulder that only added to her state of stunned horror. Suddenly a loud hissing sound filled her ears, and she realized she couldn't breathe . . .

She jolted awake, only to become aware that the hissing sound was coming from Mr. Tiddles, who had jumped onto the nearby window ledge and was bristling with feline ferocity, the hair on his back sticking up in stiff spikes of indignation.

And she really couldn't breathe.

Something had hold of her throat in a viselike grip, closing off her windpipe and inhibiting the flow of air to her lungs. And it was only as her eyes began to adjust a bit that the dark figure bending over her began to take shape in the moonlit room.

"You must forget," a voice whispered, the words resonating with an edge of silken menace. "Do you hear me? Whatever you have remembered, you must forget. Or I can promise you that your nightmares will be the least of your worries. And you won't live to tell the tale."

A pillow was slammed over her face, and she began to fight in earnest.

Slumped in the armchair next to his bed, Royce gazed unseeingly through the window at the smattering of stars that twinkled against the velvety black backdrop of the sky. It was well past midnight, and the house had long ago grown quiet and still. But after spending the past several evenings staring at the ceiling, unable to drift off no matter how hard he tried, he had learned from experience that there would be little if any rest for him.

Despite his best efforts to wipe her from his mind, it seemed that there was nothing that would serve to distract him from his obsession with the alluring young woman who occupied the guest room next door.

While he had done a quite thorough job of avoiding Aimee in the flesh for the past week, she was still all he could think about. During the day, when he was absent from the Hawksley town house and should have been concentrating on other things, he found himself going over everything that had happened between them in his head, reliving every detail of the passionate kiss they had shared. And at night, the few hours of slumber he did manage to achieve were beset by terrifying dreams in which he watched helplessly as she tumbled down a steep flight of stairs and landed in a crumpled heap at the bottom. When he ran to her and lifted her in his arms, it was to discover that it was no longer Aimee, but Cordelia. Cordelia with her eyes wide open and glazed and her neck bent at an unnatural angle, just as it had been when he had dragged her body from the wreckage of his brother's phaeton on that afternoon so many years ago.

Needless to say, the lack of sleep had left him feeling decidedly on edge. Tomorrow, however, should see an end to his torment. His business in London was concluded, and he planned on departing for Stonecliff first thing in the morning. As much as he had appreciated the chance to catch up with Hawksley, it would be a relief to return home. His remote and sprawling estate in

Cornwall, nestled along the craggy coastline, was the one place he truly felt comfortable and free to lower his defenses.

And maybe once he put a few hundred miles between himself and Aimee, he would finally be able to forget her.

Shifting in his seat, he reached up to pinch the bridge of his nose with a weary exhalation. Tomorrow promised to be a long day, and he wanted to make an early start. It wouldn't do at all for him to begin such a grueling journey already exhausted. Perhaps if he lay down and forced himself to clear his head of everything else, he would eventually doze off, if only for an hour or two.

Just as he made a move to stand, however, a slight sound penetrated his sleep-deprived senses, bringing his head up and his eyes shooting in the direction of the wall that separated him from Aimee. He had turned into such a mother hen of late when it came to her that every noise that drifted from the other side of the wall left him waiting with bated breath until he was certain that she was all right.

But this wasn't nearly as innocuous as the usual muffled footstep or creak of her bed. It was little more than a faint disturbance of the air, but for some reason it sent a chill up his spine, raising his hackles and bringing him to instant alertness. And when it came again, he realized why.

It was a choked feminine scream.

With a speed he hadn't even known he was capable of exhibiting, he flew out into the hallway, not even bothering to knock before flinging open the door to Aimee's room and barging over the threshold. Due to the moonlight spilling in through the open balcony doors, the interior of the chamber was almost as bright as day, and there was no way he could miss seeing the male figure bending over the bed.

The male figure who was pinning Aimee's struggling form to the mattress as he attempted to smother her with a pillow.

A low growl rumbled up from Royce's throat, and his hackles rose as an all-consuming wave of fury washed over him. Strong, hot, and pulsing, it misted his vision with the red haze of anger, blinding him to everything except the driving need to eliminate the threat.

He lunged forward. But before he could cross the room, the intruder bolted, releasing his grip on the pillow and hurdling over the bed to vanish onto the balcony.

Not about to let him get away, Royce followed close behind, just in time to see him scramble over the railing with the skill and precision of an experienced second-story man. Swinging away from the building, Aimee's attacker jumped the last few feet to the ground before scaling the town house's rear gate and scurrying off into the darkness of the mews.

Damnation! Royce pounded an impotent fist against the railing. If he had been just one second sooner, he would have had the bastard! Thwarted rage coursed through his veins, and that dark, feral part of him shifted like a caged panther within, prodding him to leap off the balcony himself and take off in pursuit, to track the man down and tear him apart with his bare hands.

"Stonehurst?"

Aimee's hoarse croak brought him back to his senses, and he exerted every bit of willpower he could muster to tamp the lid back down on his swiftly rising anger. He couldn't lose control in front of her. And he couldn't leave her. Not now.

Entering the room once more, he approached the bed and slowly sat down on the edge of the mattress, his assessing gaze skimming over her, searching for any visible signs of injury. She was curled into a ball, her soft brown hair coming loose from its waist-length plait and her white nightgown gaping at the neck to reveal the pale, smooth curve of her shoulder. Her expression was so very shaken and vulnerable that nothing could have kept him from reaching for her. Not even his vow to keep his hands off her.

Gathering her close, he pressed her face into his neck and closed his eyes, savoring the feel of her against him and taking comfort in the knowledge that she was safe and whole in his arms. Never before had he felt such fear or such an instinct to protect, though he couldn't quite bring himself to examine the reasons too closely.

"Shhh," he soothed, smoothing back the wisps of hair that had fallen into her face with one hand as he stroked her back with the other. He could feel her trembling, and it only roused his wrath against the unknown assailant even more for daring to put his filthy hands on her. But he managed to smother the spark of temper as he continued speaking to her, trying to calm her with his reassuring tone. "It's all right. I've got you. I've got you and no one is going to hurt you. I promise."

"Stonehurst."

"Shhh."

"No, Stonehurst, you must listen to me." Aimee's voice rose unexpectedly in volume, still sounding vaguely raspy, and she pushed away from him, lifting her head so that she could meet his gaze. "I had another dream."

He frowned at her, more than a bit disgruntled by her insistence on relating this tale at a time like this. "Aimee, as troubling as your nightmares have been, I think there are far more important matters we should be concerned with right now. In case you didn't notice, someone just tried to kill you. We need to alert your family and fetch the watch as well as your physician—"

"No, you don't understand," she interrupted him, her hands clutching at the material of his shirt as if desperately trying to convey the importance of what she had to say. "I saw more this time. Something I've never seen in my dreams before."

"What?"

"A face. I saw a face looking in through the French doors behind Lord Stratton just as the gun went off. It was blurry and I couldn't quite make out who it was, but there was someone else there. I know it."

Aimee paused, licking her lips, then went on in a rush, as if she needed to get the words out before she could think better of it. "And the man tonight. He said . . . He told me I had to forget. That I had to forget whatever I had remembered or I wouldn't live to tell the tale. I think . . . I think it must be somehow tied in with my dreams."

Royce's grip on her arms tightened as what she was telling him began to sink in. By Christ, he had known that these bloody nightmares of hers were an ill omen. He should have listened to his instincts and gone to her father with the information from the very beginning. "Goddamn it all to hell!"

She winced, but did not let his venom deter her. "That's not all," she said softly, reluctantly. "The other night, I don't think that I just lost my balance and fell down the stairs. I'm almost certain now that someone pushed me. That someone was trying to kill me then too."

A roaring filled Royce's ears as he fought to hold

on to his equilibrium. Someone had tried to kill her. Not just once, but twice. And if that person had succeeded, Royce would have been the one to blame. He had let pleas to keep her secret sway him into going against his better judgment. But not anymore.

Releasing her, he rose to his feet, his eyes never leaving hers. "That's it," he gritted out from between clenched teeth. "It's time to tell your family everything. Now."

Chapter 10

"I just don't understand why you didn't come to me with this."

Perched on the edge of the same striped damask sofa where she had been lying when she had returned to consciousness after her fall several evenings ago, Aimee balled her hands into tight fists in her lap and peered apprehensively up at her father. He was pacing before her, his mouth set in a grim line and his features drawn into a taut mask of anxiety.

It was an expression that was all too familiar to his daughters, for it was identical to the one he had worn in the days immediately following the murder of their mother.

This was all her fault, Aimee thought miserably. She was the one responsible for bringing that look to his face, and she hated herself for it.

With a heavy heart, she glanced around the parlor at the other members of her family. They had gathered together this morning in response to Lord Albright's urgent summons, and though they had all remained quiet as Aimee had told them about her recent dreams and related the tale of last night's intruder, their concern was obvious. If only there had been some way to keep from dragging the people she loved into this terrible mess. But after what had happened, involving them could no longer be avoided.

She had almost been killed. And if it hadn't been for Stonehurst, she would have been.

Out of the corner of her eye, she studied the viscount surreptitiously. He stood just a few feet away, arms crossed as he observed the proceedings with his typical stoic mien. Aimee was well aware, however, that he was far more affected than he pretended to be. When he had unexpectedly taken her in his arms after chasing her assailant away the evening before, she had been in a state of shock, unable to process much of anything except the warmth of his embrace and the fact that she was safe. But after a second or two, she had realized that she could hear his heart pounding like a drum in his chest, could feel the tremor of his hands as they stroked her hair and smoothed over her back, and the telltale signs of his fear for her had left her stunned.

No one looking at him now, however, would ever guess that his dispassionate demeanor went only skin-deep.

At that moment, Lord Albright drew her attention back to him by coming to an abrupt halt and pivoting on his heel to confront her, his troubled gaze meeting hers.

"Aimee, you know how much I love you and your sisters," he said softly, earnestly. "You are all I have left of your mother, and if anything ever happened to any of you . . ." He reached up to rake a hand back through his thick mane of graying hair, then sank down on the sofa next to her as if his legs refused to hold him upright any longer. "You should have told me what was going on."

A lump of raw emotion clogged her throat at his words, and she had to swallow several times to clear it away before she could speak. "I couldn't, Papa. I didn't want to worry you. And I thought they were only bad dreams. That I could cope with them myself."

"Even so. I deserved to know what you were going through. And evidently they are more than just bad dreams if someone is trying to kill you over them."

"But I didn't suspect that until last night. The evening of the dinner party I was so tired and confused, I couldn't be sure of anything. I never felt anyone actually push me, so I convinced myself that I was imagining it all."

"You didn't imagine those bruises around your neck."

This came from Stonehurst, whose hooded stare never wavered from the livid black and blue marks that marred the creamy skin of her throat. She traced them gingerly with her fingertips, then gave the lace ruff of her collar a self-conscious tug, disconcerted by his intent regard.

"No," she conceded. "But aside from what my instincts tell me, we still have no proof that the two incidents are even related. At least nothing that the law would consider to be at all convincing."

A muscle leaped in the viscount's squared jaw. "It seems a rather logical conclusion though, does it not?" Without giving her a chance to reply, he turned to address her father. "I must apologize again, Albright, for not informing you of all of this when Lady Aimee first confided in me. I—"

"Nonsense." The marquis cut him off with an upraised hand. "No apologies are necessary, Stonehurst. I know my little mouse better than she thinks. She may seem meek and biddable, but underneath it all, she is more stubborn than both of my other girls put together. I doubt there was any gainsaying her." He arched a brow and eyed his youngest daughter shrewdly. "And it sounds as if she wasn't entirely forthcoming with you about the matter."

"No, she wasn't," Stonehurst acknowledged in a clipped tone, his glittering gaze once again pinning Aimee in place. "I can assure you, if I'd had the slightest inkling that someone had deliberately pushed her down those stairs, she would have come to you with the information at once. I would have seen to it."

Aimee bristled, not only at being discussed as if she weren't even there, but at his high-handed declaration. The man seemed to be under the mistaken impression that he had the right to govern her actions, and she would have loved to disabuse him of the notion. However, her family's presence in the room kept her silent.

It was Connor who finally brought an end to the tension-riddled stillness that hung over them all. "This face you saw in your nightmare . . . You have no idea who it was?"

Grateful for the chance to concentrate on something else besides Stonehurst's fierce glower, Aimee faced Jillian's husband and shook her head. "It happened so fast, and I couldn't see clearly. I woke up before I could bring all of the details into focus."

"Could it have been my father?" This question came from Hawksley, who was leaning against the ornamented back of the gilt-edged love seat where Maura sat on the far side of the parlor, his forehead furrowed in brooding consideration. "We know that he was drawn here by the letter Stratton forged with your mother's signature, so it is feasible that he showed up while Stratton was still here."

"I don't think so. I can't be certain, of course, but it didn't appear to be."

There was another short hush. Then Lord Albright suddenly pounded a fist against the arm of the sofa, making everyone jump in alarm.

"By damn, just how many people were skulking about my house that evening?" he barked. "Hawksley. Stratton. And now we find out that someone else was there as well? How is it that half of London apparently showed up at my door, yet no one saw a thing?"

Racked with guilt at the pain her revelation was causing him, Aimee watched as Jillian left the circle of Connor's arm to move forward and lay a comforting hand on their father's shoulder. "Papa, there was a terrible storm that night, and it was quite late," she told him gently. "It's not surprising that no one saw anything. And you have to calm down. Working yourself into a fit isn't going to do anyone any good at this point."

He expelled a harsh breath and slumped back in his seat, looking frail beyond his years. "I know. It's just that I believed that all of this was finished and that your mother could finally rest in peace. To discover after all of this time that there was yet someone else who might have been involved only opens the door to more questions." Lifting a hand, he pinched the bridge of his nose in a weary gesture. "At the very least, this person was a witness to the crime and never came forward to clear the late Lord Hawksley's name, and at the worst . . ."

His voice trailed off, but there was no need for him to go on. Aimee knew exactly what he'd been going to say. There was a distinct possibility that whoever had been lurking outside that evening might have been an accomplice to the crime.

"This is utterly preposterous."

The snapped statement had heads swinging in the direction of the rigid figure seated on the love seat next to Maura. Lady Olivia had said very little since she had arrived with Lord Albright several hours ago and was the only one in the group who had not displayed any sort of visible reaction to Aimee's story. But her expression now clearly reflected her opinion on the matter as she surveyed first Aimee, then her brother with more than a hint of condescension.

"Really, Philip, I'm sure I don't see how you can take such rubbish seriously," she chided, her lips pursed in disdain. "There is no proof that these so-called memories of Aimee's are anything more than nightmare-induced delusions." She gave a curt shrug. "The very idea that anyone else was there is absurd. Stratton confessed, and he certainly never implicated anyone else. The girl's head is muddled, that's all."

Stung by the way her aunt so coldly dismissed all that she had suffered in the past few weeks, Aimee lifted her chin, prepared to defend herself. To her surprise, however, Stonehurst leaped into the breach before she could even open her mouth.

"Then how do you explain the attempts on her life, my lady?" he demanded, leveling the woman with a fierce frown. "Someone has tried to kill her. Not once, but twice. And her attacker last night came right out and warned her to forget whatever she has remembered. I'd say that's reason enough to take all of this *rubbish*, as you call it, quite seriously."

"Indeed." Portly and balding, Morton Tolliver strode into the parlor unannounced, his ruddy face creased with grave solemnity and his curly-brimmed beaver tucked under one arm. "Most definitely reason enough."

A longtime friend of the marquis, Tolliver had been the first person Lord Albright had contacted upon learning what had happened to his daughter, and the man had shown up close on the heels of the rest of the family early that morning, offering to do whatever he could to help. Following the disbandment of the Bow Street offices and the formation of the Metropolitan Police a few years before, the former Runner had opened his own investigative agency, and upon his arrival at the Hawksley town house, he had immediately set about using his considerable sleuthing skills to ferret out what he could from the officers who were poring over the scene.

"Tolliver." Rising swiftly, Lord Albright crossed the room to meet the other man halfway. "What have you been able to find out?"

"Not much, I'm afraid." Tolliver grimaced. "I have just finished speaking with the officer in charge of the investigation, and he seems convinced that this was only a random burglary gone awry. His men have given the bedchamber and the balcony a rather cursory examination, and they are questioning the staff even as we speak, but it is very unlikely that they will pursue the search much further. As the suspect took nothing from the premises and they are lacking a detailed description to work with, capturing him doesn't appear to rate very highly on the law's list of priorities."

Her father turned such an alarming shade of red that Aimee was certain he was going to have the apoplexy. "The monster attacked my daughter! What more do they need in order to *make* it a priority?"

Tolliver briefly clasped the marquis's shoulder. "I'm sorry, Albright. I wish I had better news to report. But regardless of what the law believes, I am at your disposal for as long as you need me. I promise you, I will get to the bottom of things, no matter what it takes." He glanced over at Stonehurst and Aimee, his gaze penetrating. "Are the two of you certain there isn't anything else you can tell me about the intruder? Nothing that stands out in your minds about him at all?"

Shuddering, Aimee flashed back to the instant she had awakened to find that dark shadow looming over her. She could still feel his hands wrapped around her neck, choking her, cutting off her air, and it filled her with a rising sense of terror, freezing her tongue.

As if sensing her inability to reply, the viscount startled her by subtly shifting his big body a bit closer to her, moving so that he stood next to the arm of the sofa. The warmth that vibrated off him surrounded her, making her feel unaccountably safe, and she gave a thankful inward sigh when he responded to the query for both of them. "He wore a long coat with the collar pulled up and a cap angled low over his face. Even with all of the moonlight flooding the room, I couldn't see his features. He was tall and wiry, and that's all I could make out."

Tolliver was quiet for a moment as he mulled things over, then advanced toward the sofa, coming to a halt before Aimee and peering down at her with compassionate brown eyes. "Lady Aimee," he addressed her kindly. "You say this man knew about your resurfacing recollections of your mother's murder. How is it that he could have come by such knowledge?"

She bit her lip. That was something she had been wondering herself, and she had yet to come up with any answers. "I don't know. I never spoke about my dreams aloud to anyone until I confided in Lord Stonehurst the night of the dinner party."

"Then if His Lordship shared that information with no one else, there is only one other solution. Someone must have overheard your conversation."

At Tolliver's words, Aimee stiffened and glanced up at the viscount. The stony cast of his features told her that he was thinking exactly the same thing she was. The two of them had been so involved in their heated discussion that evening that anyone could have wandered out into the garden and stumbled upon them, and neither of them would have been any the wiser. Why, her aunt had approached them and had practically been right under their noses before they had even taken note of her presence, so it was entirely possible that someone else could have been lurking in the shadows, eavesdropping on them without their knowledge.

The thought of it sent a shiver up Aimee's spine.

Tolliver was still talking, one pudgy finger stroking his chin in thought as he stared off into space. "I suspect that the man last night was a mere underling, hired to do the job by the real culprit."

Lord Albright spoke up from behind his friend. "What are you saying?"

"I'm saying that I don't think it is mere coincidence that the first attempt on Lady Aimee's life took place at that dinner party."

Aimee felt Stonehurst tense next to her. "You think someone who was here that night has something to hide." It wasn't a question, and the words held a chilling edge of menace.

From the other side of the parlor, Maura made a sound of protest. "But that's impossible!" she exclaimed. "The only ones in attendance were family and close friends."

"Exactly." Tolliver sent a narrow-eyed look around the room at large.

It was at that point that Lady Olivia surged to her feet, her cheeks ashen. "How dare you? That is beyond ridiculous! Why, no one we know—"

"Hush, Olivia!" Lord Albright's sharp admonition cut her off mid-tirade, and she subsided as he turned back to the former Runner. "Go on, Tolliver."

"If we rule out everyone in this room, who does that leave? Who else was invited to the party?"

"Maura kept the guest list quite small." Jillian's tone was subdued as she leaned against her husband, who had strode forward to join her next to the sofa. "The Dowager Duchess and the Duke of Maitland, Lord Bedford, and Violet Lafleur."

"It couldn't have been the dowager duchess or Miss Lafleur," Stonehurst asserted. "I saw the two of them talking to Monroe in the drawing room when I came in from the garden."

"That's right," Connor confirmed. "They never left the room the whole time."

"And what about Bedford and Maitland?"

Tolliver's inquiry flung Aimee back in time to her mad flight from the garden, when she had dashed up the steps to the terrace to find two male figures leaning against the balustrade in the darkness, smoking cheroots.

"They were outside," she whispered.

Stonehurst's head whipped in her direction, his eyes piercing her like knife blades. "What?"

"The baron and the duke. I passed them on the terrace as I was returning to the town house. I thought they both looked at me rather oddly as I went by, but neither of them said anything. What with all of the chaos surrounding my accident afterward, I forgot about it."

"So it is conceivable that they might have been privy to your revelation," Tolliver mused. "Though Maitland seems an unlikely suspect. There is no motivation there that I can see. Bedford, however . . ." He paused, lowering his brows in contemplation. "I'm sure none of us have forgotten that his prior association with Lady Albright once placed him on the initial list of suspects. Perhaps we were too quick to absolve him of any involvement in the marchioness's death after Stratton's confession."

"No!"

Her eyes flashing with diamond-hard brilliance, Lady Olivia came sweeping across the room toward them like a ship at full sail, obviously in high dudgeon. Drawing up short before Tolliver, she jabbed an accusing finger at him and leveled him with an enraged look.

"You odious little toad!" she hissed. "I won't let you do it, do you hear me? I won't let you condemn an innocent man!"

Aimee gaped at her aunt, startled by her outpouring of venom on Lord Bedford's behalf. Apparently the woman cared far more for the baron than she had ever let on.

"Even if someone else *was* there that night," Olivia continued furiously, poking her finger at Tolliver with each reproachful word, as if to emphasize her point, "it could have been anyone. A servant or someone passing by on the street. You can't have a person arrested merely on the strength of—"

"That's enough, Olivia!" Seizing his sister by her arms, Lord Albright pulled her a short distance away from Tolliver and gave her a little shake. "You must calm down. It's not as if we have proclaimed the baron's guilt and plan on throwing him in a cell at Newgate at any moment. But we have to examine every possibility. Especially when Aimee's life could be at stake."

"Yes." Clearly flustered by Olivia's attack, Tolliver tugged at the lapels of his coat, clearing his throat before going on in a gruff tone, "Well, in any case, I think it would be best for all concerned if we could spirit Lady Aimee away for a short while. Get her out of the city while we look into the matter."

The marquis gave an approving nod. "An excellent suggestion."

Overwhelming panic washed over Aimee at her father's agreement. Leave her family now, when they needed one another more than ever? She wouldn't do it! "No, Papa. I deserve to be a part of this too. I want to stay and help you."

Lord Albright released his hold on a still-fuming Lady Olivia and moved back to the sofa to lay a hand on Aimee's shoulder. "Mouse, please. That monster attacked you right here in your sister's own home. How can I rest easy when I am constantly worrying about the possibility that he may strike again?" He shook his head. "I'm sorry, but I can't take the chance. Once I can be assured that you are safely out of harm's way, I will be better able to focus on getting to the bottom of things once and for all."

"But where can we send her, Papa?" Jillian asked. "Surely Albright Hall would be too obvious a choice, and it is so large and sprawling, it wouldn't be very easily defended. The same can be said for Hawksley's country estate."

"What about Stonecliff?"

Lord Hawksley's suggestion was met with a

vast array of reactions. Lady Olivia gasped and seemed to go even paler, while the marquis frowned and appeared to be mulling over the notion. Everyone else went still, as if awaiting Lord Albright's verdict.

As for Aimee, she felt herself go numb all over, her fingers digging into her knees through the material of her morning gown as she sat in paralyzed dismay. Truly, things were getting worse with every second that passed. They actually expected her to let herself be locked away in virtual seclusion with the very man who had such a dangerous effect on her deepest emotions and her peace of mind? Why, just the idea was enough to fill her with trepidation.

She'd had a hard enough time controlling her body's response to him in the last few days, when there had been plenty of other people around to act as a buffer between them. How on earth was she to keep behaving as if he meant nothing to her if she was forced into such close and continued proximity to him?

Out of the corner of her eye, she took note of Stonehurst's severe countenance. He looked almost as unhappy as she felt. His hands were fisted at his sides, and his spine was so ramrod straight that she was sure it was going to snap in two.

"I don't think that's a good idea," he finally said aloud, sounding as if he were gritting the words out through clenched teeth.

Lord Hawksley narrowed his eyes, surveying his friend with interest. "Why not? It seems like the perfect solution to me. It's peaceful, remote, and about as far from London as one can get without leaving England's shores or heading for the Scottish border. And with the walls of the estate on one side and the natural barrier of the cliffs and the sea on the other, the house is practically a fortress."

"Which is precisely why it is no place for a young woman. Lady Aimee isn't used to that sort of isolation. She will be bored to tears outside of a week. And I am not the most sociable or genial of hosts."

"We're asking you to look after her, Stonehurst, not to entertain her." The earl left Maura's side to cross the room and clap the other man on the back in a gesture of easy camaraderie. "And in that respect, I have every faith that she will be well protected."

Stonehurst cast a quick, indecipherable glance in Aimee's direction, his gaze locking with hers fleetingly. "I wouldn't be so sure," he muttered under his breath.

She seemed to be the only one who heard him, however.

The Marquis of Albright, who had been pacing before them, hands clasped behind his back, abruptly whirled, the matter apparently decided as far as he was concerned. "Stonehurst, I would consider it a personal favor. You know how much my daughters mean to me, and you are one of the few men I would trust to see to Aimee's safety."

When the viscount remained silent, the marquis took a step toward him, his expression beseeching. "Please. I cannot lose one of my girls. I ask you in the name of our friendship."

Not even the hardest of individuals could have denied such a request. After a second, Stonehurst grimaced and inclined his head in grudging assent. "Very well."

"Thank you. I know that she will be in good hands with you."

Giving the other occupants of the room his back, the viscount strode over to stand before the parlor window, staring out through the lacy curtains at the bustling environs of Grosvenor Square. Watching him, Aimee could feel the tension coming off him in palpable waves.

"Before all of this happened, I had planned to depart for Stonecliff first thing this morning," he said over his shoulder without turning around. "Obviously it is too late for that, but I should still like to get under way as soon as possible."

"The sooner, the better," Lord Albright agreed. "We'll need to make a few arrangements and pack up Aimee's belongings, but that shouldn't take long. Hopefully you'll be able to set off without too much of a delay. Will tomorrow morning suffice?"

Aimee buried her face in her hands. Her whole life was being decided around her, and as usual she was just letting it happen. But what else could she do? She certainly couldn't explain to her father why she was so reluctant to go with Stonehurst. So it seemed she was left with no recourse other than to give in gracefully.

In the meantime, her father was carrying on as if she had never even offered a word of protest, issuing instructions right and left. "Tolliver, if you could provide me with a few of your most trustworthy men, I would be willing to pay them quite handsomely to ride along on the journey. Just as a bit of added protection and to lend their aid should Stonehurst require it. And of course, Olivia will go along as well—"

"No, I will not."

The unequivocal declaration had all eyes flying in Lady Olivia's direction.

She stood with hands propped on her hips, glaring at her brother in seething resentment. "I am tired of having my life turned upside down and disrupted because of Elise," she spat. "The woman is dead and still she manages to cause trouble for this family at every turn. Well, no longer. I refuse to be banished to the wilds of Cornwall for who knows how long while you comb the city in search of some fictional accomplice to Stratton's crime. And I will not change my mind, Philip, so don't even think of trying. If you insist on wasting your time in such a fruitless endeavor, you can do it without me."

With that, she marched from the room, leaving an awkward hush in her wake.

"What will we do now, Papa?" Maura ventured after a long moment, biting her lip. "Aimee cannot accompany the viscount to Stonecliff without some sort of chaperone."

The spark of hope her sister's words ignited within Aimee was immediately extinguished when the marquis lifted his chin in determination.

"Then we shall have to put our heads together and come up with another solution," he said, his voice rife with resolve. "She simply cannot remain here. I would never forgive myself if . . ."

When he trailed off, Jillian moved around the sofa to tuck her arm through his. "It's all right, Papa. We'll think of something. If Aunt Olivia won't come around, perhaps Connor and I could go. Or Maura and Hawksley. I'm sure they would love the chance to visit Stonecliff."

Her fingers twining nervously in her lap, Aimee watched as Lord Albright shared a veiled look with first one son-in-law, then the other, before dismissing his eldest daughter's suggestion. "I will more than likely need Connor and Hawksley to assist Tolliver and myself in our investigative endeavors. And you and Maura have your children to think about." He shook his head, a purposeful light entering his eyes. "We shall have to think of another alternative, and I do believe I already have someone else in mind."

So it seemed her fate was sealed, Aimee fumed. She was to be sent away, regardless of her wishes, and the fact left her feeling hurt and resentful. As much as she loved her father and realized he was only thinking of her welfare, she couldn't help but wonder if he would have done the same thing if it had been Jilly or Maura who had wound up in this situation.

She is nothing to worry about. A mouse, as you said. No one will pay her any mind.

Her mother's dismissive words from last night's dream echoed in her head, but she shrugged them off as the others set about making plans and turned her head to glance over at Lord Stonehurst. He was still standing in profile to her, his gaze focused on the view beyond the window glass. But as if he felt the weight of her stare, he suddenly looked back over his shoulder, his gaze colliding with hers with a stunning and almost physical force that practically knocked the breath from her. The turmoil she could see roiling in the depths of his eyes told her in no uncertain terms that she wasn't the only one who had been left reeling by this tangle.

For an unknown length of time, they were going to be forced to coexist in close proximity, side by side on a remote estate where there would be no one to act as a mediator should things spiral out of control.

She could only pray that the two of them would survive the experience.

Chapter 11

"**M**y dear child, I simply cannot fathom why you look as if you are being led to the gallows. Surely it can't be as bad as all of that."

Tucking a stray tendril of hair back behind her ear, Aimee glanced up at the Dowager Duchess of Maitland. The woman was studying her with perceptive brown eyes from her corner of the jostling carriage, the feathers in her purple satin turban bobbing rather comically with each jolt of the conveyance.

Normally the sight would have had Aimee battling the urge to smile, but not today. She was too busy trying to ignore the sharp pangs of guilt she felt at the concern that suffused those kindly features.

She was well aware that she hadn't been the most scintillating of traveling companions. Much of the weeklong journey from London had passed in suffocating silence. Partly because of her own unhappiness at being forced to make the trip, and partly due to her fear that she would forget herself and accidentally blurt out something that she shouldn't.

Upon arriving at the decision to ask the duchess to accompany his daughter to Stonecliff, Lord Albright had come to the conclusion that it was for the best if the elderly lady remained in the dark as to the real reasons for Aimee's departure from town. Not that he distrusted Theodosia, but the marquis had pointed out that the fewer people in London who knew the details, the better. There was always a chance the dowager might slip and reveal the information to an acquaintance. Not to mention that such a revelation would only serve to frighten her unnecessarily.

Aimee gave an inward grimace. Her father had assured her that they would tell Theodosia everything once they had the answers they sought, but that didn't make it any easier to keep the details to herself. Hiding it all only added to her already heavy burden, and the strain was taking its toll. With each day that passed as their little caravan wound its way along the road to Cornwall, her tangled emotions roiled ever closer to the surface of her deceptively composed façade, threatening to overwhelm her.

And it hadn't helped to have Lord Stonehurst lounging in the seat across from hers the whole time, his flinty eyes fixed on her with fierce intensity. If she had been uncommunicative, then he had been even more so. In fact, he hadn't said a word to her since the day they had set off for Stonecliff, and she had taken his brooding reticence as a sign of his own displeasure with the situation that had been foisted upon him. After all, she was about to invade his own personal sanctuary, and she doubted that he was delighted by the prospect.

She peeked at him furtively out of the corner of her eye to find him observing her now, the scarred corner of his mouth quirked upward in sardonic amusement as he awaited her response to Theodosia's query. It was almost as if he were anticipating the opportunity to watch her stumble her way through an explanation.

Apparently the truce that had existed between them while under her sister's roof was null and void.

The irritating cad, she fumed. Every time she started to believe that a caring human being existed behind that hard exterior, he proved her wrong. Well, let him smirk all he wanted. She would not allow him to discomfit her any further.

Tearing her gaze away from his, she turned to the dowager, doing her best to appear calm in the face of the woman's thorough examination. "I'm sorry, Your Grace. I suppose I'm a trifle homesick. I'm not used to being away from my family for such an extended period of time."

Theodosia tilted her head, considering Aimee for several long seconds before giving a sympathetic nod. "That is understandable," she acknowledged. "But after your dreadful experience the other night, your father was right in wanting to get you away from the city for a while. Why, it's just appalling! A person isn't even safe in her own home anymore. And to be accosted so soon after your accident . . ." A shudder racked her matronly figure. "I hope the law succeeds in catching the miscreant and punishes him most severely for his foul deeds."

Another shard of guilt pierced Aimee. The marquis had told the dowager about the break-in at Maura's town house and Aimee's brush with the intruder, but he had let the woman believe that it had been nothing more than the unsuccessful burglary attempt that the law had proclaimed it to be. Such subterfuge did not sit well with Aimee, however, especially when the duchess had always been so good to her in the past.

Before she could think of a word to say to fill the suddenly awkward silence, Theodosia forestalled her by facing Stonehurst. "It was most kind of you, my lord, to offer your home so that Lady Aimee could recuperate in peaceful surroundings," she said approvingly.

The viscount lifted a shoulder in an indolent shrug. "Lord Albright has been most kind to me. It was the least I could do in return."

His less than subtle message couldn't have been any clearer if he had shouted it. He was doing this for her father. Not for Aimee. And if the meaningful look he slanted in her direction was any indication, he wanted her to know it.

For some reason, his deliberately callous dismissal of her stung.

The dowager duchess pursed her lips, her gaze darting back and forth between the two of them as if weighing and measuring their reactions. "I see," she murmured, her tone intimating that she did indeed see far more than they would have liked.

In an effort to distract herself from the tension inside the carriage, Aimee whipped her head about and peered out through the window at the leaden sky overhead. With each mile that brought them closer to Stonehurst's estate, the landscape grew rockier and more remote, and the scent of rain as well as the sea drifted to her on the occasional breeze. One of the men Tolliver had appointed to guard duty rode next to the coach on horseback, and he doffed his cap in a show of deference before prodding his mount into a faster gait with a nudge of his heels, trotting ahead on the dusty trail.

The sight of him and the other riders who surrounded them brought the reality of her circumstances home to her with painful clarity, and she released a shaky sigh. She longed to be back at home with her family, to believe that this was all part of just another nightmare that she would wake up from any second. But she was very much afraid that wasn't going to happen.

Despite her repeated pleas to be allowed to stay in London, Lord Albright had remained adamant in his refusal to give in. Nothing would do but for Aimee to be whisked away from danger with all due speed, and while she understood his need to protect her, that didn't lessen her frustration.

"It's for your own good, darling," he had told her as he had kissed her good-bye and handed her into the waiting coach. "I was helpless to prevent it when Jilly and Maura's lives were threatened because of the intrigue surrounding your mother's death, but I'm not helpless now and I won't stand by and watch you become embroiled in all of this. In the meantime, you must try to view this as a holiday of sorts. I promise you, you can return to town as soon as Tolliver and I have this scoundrel in custody."

But who knew how long that would be, she reflected dismally. Though they appeared to be focusing most of their attention on Baron Bedford, there were any number of scenarios that had to be looked into and ruled out before they could be certain of anything. Maura's staff would have to be closely monitored, just in case one of them had been involved or had perhaps overheard Aimee's confession to Stonehurst and had inadvertently repeated the news to someone else. Even Theodosia's stepson, the Duke of Maitland, would receive his share of scrutiny. The marquis had made it clear that no one could be entirely eliminated until the true fiend was caught, and that meant Aimee would have to stay on her guard.

At that moment, she heard someone call out, and the coach drew to a halt before a pair of heavy iron gates set in a high stone wall. The man who had been riding alongside them reined in and climbed down from his horse, swinging the gates wide, then motioning their driver on through. Once again, they lurched forward, following a narrow track that circled a dense grove of trees before veering onto a slightly wider path that ran parallel to the coastline. On Aimee's side of the carriage, the ground abruptly fell away, and she found herself staring out over the churning waters of the sea.

And just up ahead, perched on a rocky promontory that was a jagged extension of the surrounding bluffs that gave the estate its name, was a sprawling and forbidding structure built of gray stone that seemed to blend in with the very harshness of its environs.

Stonecliff.

Aimee shivered. With the somber backdrop of the sky and the waves crashing against the base of the cliffs far below, it made for a bleak and desolate picture. The house itself loomed like some im-

penetrable medieval stronghold from which there
was no escape.

This was to be her safe haven for the next several weeks? Good heavens, she might as well have
been banished to the ends of the earth!

The rutted drive sloped steadily upward, leading the coach on a circuitous route around to the
back of the house, where they finally rolled to a
stop in the courtyard. A pair of groomsmen came
scurrying from the stables nearby, one catching
the horses by their halters while the other moved
to open the carriage door with a flourish.

Rising from his seat, Stonehurst stepped down
and reached back for first Theodosia, then Aimee.
When he handed her out, Aimee noticed that he
took great care to avoid her gaze, and she couldn't
help but wonder if he had felt the same frisson of
awareness that had stolen up her arm the instant
he had taken her hand in his. If he did, he showed
no sign of it, and he released her as soon as she
stood on the cobblestones next to him.

His lack of reaction nettled her pride. Why was
it such a struggle for her to distance herself from
the blasted man when he seemed to have no trouble at all?

"Welcome to Stonecliff, Your Grace, Lady
Aimee," he said, offering them a coolly polite
smile before indicating a thin, bespectacled man
who had emerged from the house at the carriage's
approach and now hovered at his elbow, awaiting

instructions. "This is the butler, Whitson. He will be showing you to your rooms and helping you to get settled in."

His aloof tone when she was feeling so very disconcerted roused Aimee's ire, and she lifted her chin, propping her hands on her hips in a challenging stance. "And just where will you be, my lord?"

He eyed her dispassionately, but a muscle began to tic in his jaw, a betraying signal that let her know he wasn't nearly as immune to her prodding as his detached air might suggest. "As much as I hate to abandon you so soon after our arrival, I'm afraid I have some rather urgent matters that need my attention after such a long absence. But Whitson is at your disposal should you need anything at all, and I shall see you both at dinner." He sketched them a perfunctory bow. "If you will excuse me?"

With that, he pivoted and strode off across the courtyard toward the stables, leaving Aimee seething as she glared after him. Urgent matters indeed! He simply didn't want to spend any more time in her presence than he had to. And if she was honest with herself, she had to admit that his reasoning was sound. What with the constant tension between them, it would be wise if they continued to avoid each other as much as possible during their enforced imprisonment together.

Brushing aside her temporary fit of pique, she

glanced over at Theodosia, who was regarding her with one eyebrow raised in speculation. But before the elderly woman could comment, Whitson stepped forward, drawing their attention.

"Your Grace, my lady," he intoned. "If you would follow me?"

Amid the sudden commotion as several footmen descended upon the carriage and set about the task of unloading their luggage, he led the way inside.

To Aimee's dismay, she discovered upon entering the house that the interior was every bit as dark and dreary as the exterior, with flagstone floors, tapestry-covered walls, and narrow, arched windows that let in little light. And though the connecting rooms the butler showed them to were spacious and elegantly furnished, the minute traces of dust and the stale scent of disuse that pervaded the air gave ample evidence that they had only recently been opened up and hastily prepared for occupation.

It was quite obvious that the viscount rarely entertained guests.

Once the footmen had delivered their trunks and Whitson had left them to unpack with the assistance of one of the maids, a clearly exhausted Theodosia opted to lie down and take a short nap to refresh herself before the evening meal. But after changing out of her wrinkled traveling dress and spending a quarter of an hour tossing and turning on top of her coverlet, Aimee came to the conclusion that sleep was going to prove elusive as far as she was concerned. Not that she wasn't just as tired as her companion. Her churning thoughts simply wouldn't let her rest. Every time she closed her eyes, she couldn't help but wonder whether the nightmare would revisit her. Whether this was the time when it would reveal far more than she was prepared to deal with.

So, with a vague notion of doing a bit of exploring, she rose and splashed her face with some tepid water from the porcelain basin on the washstand before quietly letting herself out of the room.

There was no particular destination uppermost in her mind, but eventually her wanderings through the dimly lit, labyrinthine corridors led her back outside to the courtyard, where she paused to observe the activity taking place around her. The stable appeared to be the center of most of the bustle, as two of the Stonecliff grooms and Tolliver's men rushed to get the horses unbridled and quartered before the coming storm struck.

There was no sign of Stonehurst, and Aimee couldn't help but wonder what had been so very urgent that he had all but deserted his guests at the first possible opportunity, leaving them to their own devices.

Unable to stifle her curiosity, she lifted her skirts and crossed the cobblestones, weaving a path through the knot of men who blocked the entrance to the stable. Her presence went unnoticed, as usual. The wind had picked up a great deal and was much chillier than it had been when she had first arrived, and she was glad of the building's sheltering warmth as she ducked inside.

Within, things were a trifle less chaotic, and she halted for a second to get her bearings. It was as she lingered there, her gaze searching the shadows for some sign of her errant host, that a soft, snuffling sound reached her ears. It came from so close to her shoulder that it startled her, and she whirled about to find herself nose to nose with a big bay gelding who had poked its head out from a nearby stall.

Aimee knew next to nothing about horses, but she had always loved animals, and the gentleness in those faded brown eyes reassured her. Reaching up, she stroked the gelding's graying muzzle and gave a delighted laugh when it nickered in contentment and nudged her palm.

"He likes you." A stocky, barrel-chested groom with thinning, reddish-brown hair approached her from the rear of the stable, an infectious grin wreathing his weather-beaten face. "Balthazar doesn't take to just anyone that way."

His comment had her smiling at him in return. "He's so sweet."

"Shhh." The man laid a finger over his lips, his expression becoming one of mock horror. "You mustn't let him hear you say that, my lady. Balthazar here was quite the bold high-stepper in his day, and being described as sweet could permanently wound his ego."

"I see." Struggling to maintain a serious countenance, Aimee nodded sagely. "I'm sorry. I certainly wouldn't want to offend his male pride."

"That's all right. I'm sure he'll forgive you if you promise to bring him a lump of sugar the next time you visit."

"Ah. Thank you for the advice. I'll try and remember that, mister . . . ?"

"Just O'Keefe will do. And you must be Lady Aimee." The groom leaned back against the stall and crossed his arms, surveying her with his bushy eyebrows raised in inquiry. "Is there something I can help you with? I'm afraid it isn't the best time to take one of the horses out. There's a tempest brewing, and it looks to be a pretty fierce one. These late September storms usually are."

She shook her head. "Oh, I wasn't wanting to go riding. Actually, I was looking for Lord Stonehurst. I saw him come in here earlier, though I can't seem to locate him now."

"He was here, but he left a short while ago." Lifting a big, square hand, O'Keefe scratched behind one of Balthazar's pointed ears, and the horse gave another contented snuffle before shifting closer and lowering his head so that the groom could better reach the spot. "This poor old fellow is getting on in years and has been under the weather of late, and His Lordship has been most concerned about him. He wanted to check and make sure that all was well."

"Oh?" Aimee regarded the gelding with increased interest. The normally taciturn Stonehurst had never seemed the sort to let himself get overly attached to an animal, and the revelation surprised her, to say the least.

"Mmm. There's quite a strong bond there, seeing as how Balthazar was the viscount's mount during his time with the cavalry. Of course, they had no further use for him after his injury."

At first Aimee thought the man was referring to Stonehurst. It wasn't until he ran his hand back along Balthazar's side that she noticed the livid scar that cut across the horse's left flank. It was a jagged slice and looked as if it had gone straight to the bone, and the sight of it rendered her speechless.

"There were those who believed he should be put down," the groom continued, oblivious to Aimee's state of shock. "But His Lordship would have none of it. He brought Balthazar back to England and fought hard to save his life, even when he was in bad shape himself." A sorrowful look crossed his wrinkled visage. "I don't know what he'll do when Balthazar's time comes. I have little doubt he'll be devastated, though he'll do his best to deny it."

Positive that her amazement must show on her face, she avoided the groom's gaze by focusing on the soothing motion of her hand as she continued to stroke the animal's nose. "How sad," she finally managed to say, forcing the words out past the lump that clogged her throat.

"Sad indeed. And though I'm loath to say it, I think that day is coming sooner rather than later. Balthazar is old and tired, not to mention half blind and sickly most of the time." The groom shook his head. "Lord Stonehurst has already lost so much. I'll hate to see him lose something else he cares about."

Aimee jerked her head in the man's direction, her instincts on alert. Before she could ask him what he meant, however, one of the other grooms called out to him, and he doffed his cap before excusing himself and striding away.

As soon as he was out of sight, Aimee turned back to the horse, biting her lip in contemplation. For some reason, she couldn't quite equate her own view of the viscount with what O'Keefe had just told her.

After everything that had happened between them in the past year, she had convinced herself that the Lord Stonehurst she had once befriended had never existed. That the gruff kindness and gentle understanding that had made her fall in love with him had been nothing more than a façade, hiding the harsh and unfeeling man he truly was underneath. She'd had to believe that in order to survive his rejection.

But would someone who was incapable of caring fight so hard to save a mere horse's life? Would he continue to look after the animal, even when the naysayers around him seemed to believe that it was hopeless?

And what had the groom been talking about when he had mentioned that Stonehurst had already lost so much?

It definitely gave her food for thought.

Chapter 12

Well, this ordeal had certainly been less than pleasant.

The unscarred corner of his mouth quirking upward at a sardonic angle, Royce contemplated his guests from his place at the head of the table. They sat one to each side of him, their heads bent over their plates. Conversation had been scarce, but he supposed he couldn't blame them for that. The gloomy atmosphere was enough to quell even the most lively of souls.

He sent a quick glance around at the dreariness of his familiar surroundings. Though he was used to the dark and dismal aura of his childhood home, he could see how it could be off-putting to others. The flickering flames from the candelabras cast an eerie, almost otherworldly glow over the massive dining hall, their meager light doing little to dispel the shadows that lingered at the edges of the room. And over the clink of china and cutlery, the intermittent roll of thunder from outside shook the very foundations of the house, making his companions flinch with each rumbling growl and adding to the tension that hung over them.

It reminded Royce of the interminable family dinners he had suffered through in his youth. Of the suffocating silences and the sense of strain that had pervaded the air as his father had glowered at him from this very chair and Alex had eyed them both warily down the length of the table, as if expecting them to leap for each other's throats at any second.

It was a stark contrast to his memories of the meals he had shared with Alex and Cordelia in the years before he had left Stonecliff. On those occasions, laughter and high spirits had prevailed. And that had been thanks to Cordelia. She had brightened this room the way she had brightened their lives, bridging the gap between the brothers, if only for a short while, and Royce looked back on that time as one of the rare periods of contentment in his life.

But it had been all too fleeting.

"My lord, you simply must pass my compliments along to your cook."

The crisp voice yanked him from his melancholy ruminations, and he glanced over at the Dowager Duchess of Maitland, who was peering at him over her glass of wine as if attempting to discern the direction of his thoughts.

"Dinner was superb," she went on, dabbing at her lips with her napkin. "Especially the roast pheasant. Why, I cannot recall the last time I tasted anything so delicious." She turned to the girl seated across from her, her eyebrows raised expectantly. "Don't you agree, Aimee?"

Appearing startled at being brought into the discussion so abruptly, Aimee blinked and put down the fork she had been clutching in one white-knuckled hand.

"Yes, Your Grace," she concurred, though she sounded far from enthusiastic. "It was most delicious."

An interesting observation, Royce mused, considering she had barely touched anything on her plate. He didn't call her on it, however. Instead he focused his attention on the duchess. "I am glad that you enjoyed it, and I shall be happy to let the kitchen staff know that you were impressed with their efforts."

"Excellent." The elderly woman laid aside her napkin and beckoned to Whitson, who hurried forward with her cane. "Now I'm afraid I shall have to excuse myself. As much as I hate to retire so early, I fear my old bones haven't quite recovered from our journey."

Royce stifled the sudden urge to chuckle at the eagerness that suffused Aimee's features as she pushed back her chair without waiting for a servant to assist her and prepared to stand. It was obvious she was ready to seize upon any excuse to get away from him.

But the dowager halted her with a wave of her hand. "No, Aimee, you mustn't cut your evening short because of me. None of us has ever been the sort to be concerned with the proprieties, and I see no reason to start now. You should stay and chat with Lord Stonehurst."

Royce frowned as he surveyed the woman, taking note of the avid gleam in her eyes. He didn't know Theodosia Rosemont very well, but he had heard stories from Hawksley and he had been warned about her predilection for playing match-maker. She was more than likely hoping that her absence would somehow succeed in pushing him and her young charge together, placing them on the path to matrimonial bliss.

Of course, he could have told her that she was doomed to disappointment. Even if Aimee could bring herself to forgive him for turning his back on their friendship, he couldn't and wouldn't allow the attraction that had sparked between them to go anywhere. He was not a proper hus-band candidate for any young lady of good breed-ing, and most especially not Aimee. In the end, he would only end up hurting her far worse than he already had.

Visibly deflated, Aimee sank back into her seat, though the defiant angle of her chin gave mute tes-timony to the fact that she hadn't given up on the prospect of escaping just yet. Royce could almost see her mind working frantically, clearly trying to come up with another plan of attack.

"But will you be able to find your way back to your chamber alone, Your Grace?" she persisted, a vague hint of desperation threading her tone. "You were just saying as we came down to dinner earlier that all of the corridors looked alike to you."

The duchess hesitated, then wrinkled her nose in a wry grimace. "I must confess that my sense of direction is not what it once was." She faced Royce, her countenance reflecting her uncustomary sheepishness. "If a member of your staff would be so kind as to escort me, Lord Stonehurst, I would be most appreciative."

"Of course." With a nod to Whitson, Royce rose, moving around the table to pull back the dowager's chair. As she got to her feet with the support of his hand at her elbow, her stern gaze locked with his, conveying a message that he had no trouble interpreting.

This woman was no one's fool, and while she might have made the decision to place her trust in him for the time being, that didn't mean he had gained her wholehearted stamp of approval. Her eyes warned him in no uncertain terms that she would make sure he regretted it should he prove himself unworthy of her confidence.

Little did she know that her warning was completely unnecessary. As far as he was concerned, Aimee was strictly off limits.

"I hope you have a most restful evening, Your Grace," he said solicitously.

"I'm sure I will." The duchess returned his bow with a polite inclination of her head before pinning Aimee to her seat with a pointed look. "Now, you see, my dear? I shall be fine, and there is no reason to interrupt your meal. In fact, I insist that you stay and finish every bite."

Her words were infused with a meaningful emphasis that had Aimee's checks flushing a dull red. Despite his amusement at her predicament, Royce couldn't help but sympathize with her. It wasn't every day that your chaperone practically threw you at the head of a man you loathed.

Leaning heavily on her cane, the elderly eccentric left the room with the butler following close at her heels.

In the wake of her departure, an icy silence descended, punctuated only by the ticking of the clock in the corner. As Royce made his way back to his seat, he could feel Aimee's hostile stare burning into him like a brand, willing him to look in her direction. But some devil on his shoulder prodded him into waiting until he was settled at the head of the table once more before finally deigning to meet her furious gaze.

"Far be it from me to point out the obvious," he drawled with a careless nonchalance that was certain to rile her even further, "but your words of praise for this evening's repast somehow don't quite ring true." He indicated her nearly full plate with a sweep of his hand. "One could be excused for thinking the meal wasn't to your liking."

"Perhaps it is the company and not the food that is responsible for robbing me of my appetite, my lord."

Her waspish retort had Royce arching an eyebrow in mocking amusement. "Well, that certainly puts me in my place, doesn't it?"

She glared at him, drawing herself up stiffly. "Laugh if you must, but I find this entire situation untenable! I don't belong here. I should be at home with my family, helping them to pursue the investigation into the night of my mother's death, and it isn't fair—"

Her words choked to a halt and she slumped in her seat, her rebellious expression fading away, to be replaced by one of such misery and despair that Royce was seized with the abrupt urge to take her in his arms, to hold and comfort her as he had after her close call with the intruder.

A dangerous impulse, and one that had to be resisted at all costs. For each time he had Aimee nestled in his embrace, it grew more and more difficult to let her go.

"I apologize, my lord," she said quietly, oblivious to the riotous emotions that had surged to life beneath his seemingly aloof façade. "I must sound like a spoiled child, and I had no right to lash out at you like that. Especially when you are only trying to oblige my father. But I cannot help how I feel. I am the one to blame for all of this, yet I have once again been relegated to the background as if I am incapable of contributing anything useful."

Her unexpected apology caught Royce off guard, and he winced at the shard of guilt that pierced him. In truth, he deserved her ire, for he had to admit that he had been deliberately goading her, and not just for the sheer pleasure of seeing her golden eyes spark with temper, though that had definitely been an added incentive. Underneath his display of cynical bravado had been a desire to reestablish the distance that he was having so much trouble trying to maintain between them.

"I'm sure your father doesn't see it that way at all, my lady," he assured her, his voice softening with sincerity, even as he gripped the edge of the table against the continued compulsion to reach for her. "And you are not to blame for what's happened. I have no idea how you came by such a conclusion, but you've done nothing wrong."

She bit her lip and glanced down at her hands in her lap. "It was the return of my nightmares that set things in motion again. I never should have told you about them. Then everyone would be safe."

"You can't be sure of that. And keeping such

a secret was already torturing you to the point of illness. It had to come out. There was no other option."

Royce's words carried an authoritative conviction, but they didn't seem to sway Aimee.

"I suppose we shall have to agree to disagree on the subject," she said, lifting one delicate shoulder in a slight shrug. "In any case, you can't be any happier at having me here than I am to be here. I saw your face when Hawksley first made the suggestion that I seek refuge at Stonecliff. You wanted no part of it."

He couldn't deny that. But whatever his initial inclination, he hadn't been able to refuse Lord Albright's request. How could he when Aimee's very life was in jeopardy? Regardless of how awkward it was to have her here, he would never have been able to forgive himself if he had walked away and something had happened to her as a result.

For a brief instant, he was thrown back to the moment when he had burst into Aimee's bedchamber to find that dark, menacing figure bending over her, hands wrapped around her neck, and an overwhelming wave of remembered rage washed over him. The mere recollection of the incident affected him just as powerfully as it had that night, but he somehow managed to push it away and concentrate on the conversation at hand.

"Maybe not," he said aloud, striving for a neutral tone. "But you are here now, and there is nothing to be done about it except resign ourselves and try to muddle through the best we can."

With that, he gestured to Whitson, who had returned from escorting the dowager duchess to her room and hovered unobtrusively just inside the door. At his master's signal, the butler immediately sprang into motion, clapping his hands to summon the footmen who had been waiting in the background for their instructions.

As the servants converged upon them, Royce kept speaking, more than ready to put some distance between himself and this unnerving female who was far too skilled at unearthing his most deeply buried emotions. "As it seems that neither one of us is in the mood to do justice to what is left of the meal, I propose we follow the dowager's example and retire for the evening. The trip from London wasn't easy for any of us, and an early night will do us both good."

Aimee didn't reply, but watched quietly while the footmen darted and scurried about, clearing away the trays and dishes from the table and nearby sideboard. When they had all disappeared back toward the kitchens once more, she looked up at Royce, a flicker of humor suddenly lighting the melancholy depths of her eyes.

"I assume you realize that your servants are terrified of you."

Her candid observation startled him. Over the years, he had become so used to the furtive glances and fearful demeanors of his servants whenever they were in his presence that he rarely even noticed it anymore. It was a fear that his father had planted the seeds for and nurtured long ago. Many members of the household staff had worked at Stonecliff for a generation or more, and the late viscount's ravings about his youngest son's curse, coupled with Royce's involvement in Cordelia's tragic death, had shaped their opinion of him before he had even returned from the war.

But it would do little good to try and explain such a thing to Aimee. Coming from such a loving family, she would never understand. So he brushed aside her remark with a dismissive flick of the wrist.

"I assure you, I have given them no reason to be," he told her coolly. "They've always tended to tread carefully in my vicinity. I suppose they find me intimidating."

She studied him in silence for several seconds, then shook her head. "I don't think you are nearly as hard as you would like people to believe," she asserted with a surprising firmness. "O'Keefe certainly seems to like you well enough."

"O'Keefe?" Royce felt a frisson of alarm at the mention of the red-haired stable hand. The last thing he wanted was for Aimee to become acquainted with the one man at Stonecliff who knew everything there was to know about him. "When did you speak to him?"

"Earlier this afternoon, when I went out to the stables to find you."

"I wasn't aware that you had been looking for me."

"I didn't need anything in particular. I was just feeling restless and decided to do some exploring." Aimee paused, her gaze skimming his features as if searching for something in his expression before she went on a bit tentatively, "He introduced me to Balthazar."

Royce struggled to keep his visage blank. Just thinking about his former cavalry mount was enough to bring all his anxiety and concern for the animal racing to the forefront of his mind, along with memories of another terrible day from his past that he had no desire to revisit. "Did he?"

She nodded. "He told me that Balthazar was wounded at Waterloo and was in a bad way when you first brought him back to Stonecliff. That you saved his life when everyone else believed he should be put down." Unable to hide her interest, she peered up at him, curiosity in her eyes. "Not many people would go to such lengths for a horse. He must mean a great deal to you."

To his consternation, her comment brought a lump to his throat, and he had to swallow several times before he finally managed to clear it away. It was true. Balthazar was the only living being he had allowed close to him since Garvey's death. He had never meant for it to happen, but somehow his determination to pull the animal through the worst of his injuries had aided him in his own recovery and had forged a connection to the gelding that he couldn't seem to bring himself to sever. Now he cared far more than was good for him.

Of course, he had no intention of confessing any of that to Aimee. But when he failed to respond to her less-than-subtle probing, she leaned forward in her seat, evidently not quite ready to give up. "How was he injured?"

His fingers closing spasmodically around the linen square of his napkin, Royce crumpled it in his fist as her question sent images flashing through his head. The French solider emerging from out of the smoke on the battlefield, weapon upraised and poised to strike. The ground rushing up to meet him as Balthazar went down with a shrill whinny. The red haze that had misted his vision as the tip of the bayonet had sliced across his cheek, ripping the flesh open and leaving a trail of searing agony in its wake. And Garvey's face, rife with horror as he ran to intercept that final, killing blow . . .

God, he didn't want to think about it! However, it was obvious Aimee wasn't going to relent until he told her something, so he decided it couldn't hurt to part with just a few details. Perhaps if he appeased at least some of her inquisitiveness, she would let the subject drop.

"It was a French bayonet," he informed her gruffly. "It caught Balthazar across the hindquarters and damaged the muscles in his left flank."

"Was it the same bayonet that gave you your scar?"

He felt a muscle jump in his jaw at the query, and the napkin he had been clutching fluttered to the floor unnoticed as he got to his feet, fighting to hold on to his mask of control.

"That is not something I wish to discuss," he gritted out from between clenched teeth.

Aimee stared up at him, her gaze troubled. "But perhaps you should. You've never spoken about any of it, and it can't be good to keep so much bottled up inside. O'Keefe says—"

"It sounds as if O'Keefe said entirely too much. And you are prying into matters that are none of your business. I told you I don't wish to discuss it and I meant it."

A stunned hush followed his harshly grated admonition. Blinking, Aimee reeled back as if she'd been slapped. Then, just like a candle being snuffed out, every bit of emotion abruptly disappeared from her expression, leaving her face cold and remote.

"Of course," she said stiltedly. "Do forgive me for prying. Like a fool, I thought I might be able to help." Pushing back her chair, she rose and faced him with an air of haughty composure that would have made her aunt Olivia proud. "I must have been mad to feel any compassion for you whatsoever. After all, one has to be human in order to suffer from human emotion, doesn't one? But that's a mistake I shan't make again."

With that, she turned and marched from the dining hall in a flurry of skirts, leaving Royce staring somberly after her.

Chapter 13

Royce swirled the dregs of his drink around the bottom of his snifter as he peered out through the library's narrow window at the cliffs surrounding his home. Though the worst of the recent storm had passed, an occasional growl of thunder could still be heard in the distance, rolling across the onyx sky at a low-pitched rumble.

After the disastrous turn of events that had taken place at dinner, the chaos of his thoughts had made it impossible for him to even consider attempting to settle in for the night. So instead of retiring to his bedchamber, he had retreated to the one place that had always been his sanctuary, in the hope that a bracing shot of brandy would help quell his edginess as he mulled over the best way to mend fences with Aimee. Whether they liked it or not, the two of them were going to have to accept that she was going to be here for an indefinite amount of time, at least until her attacker was caught. Things were already strained enough without letting matters stand as they were.

He mentally cursed himself as he recalled the hurt that had flitted across her elfin features in response to his snapped reprimand, before she had swept from the dining hall. He was well aware that his behavior had been inexcusable, and his only justification was the fact that she had been probing at wounds that were still far too raw. Dredging up the past was something he needed no help doing. Here at Stonecliff, reminders of some of the most tragic moments in his life lurked around every corner, waiting to pounce with alarming frequency.

Turning away from the window, he let his brooding gaze travel around the room. If he closed his eyes, he could picture himself as a small boy, playing at soldiers with Alex as they ran up and down the aisles formed by the rows of towering bookshelves, their laughter echoing off the walls.

At thoughts of his elder brother, Royce couldn't help but feel a sharp pang of remorse. Throughout the years, Alex had tried on numerous occasions to reach out to him, to reestablish the closeness the two of them had once shared as children. But their father's machinations and Royce's envy of his sibling's position as favored son and heir had brought a swift end to that. As if they were pawns on a chessboard, the late viscount had set his sons against each other, manipulating them into a competitive game of one-upmanship that had finally succeeded in destroying whatever fragile bond had once existed between them.

It hadn't been until Alex had inherited the title, until Cordelia had come into their lives and insisted on playing the role of peacemaker, that they had taken the first tentative steps toward repairing their relationship. But Royce's reckless actions on the day Cordelia had been killed had ended up pushing his brother away for good.

At that moment, a faint sound from the direction of the library door yanked him from his ruminations, and he looked up to see a shadowy figure hovering uncertainly on the threshold. Though he strained his eyes against the dimness, the glow from the lamp on his writing desk did not quite reach that side of the chamber, and he could make out nothing other than a vague silhouette.

"Who's there?" he called out, a thread of impatience in his voice.

The figure hesitated, as if debating whether to answer him or bolt, then took a step farther into the room. Light spilled over a heart-shaped face etched with trepidation.

Aimee.

Framed in the doorway, clad in a white dressing gown of cambric and lace, and with her light brown hair free and tumbling over her shoulders, she made a picture far removed from that of the plain and proper young miss she normally seemed intent on presenting. In fact, to him she looked as ethereal as a fairy sprite that had stepped from the pages of a children's storybook. Her amber eyes were even larger than usual, wide golden pools so luminous, he could easily drown in them.

"I'm sorry," she murmured. "I couldn't sleep because of the storm, so I thought I would see if I could find a book to while away the hours. I didn't realize anyone would be in here."

Tossing back the rest of his drink, Royce took a second to make sure that none of the disconcertment he felt at her unexpected appearance betrayed itself when he addressed her. "And if you *had* known?"

Her chin went up, and a distinct spark of temper lit those long-lashed eyes. "If I *had* known, I can assure you that I would have stayed in my room."

Royce grimaced at her scathing reply. He was being an ass, and no mistake. For some reason, however, he couldn't seem to help himself when it came to Aimee. As if recognizing the threat she posed to his much vaunted control, his defenses involuntarily slammed into place whenever she was in the vicinity, without any bidding from him.

Even as his conscience cringed at his behavior, he set his snifter down on the polished surface of the desk before sweeping an arm out before him in a mocking gesture of welcome. "As you are already here, you may as well come in. I don't bite, contrary to the opinions of my staff."

Aimee frowned and pulled the lace-trimmed edges of her wrapper more closely together over the sheer fabric of her nightgown. "I'm not precisely dressed to join you," she pointed out in hushed tones, casting a quick glance back toward the hallway behind her as she wrapped her arms about her waist self-consciously.

He lifted a shoulder in a careless shrug. "As the dowager duchess noted at dinner, I've never been the sort to stand on ceremony. And I highly doubt that there is anyone left awake to stumble upon us." Arching a brow, he crossed his arms and regarded her with a touch of cynicism. "Or perhaps that is the plan. Have you decided that I am to be the solution to your matrimonial woes?"

His words had her forehead wrinkling in confusion. "I beg your pardon?"

"Your chaperone seemed rather eager for us to spend some time alone together earlier." Shoving his hands into his pockets, he made a great show of strolling forward to peer past her out into the corridor. "Is she waiting out there to pounce, to catch us in a compromising situation so you can force my neck into the parson's noose?"

It sounded preposterous, even to his own ears. What sane young miss with an eye toward ensnaring a husband would ever deem him to be a worthy enough candidate that she would attempt to trap him into wedlock? After all, he was the reclusive, half-mad Viscount Stonehurst, and his days of being considered a prime catch on the marriage mart were long over. But it was too late to call the allegation back, so he waited for Aimee to take him to task, fully expecting her to deliver the dressing-down he so richly deserved.

Instead, she shook her head and stared up at him as if she had never seen him before. "I don't understand what's happened to you," she whispered, her expression a mixture of sadness and bewilderment that made even his hardened heart give a painful squeeze. "You didn't used to be like this, so callous and antagonistic. Perhaps you were a bit surly on occasion, but even when you were angry, you were never deliberately cruel. It makes me wonder if the man I once believed you to be ever existed in the first place."

She wheeled about, obviously intending to leave him to his own devices. But as she did so, a wave of panic washed over him. He couldn't let her leave like this. Not with so much anger and tension simmering between them.

Reaching out, he caught her by the wrist, pulling her to an abrupt halt. "Wait," he entreated, the plea emerging as little more than a hoarse croak. "Please."

She paused, surveying him over her shoulder with marked coolness. "Yes?"

Just as always, the satiny texture of her skin

beneath his fingers played havoc with his senses, making it difficult for him to concentrate. But somehow he managed to ignore the heated tide of awareness that surged through him and focus on what he wanted to say.

"You're right," he conceded. "I'm being a colossal boor."

"Yes, you are."

Her clipped agreement startled a bark of laughter from him, but he sobered almost immediately and continued on, determined to convince her of his earnestness. "Please, accept my apology. As you've no doubt surmised, I'm not used to having guests at Stonecliff. It's put me on edge, and I tend to become rather ill-tempered as a result."

Aimee narrowed her eyes, examining him as if to ascertain the depth of his sincerity. Then, to his relief, she gave a nod, her lips curving in a rueful smile. "I suppose I can forgive you if you can forgive me for prying earlier," she relented. "I had no right to push you to talk about things that you clearly aren't ready to share."

"There is nothing to be forgiven. You meant no harm, and I never should have lashed out at you. And despite my ridiculous accusations, I realize that I am not precisely at the top of your list of potential husbands. It was foolish of me to suggest that you would resort to tonnish games in order to secure a proposal from the likes of me."

To Royce's puzzlement, a shadow crossed Aimee's face at his words, stealing her smile as it went. "Not so foolish, really. It's not as if suitors are queuing up to beg my father for my hand, and I would imagine that some young ladies in my position would feel justified in stooping to such desperate measures." She took a step back from him, tugging her hand free from his grasp as she did so. "It's all right, you know. I can quite understand why the thought of being tied to me for the rest of your life would be so abhorrent to you."

Temporarily stunned by her matter-of-fact statement, he stood as if paralyzed, so astounded that he almost didn't notice when she started to turn away. Just before she reached the door, however, he came to his senses and caught her once again, this time by the arm. "Wait a second," he growled, his forehead furrowed in a fierce scowl. "Abhorrent? What is that supposed to mean?"

"It means that I am well aware that I am not the sort of female that gentlemen find attractive or would ever want as a wife."

He gaped at her, nonplussed. That she could honestly believe herself to be anything less than desirable boggled the mind. No, she was not a raving beauty, but she possessed a sweetness and strength of spirit that many a gentleman would find far more appealing if she ever lowered her guard enough to let a man truly know her.

Drawing her toward him, he clasped her hands in his. "Why would you say something like that?"

he asked softly, even as he felt her stiffen at the gentle grip of his fingers.

Her gaze never wavered from his, though a despondency she couldn't quite conceal flashed behind her eyes. "Because it's the truth. I've always known it. I am plain and dull, altogether uninspiring in appearance and in personality. Utterly forgettable in every way."

Royce had to restrain the urge to laugh wildly at her self-description. Forgettable? He didn't think so. He had been trying for well over a year to forget about her, with little success.

She was still speaking, completely oblivious to the thoughts racing through his head. "But it's all right," she was saying, sounding as if she were trying to convince herself as much as him. "I've more or less reconciled myself to the fact that I am not meant for love or marriage, and I can accept my lot and be content."

At a loss for words, he groped about for something, anything he could say to make her see reason, though he was the last one who should be counseling her. "Aimee, you are so young," he began cautiously. "Far too young to be making such a sweeping decision about your future right now. You may meet someone who will change your mind. Someone who will care for you in the way that you deserve."

Even as he smothered an unwanted niggle of jealousy at the thought of her with any other man but him, Aimee gave a scornful sniff. "Now you sound like my sisters. Really, Stonehurst, I hardly think that my age has anything to do with it. Aunt Olivia says that some women are simply destined for spinsterhood."

"Well, she's wrong. Especially if she is implying that such a destiny is to be yours."

"You'll have to pardon me if I beg leave to doubt it. It's difficult to stay optimistic regarding your romantic prospects when most men tend to look right through you."

Unable to suppress his growing exasperation at her stubbornness, Royce gave her a shake. "Why in bloody hell would you listen to such rubbish? Just because your harpy of an aunt has resigned herself to being alone and unhappy doesn't mean that you have to as well. You are nothing like her. You are a warm and lovely young woman that any man would be proud to claim as his wife."

"Yet *you* walked away after I all but offered myself to you." Slipping from his grasp, Aimee moved to stand before the window he had been looking out of just a short while before, her hands fisting at her sides so tightly that her knuckles turned white. "And who could blame you? It must have made for a most awkward situation. You were a grown man, and I was a silly little girl who hounded you incessantly, following you about and—"

"Don't," he interrupted her, his voice harsh

with suppressed emotion. "Whatever you might believe, I promise you that I never saw you as a silly little girl. And the reason I left had nothing to do with you."

At least not in the way she suspected, he silently amended. But it would be better if she never found out that his departure had stemmed from his own obsessive and entirely inappropriate fascination with her. It would only serve to complicate the matter.

"There is nothing wrong with you," he went on, his pronouncement ringing with utter conviction. "Nothing at all."

She ducked her head, and the light from the lamp on the desk played over her, highlighting the subtle curves of her form beneath her wrapper and delineating the delicate bone structure of her piquant face. Her fragile loveliness was enough to make his mouth go dry with need. If only she could see herself now, she would never, ever again doubt her allure.

"Please don't lie to me, just to spare my feelings," she said tonelessly. "I've already told you that I have no illusions as far as my shortcomings are concerned. Why should you be any different than any other man?"

Her refusal to see in herself what was so evident to him sparked his temper. Taking a long stride forward, he seized her in his arms and pulled her to him, his eyes blazing down into hers.

"Damn it, what will it take for you to cease belittling yourself?" he grated. "You're perfect! So bloody perfect that I can't keep my hands off you!"

Her audible gasp was followed by a heartbeat of stillness.

"Wh-what?" she finally managed to stammer in a breathless squeak.

Well, so much for keeping his attraction to her to himself, Royce mused grimly. And now that he had blurted out the truth, there was no use in evading the issue. "You heard me. If you are so very undesirable, then why can't I seem to get you out of my head? Why do you think I kissed you the way I did the night of the dinner party?"

"I don't know." Her cheeks flushing, Aimee clutched at the sleeves of his coat, her fingers digging into the material, not even seeming to realize that she was doing so. "You were angry and frustrated and wanted to prove a point, that's all. You didn't— You couldn't possibly ever want me."

"I can and I do. I have for over a year now."

She made a sound of denial at Royce's claim, but he nudged his hips forward insistently, fitting the suddenly rigid and aching length of his arousal into the warm, shadowy notch between her thighs.

"Do you feel that, Aimee?" he ground out through clenched teeth, trying desperately to resist the urge to continue rocking against her, to slide himself back and forth over that most secret, sensitive part of her until they both shattered from the pleasure of the contact. "Deny that, if you can. That's what happens to me whenever I'm around you, and all I want to do is bury myself in your liquid heat. To plunge into you until everything around us ceases to exist and we lose ourselves in each other."

If he had hoped that the blatant earthiness of his declaration would shock her into acceptance, it had exactly the opposite effect. Her spine went ramrod straight and she glared at him, her palms spreading out over the broad wall of his chest as if to hold him at bay.

"I imagine that is more or less the typical male response to being in such close proximity to a female," she informed him imperiously. "Particularly if she happens to be in a state of undress. It wouldn't matter what woman you held in your arms. You would still have the same reaction."

Her haughty assertion finally succeeded in pushing him beyond the boundaries of his patience.

"Is that really what you believe?" he rasped low in his throat. "I suppose I'll just have to prove you wrong, won't I?"

Then, despite the fact that he knew it was a mistake and he would despise himself for it later, he cupped her face in his hands and swooped in to kiss her with a savage intensity.

It was like going up in flames. The instant his mouth touched hers, the fire that had been smoldering just beneath the surface of his skin flared up and turned into a conflagration, burning away all logic, all reason. He was consumed by the woman nestled against him, and there was nothing beyond this moment. No past, no future. Only the sweetness of her lips as he devoured her with all the fierce yearning he had fought for so long to hide.

And apparently he wasn't the only one caught up in the power of their embrace. To his delight, Aimee made no move to push him away or to try to escape his hold. In fact, after an initial hesitation, she tentatively slid her arms around his neck and kissed him back with equal fervor.

Over and over their mouths met, melded, and clung in an ardent exchange, each kiss blending into the next with a deceptive languidness that belied the urgency Royce could feel churning at his very core. It drove him, whispering in his ear to take what he had been waiting for all this time, and he had to struggle to keep his lust for her from prodding him into going too fast.

"Do you believe me now?" he muttered between kisses, his tongue darting out to trace the seam of her lips before skimming along the line of her jaw. "Do you believe me when I tell you that I want you?"

She shivered and closed her eyes as if attempting to avoid his probing gaze, but he wasn't about to let her do so.

Delving his fingers into her hair, he wrapped a light brown skein shimmering with strands of gold around one hand and gave it a gentle tug. The heavy mass was much longer than he had imagined it would be in his daydreams, falling almost to her waist in a shiny curtain of spun silk.

"Tell me," he prompted, nipping at the dainty outer shell of her ear. "Do you?"

A muffled moan was her only reply. But it was enough for Royce. The way she clutched at his shoulders, holding him to her as if afraid he would try and pull away, gave mute testimony to the depth of her own desire for him.

Filled with a sense of elation, he swept her up into his arms and carried her to the velvet-upholstered love seat that was tucked into the most shadowed corner of the room, where he lowered her to the cushions and followed her down. All the while, he kissed her, his lips ravaging hers with devastating mastery. When he finally lifted his head to look at her, it was to find her staring up at him through passion-glazed amber eyes that glowed with a molten light, her expression one of slumberous invitation.

No mouse this, Royce thought in satisfaction, but a golden girl. *His* golden girl. A woman of rare inner beauty who never failed to warm his soul and who wanted him just as much as he wanted her.

Needing to see her, all of her, he loosened the belt on her wrapper with an unsteady hand, then reached up to slide his fingers under the lacy strap of her nightgown. She didn't protest, though she stiffened infinitesimally and bit at her already kiss-swollen lower lip in obvious apprehension.

"It's all right," he soothed her, nuzzling her temple. "It's going to be all right, sweetheart. I just want to look at you. I've wanted to see you like this for so long."

Easing the strap down over the slope of her shoulder, he tugged the material aside to reveal one creamy bare breast in all its glory. Small and pert, its rose-colored nipple visibly hardened as the cool air of the chamber brushed it, and Royce let out a harsh groan at the sight before cradling the slight weight of her in his palm.

When Aimee jolted at his touch, he rushed to calm her, his voice a seductive croon. "Shhh. It's all right, I promise. You're beautiful, sweetheart. So beautiful."

She swallowed, the pale column of her throat moving convulsively. "I'm too small."

"No." He stroked his thumb over the velvety underside of her breast, tracing the pink flesh of her aureole, then flicking over the pebbled tip in its center, making her quiver. She was so soft and so very responsive. Everything he had ever dreamed of. "You're perfect for me."

And she was. True, she didn't possess the ripe,

overly abundant curves of the nameless, faceless women he had bedded in the past. But somehow he found her slender form far more pleasing. Next to the temptation she presented, every other female he had ever made love to faded into obscurity.

Intent on showing her that he meant what he had said, he leaned forward and took the distended peak of her nipple into the scalding heat of his mouth, reveling in the choked cry she uttered when he laved the sensitive crest with his tongue. Arching her back, she sank her fingers into his hair and held him to her, her lashes fluttering against her cheeks as he suckled voraciously.

God, she tasted so delicious. Even if he gorged himself on her for a month, he would never get enough of her.

"Please, Royce," she panted, and he doubted that she was even aware that in her state of dazed bliss she had abandoned the use of his title in favor of his given name. It sounded so right falling from her lips. "Royce, make me yours."

The plea echoed in his head, tolling a vaguely ominous warning, and it wasn't until after he had spent several minutes lost in the intoxicating flavor of her that the reason gradually began to register with him.

Royce, make me yours.

What the bloody hell was he doing?

He set her from him with a violent oath and

levered himself to his feet, rapidly striding to the far side of the room to escape the sensual spell she was weaving so effortlessly. His chest heaving, he took several deep breaths in an effort to rein in his wildly teetering emotions and regain what he could of his composure before attempting speech.

"Forgive me, my lady," he finally said aloud, his tone stilted, almost formal. "That never should have happened."

There was a faint rustling noise, and he glanced back at Aimee just in time to see her sitting up, drawing the strap of her nightgown into place to cover her breast as she did so. A muscle jumped in his jaw when he noticed even from this distance that a patch of dampness quickly appeared on the fabric over her nipple, seeping through from the moist ministrations of his mouth.

"I don't understand," she ventured uncertainly. "I thought you wanted me."

"I do."

"Then why did you stop? Surely there is no shame in it if we want each other?"

Royce shook his head at her naïveté. If only it were that simple. "There are too many things you don't know. Things that I haven't told you."

"Then tell me now." She leaned forward in her seat, her troubled countenance and air of concern urging him to confide in her. "Please."

His shoulders slumping with abject weariness,

he turned to gaze out through the window at the inky blackness of the night sky. How could he have forgotten himself so completely? He'd let his weakness rule his actions, and it had led him dangerously close to crossing into forbidden territory. Only Aimee's husky entreaty had saved him, yanking him back from the edge before it was too late.

And now he had to find a way to tell her that what had just happened between them could never happen again.

"This is why I left." The ragged confession burst forth without his volition, forcing itself out past the constriction of his throat. "Why I distanced myself from you for so long. This damnable need for you follows me wherever I go. But no matter how much I might want you, nothing can ever come of it. Not now. Not ever."

There was a long, drawn-out pause, and Royce could practically feel the weight of Aimee's watchful stare boring into him from behind, causing the nape of his neck to prickle with awareness. When she spoke again, it was in a halting voice that held a note of genuine bewilderment. "But why?"

"Your father has been a good friend to me, and he has placed you under my protection. I will not abuse his trust by seducing his daughter. Especially when I have no intention of making an offer for her hand."

"I see."

The wounded resignation in those two words had Royce swinging about to face Aimee once more, his hands clenched into fists of frustration. "No, you don't see, and I have no idea how to explain it to you. It has nothing to do with you, Aimee, for I stand by what I said earlier. Someday you will make someone a most admirable wife. I'm the one who is lacking, not you. This is about me and my failings."

She blinked, appraising him from under lowered brows. Then, rising with a regal dignity, she pulled her gaping wrapper closed and marched across the chamber, coming to a halt in front of him.

"Exactly what failings are you referring to?" she demanded to know, her peremptory manner leaving no room for equivocation.

Dear God, how could he tell her? Royce agonized. His sins were too numerous to even begin to list them all. And if she had any inkling of the destruction he had wrought on those he had once cared about, she would run from him in horror.

"Suffice it to say that I don't deserve you. I don't deserve to have a wife and family. To be happy." Raking a hand back through his hair, he began to pace before her, jerking at the knot of his cravat in increasing agitation. "You accused me of being less than human at dinner this evening, and you were more right than you know. There is a darkness in me that you can't even conceive of, and I won't expose you to it. I've hurt so many people. I don't want to hurt you too."

"You could never hurt me," she stated with an unswerving faith that would have flattered him under different circumstances.

"Oh, but I would," he assured her bleakly. "Sooner or later, I hurt everyone."

"I don't believe that."

"It doesn't matter what you believe. This is the way it is. The way it has to be." Pushing past her, Royce advanced on the nearby desk, where he uncorked the decanter of brandy he had left there earlier and dashed another finger or two of the liquor into his empty glass. "Now, if you will excuse me, I think it best if you return to your room while I see just how long it takes for me to get well and truly soused."

"But—"

"Go, Aimee." His brusque and authoritative command cut her off mid-protest. "And if you know what is good for you, you'll stay far, far away from me."

He gave her his back, not wanting to see the pain in her eyes at his curt dismissal. Fingers biting into the fragile crystal of his snifter, he waited with bated breath until he heard the door close behind her with a soft and final-sounding click.

Then he hurled the glass across the room with all his might. It shattered against the far wall, amber liquid spilling down the plaster to drip onto the floor.

Damn it, sending her away had been the right thing to do! He knew that. So why did he feel more alone right now than he ever had in his life?

Chapter 14

For the next several days, Aimee heeded Stonehurst's advice and did what she could to stay out of his way. It wasn't hard to do, for he seemed equally determined to avoid her as well. In fact, she rarely caught a glimpse of him except on the infrequent occasions when he decided to join his guests for dinner. Most of his time was spent closed up in the library or in his second-floor study, ostensibly attending to estate business.

But Aimee knew better.

It's for the best, she reflected one morning on her way down to breakfast, a week after her arrival at Stonecliff. As much as she hated the distance between them, the mere possibility of being alone with the man, of trying to carry on a polite conversation with him after all she had learned the other night, filled her with an almost overwhelming sense of panic.

A blush scalded her cheeks as she recalled the feel of Royce's strong, muscled frame pressed up against her, the wet heat of his mouth on her bare breast. The way he had touched and kissed her, as if he could never get enough, had awakened sensations deep within her feminine core that she had never before experienced.

And to her utter astonishment, he had admitted that he wanted her. Even now, a secret thrill went racing through her at the memory of his confession. She had been stunned at the revelation, unable to believe what she was hearing. But there had been no denying the evidence of his arousal. No denying the hunger burning in his eyes for her.

How often had she fantasized that he would look at her in just that way? That he would take her in his arms and kiss her with the same sort of passionate need that he had exhibited that night? No sooner had he brought all her girlish dreams to fruition, however, than he had snatched them all away. His abrupt dismissal of her after what they had shared had hurt more than he would ever know.

For some reason, he was convinced that their attraction to each other could lead nowhere, and it was apparent that nothing Aimee said would change his mind. She didn't understand it, but it was clear that he wasn't about to offer her a detailed explanation. In any case, fretting over the problem would do her little good. She had to remember that for all his talk of wanting her, he had

never once mentioned love. Perhaps his reluctan
to pursue her had nothing to do with his past a
everything to do with a lack of any true emoti
on his part other than lust.

It was a wrenching realization.

Reaching the bottom of the stairs, she shov
her depressing ruminations away and paused
glance in a nearby mirror, making sure she w
presentable before starting down the dimly
hallway toward the dining room. While she w
feeling more than a trifle famished, she was in
hurry to join the dowager duchess, for Theod
sia had an uncanny knack of knowing whenev
something was troubling her. Sensing the tensi
brewing between her young charge and their ho
the elderly lady had been trying for days to fer
out the truth of the matter, poking, prodding, a
asking questions. Questions Aimee had no des
to answer. Not right now.

As she meandered along at a sedate pace, s
let her gaze travel over the Grenville family p
traits that lined the walls on both sides of her. S
had perused them once or twice before, and t
grim, unsmiling faces that had stared back at h
from each canvas had been disconcerting, to s
the least.

One picture in particular had caught her atte
tion. Surrounded by an ornate frame and occup
ing pride of place at the very end of the corrid
overlooking the scrolled archway into the foy

it would have been hard to miss. The subject was a large, intimidating man who bore a striking resemblance to Stonehurst, though his thick dark hair was graying and no scar marked his forbidding visage.

It had to be Royce's father, Aimee concluded, lingering before it. And the smaller painting next to it must be of Royce and his elder brother. In it, the two of them stood side by side in an outdoor setting, dressed in hunting jackets with riding crops held at their sides. They were both little more than boys, perhaps sixteen or seventeen years of age, and while Royce looked stiff and sober, there was a youthful innocence and expectation in those gray eyes that had long ago been leeched out of the gruff and jaded man he had become.

"Ah, here you are, my dear."

The sound of the voice coming from so close to her ear surprised a gasp from her, and she jerked her head about to find Theodosia standing at her elbow. So absorbed had she been in studying the portraits that she hadn't even heard the woman approach.

How embarrassing, to be caught gaping up at Royce's likeness as if entranced!

Lips pursed as she examined the paintings, the dowager duchess didn't appear to be aware of Aimee's discomfiture. "A rather dour lot, aren't they?" she mused aloud, gesturing toward the portraits with a plump, beringed hand.

Aimee cast another glance up at the picture
Royce's father, suddenly overcome by a wave
curiosity. "Did you know them?" she asked he
tantly. "Lord Stonehurst's family, I mean."

"Not well, I'm afraid. I was acquainted with I
father and mother, as we used to attend many
the same social events in my younger years. T
viscountess was sweet, if a bit too biddable for
taste. The viscount, on the other hand . . ." The
dosia frowned and wrinkled her nose in clear d
dain. "Well, suffice it to say that he was not
most charming of gentlemen. A more coldly a
tocratic individual I have yet to meet. And fro
what I understand, his temperament only wo
ened after his wife passed away giving birth
the current Lord Stonehurst."

Poor Royce, Aimee thought, biting her lip. Sh
had no idea that the late viscountess had died
childbirth. It must have been difficult, growing
with no mother and such a harsh and domine
ing father.

Her gaze went to the rendering of Royce's s
ling. A tall, golden-haired man with bright b
eyes, his was one of the only smiling faces amo
the many portraits that hung on the walls. "A
what was your impression of Lord Stonehur:
brother?" she prompted, keeping her tone delib
ately nonchalant in an effort to make her inter
seem nothing more than casual.

"An affable fellow, I suppose. Not at all like

father. He was the elder by a year or two and the heir, you know." The dowager's lined features took on a somber cast. "I believe he and Stonehurst got along well enough, but something happened between them not long after their father's death that resulted in a rift. Something involving the elder brother's fiancée."

"Fiancée?"

"Mmm. There was some sort of accident and the gel was killed. A bad business it was and quite tragic. Rumors abounded, but I don't think anyone knows the whole story aside from those who were directly involved in the incident."

This new information set the wheels of speculation turning in Aimee's head once again. Was this the missing piece of the puzzle that she had been looking for? Could the death of his brother's fiancée somehow be playing a role in Royce's determination to keep her at a distance?

"Child, I can't help but notice that you've been even quieter than usual the last few days. Is everything all right?"

Theodosia's query brought her out of her momentary reverie with a jolt. "I'm fine, Your Grace," she said, offering the elderly lady a reassuring smile. "Just missing home, and wishing that Papa would write to let me know how things are proceeding in the search for my attacker."

That much was true. There had been no further nightmares while she had been at Stonecliff, and while part of her was glad of that, another smaller part of her was disappointed. She wanted to see more. Wanted to know who had been lurking outside on that stormy night. Right now she felt helpless to do anything to aid in the investigation, but if she could only bring that pale, blurry visage into focus, she might finally have the answer as to who might want to be rid of her.

The dowager reached out to cover Aimee's hand with her own. "You must try not to worry. I'm sure your father will send along a message as soon as the scoundrel is in custody."

A shaft of guilt arrowed through Aimee. Here she was, taking advantage of Theodosia's generosity, and conversing as if nothing were out of the ordinary, all the while keeping her in the dark as to the true nature of the danger that surrounded them.

Fighting back the urge to blurt out the truth about everything, she gave the dowager's fingers a grateful squeeze. "You've been so kind, Your Grace. I can't tell you how much I appreciate all you have done."

"Pshaw!" Theodosia linked her arm through Aimee's, drawing her away from the portraits. "Your mother was one of the dearest friends I ever had. She was there for me in those dark and difficult days when my husband first became so ill. And when he passed away and my buffoon of a stepson seized his inheritance and went along his merry way without a hint of concern for my welfare, Elise was the one who made me see that I couldn't just give up. That I had to go on living, even if it was without my Randall. The least I can do in return is be here for her daughters should any of you have need of me."

Aimee studied her chaperone's regal profile as they started back along the corridor toward the dining room, their steps slow and measured to accommodate the dowager's reliance on her cane. For as long as she could remember, this woman had been a benevolent and grandmotherly figure in her life, practically a member of her family. But she suddenly realized that she had never really questioned how such a state of affairs had come about. She had no idea what had led to her mother's friendship with Theodosia or even when they had first met.

"It occurs to me that I don't really know how you and Mama became acquainted," she said aloud, ashamed that she had never taken more of an interest. "On the surface, it doesn't seem as if the two of you would have had much in common. A duchess and a former actress."

A twinkle entered the elderly lady's brown eyes. "More than you might suspect. You see, my father was a mere mister, so my marriage to the duke created quite the stir. Randall's first wife was widely adored by the ton, and they never missed an opportunity to let me know that I was an unworthy replacement. I suppose when I met your mother, I recognized a kindred spirit." She paused and peered up at Aimee, eyebrows lowered in thoughtful appraisal. "You remind me very much of her."

Aimee eyed Theodosia dubiously. She found that observation rather difficult to credit, considering that the Marchioness of Albright had been a bold, beautiful, and dazzling woman who had never cowered from anything. A far cry from her dull and ineffectual youngest daughter.

Her skepticism must have been obvious, for the duchess stopped with unexpected abruptness in the middle of the hallway, pulling Aimee to a halt next to her.

"You are more like Elise than you think, my dear," the woman insisted, her expression earnest. "You have a stubbornness and a quiet determination that comes directly from her. And I suspect behind that shy exterior of yours lurks a reserve of passionate strength you may not even be aware of. When something finally comes along that is of enough importance to you to fight for it, however, that strength will be there for you to call upon." She patted Aimee's hand where it rested on her arm, the gesture brisk and comforting. "Just you remember that the next time you begin to doubt yourself."

With that, she began to march forward once again, towing Aimee along with her.

You are more like Elise than you think, my dear.

Theodosia's staunch and unequivocal statement reverberated persistently in Aimee's head,
making her yearn to believe that the dowager's
faith in her was warranted. That she was stronger
than she had ever imagined she could be. But the
demeaning little voice that had always lurked at
the back of her mind—and that sounded rather
alarmingly like her aunt Olivia—wasted no time
in disabusing her of such a notion.

*Come now, Aimee, you must see that you are simply
deluding yourself. The only thing you inherited from
your mother, aside from the color of your eyes, is an
indisputable weakness of character. To pretend that you
are anything other than a pathetically inept little mouse
would be the height of foolishness.*

Just outside the dining room door, she pulled
up short as an icy weight settled in the pit of her
stomach. Her appetite had completely abandoned
her, and she had no wish to don a mask of pleas-
antness and behave as if all was well while she
indulged in idle conversation over the breakfast
table.

Carefully schooling her features into an unreadable expression, she turned to her companion. "I apologize, Your Grace, but I fear I'm not
feeling particularly hungry. If you will excuse me,
I think I shall retire to the library and see if I can
find a book to pass the time."

"Are you certain, my dear?" Theodosia's gaze

met hers, rife with worry. "You haven't eaten well since we arrived here, and you are bound to make yourself ill again if you continue like this. You are already looking far more peaked than I would like."

Aimee gave her a quick hug, touched by the duchess's genuine concern. "Please don't fret so over me. There is no need. If it will ease your distress, I promise I will more than make up for it at dinner."

Eager to forestall any further objections, she freed herself from the elderly woman's grasp and bussed one wrinkled cheek before hurrying off, leaving the dowager staring anxiously after her.

More than an hour later, however, ensconced in an armchair in the library with a dusty tome of poetry, Aimee expelled a gusty sigh and wearily conceded defeat. Trying to force herself to concentrate on reading right now was proving to be an exercise in futility. For the first time in memory, she was finding it impossible to lose herself in a book, and it was a disquieting discovery.

Perhaps it had to do with the fact that everywhere she looked in this room were reminders of her encounter with Royce. All it took was one glance at the love seat in the far corner to fling her back to that night and the way it had felt to lie in his arms, to have his hands and lips and tongue stroking and caressing her, moving over her bare skin . . .

Smothering a moan, she pushed away the titillating images and rose to replace the book on the shelf. It had been a mistake to come in here. But if she couldn't escape from her turmoil here in the library, where else did that leave?

Her gaze strayed in the direction of the window and the strip of blue sky she could see beyond the glass. As the weather appeared to be fair for a change, maybe she would take a short walk and then stop by the stables to see Balthazar. With so much spare time at her disposal, she had taken to visiting the horse on a daily basis, and she had swiftly grown just as attached to him as she had known she would. Despite his age and failing health, he was a noble and affectionate animal, and she could well understand why Royce had worked so hard to save him, for she would have done the same.

Surely a breath of fresh air could only do her good, Aimee concluded decisively. And it had to be better than mooning about in this monstrous monolith like a sad little ghost for the rest of the afternoon. So, smoothing the wrinkles from the skirt of her dove-gray day gown, she left the chamber with purposeful strides, stopping in the kitchen only long enough to procure a cube of sugar from the cook before heading outside.

The moment she emerged from the house into the bright sunlight, her assigned guard, a burly former Runner by the name of Edmundson, fell into step behind her with a polite nod. She smiled at him cordially in return. In the past week, she had grown rather used to having Tolliver's men trailing about after her whenever she ventured outdoors, though it had initially annoyed her to no end. As much as she would have liked to stroll along alone, she realized that they were only there for her protection, and she had more or less resigned herself to their presence.

Crossing the cobblestones with Edmundson at her heels, she suddenly became aware of a commotion coming from within the stables as she drew near. Few horses were kept at Stonecliff and only a handful of grooms were employed to see to their care, so the hay-strewn building was normally relatively quiet. Not now, however. The muffled hum of anxious voices met her ears, sending a frisson of alarm racing through her.

She quickly ducked inside through the partially closed door, her heart skittering at the loud, agonized whinnies of a horse in obvious distress. Several men stood gathered around Balthazar's stall, and she could see Royce, his features drawn into a mask of grim severity, speaking to a plump, gray-haired man who was holding a large black bag clutched in one hand.

"I'm sorry, my lord, but it doesn't look good," the man was saying, his expression every bit as serious as Royce's. "The animal is not in the prime of health as it is, and such a condition is not easy to deal with in the best of circumstances. He's very weak and having difficulty staying on his feet, and I'm sure I needn't tell you that is a bad sign. Especially when it is crucial at this point that we keep him walking."

Merciful heavens, was he talking about Balthazar?

Catching sight of O'Keefe at the edge of the group, Aimee darted ahead of her guard, who remained hovering just inside the stable door, and seized the groom by his arm to gain his attention. When he turned to look at her, the despair in his eyes slammed into her with the force of a blow.

"What is it?" she whispered, her fingers digging into the material of his sleeve.

"Colic." He spat the word as if it were a curse. "Some blasted fool wasn't careful enough when doling out the grain yesterday, and Balthazar and one of the mares got hold of some moldy feed."

Aimee's mouth went dry. She wasn't very knowledgeable when it came to colic, but she had heard of it before and knew it was a malady that horse owners dreaded. "It's serious?"

O'Keefe nodded. "It can be. We were able to nurse the mare through the worst of it and she should be fine, but she's younger and stronger than Balthazar." A muscle jumping in his jaw, he jerked his head toward Balthazar's stall, where the shrill whinnies continued. "He's been in a great deal of pain since late last night, and he doesn't seem to be getting any better. The horse doctor we brought in from Ipsley isn't holding out much hope."

There was a long span of worried silence as the two of them stared at the ring of men who blocked their view of the gelding. Then O'Keefe raked a hand back through his hair in an abrupt motion, breaking the spell.

"After everything he's been through, everything he's done to keep that horse alive, it can't end like this," he grated, his gaze focused on the viscount. "If Balthazar doesn't make it . . . well, that's something I don't even want to consider."

Her eyes blurring with tears, Aimee stared at the pale, taut face of the man who was slowly but surely chipping away at the barriers around her heart. A heart that was now breaking for him.

That was something she didn't want to consider either.

Chapter 15

The hours seemed to crawl by as the struggle to save Balthazar's life stretched well into the afternoon.

For Aimee, who could do nothing to help except try her best to stay out of everyone's way, it was pure torture to be relegated to observing the proceedings from the shadows, though she couldn't quite bring herself to retreat from the situation. Her own fondness and concern for the animal who had come to mean so much to her in so short a time made it impossible to do so.

Clearly in pain, Balthazar paced his stall, eyes rolling and tail swishing, his sides gleaming with sweat. Several times he attempted to lie down and roll around in the straw, but the viscount and O'Keefe were able to get him back on his feet and keep him walking. As any thrashing about could well prove dangerous to a horse with colic, it was imperative that they made sure he stayed upright as much as possible.

All the while, Royce's face remained set and stoic, giving no hint of his true emotions. But Aimee, far too attuned to him for her own comfort, caught fleeting glimpses of the torment he tried so hard to hide lurking in those slate-gray eyes. If he lost Balthazar, something inside him would shatter, and she doubted if anyone would be able to put the pieces back together.

Never had she felt so useless.

It wasn't until the sun had started to sink below the edge of the cliff line that Aimee recalled her earlier promise to Theodosia and reluctantly made her way back to the house long enough to join the dowager duchess for a light supper. Her appetite was nonexistent, however, and once she had finished telling the elderly lady about Balthazar, she wasted no time changing into warmer clothing and returning to the stables. Royce might be completely oblivious to her presence, but for reasons she didn't want to examine too closely, she needed to be there for him should the worst happen.

The sky was pitch-black and the wind had picked up considerably by the time she stepped out into the courtyard once again. Drawing her cloak more closely around her against the evening chill, she let Edmundson lead the way with a lantern held high. But as they approached the stable, one of the grooms who had been standing just outside the doors unexpectedly blocked her path.

"I'm sorry, my lady," he began in a deferential manner, "but it might be best if you don't go in right now. Things have gotten worse and—"

Not waiting for him to finish, she pushed past him and hurried into the dimly lit building, fear racing through her veins. If circumstances had become that dire, she certainly had no intention of waiting outside.

Within, only O'Keefe and Royce were still attending to Balthazar. The gelding was on the ground, tossing his head wildly and nipping at the viscount with bared teeth whenever he ventured too close, evidently in far too much agony to recognize his owner. Once, the horse tried valiantly to stand on his own in response to Royce's prodding, but hours of walking had weakened his scarred rear leg even further, and it refused to hold him, shaking under the strain before collapsing.

"Damn it, man, you know what has to happen," O'Keefe was saying, his jaw taut as he watched from a spot outside the stall, away from the animal's flailing hooves. "This is bloody madness."

It surprised Aimee to hear the groom address his employer so familiarly, though she supposed it shouldn't have. From the way O'Keefe had spoken of Royce the first day she met him, she had guessed that there was some sort of bond between these two that had been born from long years of association, and it seemed she had been correct.

Creeping a bit closer, she peered around one of the wooden struts near the entrance as the red-haired man went on, his voice heavy with regret. "I don't like it any more than you do, but it's time to end this. Doc Finnerty said there is nothing more to be done."

Royce, who had been murmuring to Balthazar in a soothing manner, stopped and glanced back over his shoulder at the groom, his contemptuous expression conveying his opinion of the good doctor. "Finnerty is an ass who admitted he didn't want to waste his time trying to save a horse who should have died eight years ago."

"An ass he may be, but that doesn't change the facts." O'Keefe swept off his cap and swiped at the perspiration that coated his forehead before flinging his arm toward the exhausted gelding. "Sweet Christ, look at him! He's too weary to keep fighting! Do you truly want to prolong his suffering just because you're too stubborn to see the truth?"

Her gaze transfixed on Royce's strained features, Aimee could almost imagine the battle that was being waged within him at that precise moment. After struggling so hard for so long to keep Balthazar alive, she was sure it went against his every instinct to just give up. It simply wasn't in him to surrender unless there was no other recourse, but there could be no denying that putting off the inevitable was only drawing out the animal's misery.

"You're right," he finally said aloud, the acknowledgment sounding stiff and unemotional. Only the most discerning of observers would have noticed the tightening of his jaw and the slow clenching and unclenching of his fists at his sides and realized that he wasn't nearly as removed as he appeared.

His craggy face solemn, O'Keefe leaned over to retrieve something that had been propped up against the wall next to him. When he lifted it, the lantern light glinted off a long, metal barrel, and Aimee's stomach did a heaving roll.

A hunting rifle.

Cradling the weapon in the crook of his arm, the groom entered the stall and lifted a square, freckled hand, clasping his employer on the shoulder in a show of support and compassion.

"I'll do it," he offered quietly.

"No." Royce's response was immediate and unequivocal as he reached out to take the rifle from the other man. "I'll do it. He's my responsibility."

Then, to Aimee's astonishment, his brooding gaze traveled across the stable to lock unerringly with hers. She'd had no idea he even knew she was there.

"If you want to do something to help me," he told O'Keefe, jerking his head in her direction, "take her out of here."

She gasped and started to protest, but the groom came striding toward her, the look in his eyes warning her not to make a fuss.

"Come along, my lady," he murmured gently. "Please. He won't want you to see him do this."

Without another word, she reluctantly let O'Keefe lead her out into the moonlit courtyard, where the other grooms had congregated with Tolliver's men, caps in hands and expressions sober, as if they knew exactly what was coming.

There was a long silence. Then the loud crack of a gunshot rang out.

For several seconds, no one spoke. The only movement came from the steadily increasing wind that was blowing in off the sea to tear at their hair and clothing. Her teeth sinking into her lower lip so hard she was sure she had drawn blood, Aimee stared at the stable doors with focused intensity, desperately wishing she could see through them. Behind that wooden barrier, she could hear the rest of the horses whinnying nervously, startled by the shot, but there was no other sound to offer a clue as to what was going on within.

Even though she had been waiting with bated breath for them to do so, she wasn't at all prepared when the doors finally swung open with a force that made them all jump. The man who emerged from the darkened interior looked tired and old beyond his years. His scar stood out against the whiteness of a face frozen into a mask of deliberate blankness, though midnight shadows shifted in the depths of his eyes, hinting at the volatile emotions that swirled just beneath the surface of that impassive veneer, straining to break free.

Aimee blinked away the moisture blurring her vision and took a stumbling step toward him, her hand extended as if to touch him, to offer whatever small bit of comfort she could.

"My lord?" she ventured, but he gave no indication that he had even heard her. He stalked by, looking neither left nor right, his gaze focused straight ahead, and she was left staring after him helplessly until he had disappeared into the house.

"Don't take it to heart, my lady," O'Keefe said in a consolatory tone as he moved to stand at her side. The rest of the group had already returned to their previous posts in the stable and around the courtyard. Of Tolliver's men, only Edmundson still lingered nearby, ever mindful of her safety.

"He's always had a habit of closing himself off as tight as a clamshell whenever he's hurting," the groom explained, his countenance troubled. "This has been quite the blow, even though a part of him was more than likely expecting it, and he'll be blaming himself for the whole thing."

"Blaming himself?" Aimee echoed, frowning. "But why? It wasn't his fault."

"Try telling him that. Around here, *everything* is his fault. His curse at work again, you know."

O'Keefe's words held an edge of something Aimee couldn't quite put her finger on, and it had her wrinkling her forehead in confusion.

"What do you mean?" she asked him. "What curse?"

The groom's eyes grew shuttered. "That's something you'll have to be discussing with him, my lady. But I will say this. That demon of a father of his has a lot to answer for."

With one last enigmatic look in the direction of the house, O'Keefe pivoted and loped off, abandoning her to the unanswered questions buzzing in her head.

Chapter 16

Two hours later, Aimee still couldn't get the groom's puzzling statement out of her thoughts. Lying in bed, staring up at the ceiling, she sifted through various possibilities, but the only thing she succeeded in doing was frustrating herself further.

That demon of a father of his has a lot to answer for . . .

What had Royce's father done to warrant being referred to as a demon? she wondered. She knew that Theodosia had described him as a hard man, but had he truly been as terrible as all that? And what sort of curse had O'Keefe been alluding to?

It was all very confusing, and she had no idea what to make of any of it. All she knew for certain was that somewhere in this house, Royce was mourning the passing of Balthazar alone. And suddenly that knowledge was more than she could bear.

She threw back the covers and climbed out of bed, stopping only long enough to slip her dressing gown on over her nightclothes and to assure herself that the dowager duchess was still snoring loudly in her connecting room before furtively creeping out into the hall.

There were only two places Aimee could think of where the viscount might retreat to nurse his wounds in private. And as it happened, her first guess turned out to be the correct one. As she approached his second-floor study, faint noises drifted to her through the closed door.

Screwing up her courage, she lifted her hand and rapped sharply on the oaken panel, then waited with bated breath for a reply.

There was a second of hushed silence.

"Go away."

There could be no mistaking the peremptory command in the harsh voice, but she wasn't about o be discouraged and she knocked again, a bit nore insistently.

"I said go away!"

This time the directive was delivered in a slurred shout, and it was followed by a particularly virulent curse and the crash of breaking glass.

Her heart leaping in alarm, Aimee didn't hesitate, but pushed the door open and threw herself into the room.

Within, all was dark and still, the only light coming from the faint glow of the fire that had been laid on the hearth to ward off the evening chill. At first, she could make out nothing but indistinct shapes against the gloomy backdrop, and she had to strain her eyes to see through the dimness.

"Royce?" she ventured uncertainly.

On the far side of the room, a figure detached itself from the shadows that danced on the walls and moved into the circle of firelight. The flickering flames illuminated a pallid face, marked by weariness and the ravages of grief.

His coat discarded and his clothes stained and rumpled, Royce was studying Aimee through bleary eyes, his fingers wrapped tightly around the neck of what looked like a half-empty bottle of scotch.

"I do hate to be rude," he began, his offhand tone a stark contrast to the barked orders he had issued when she had been on the other side of the door, "but it appears that your education has been sorely neglected. You seem to be under the mistaken impression that when someone says go away, it means come right in, regardless of whether you have been invited to do so or not."

Aimee drew herself up stiffly, determined not to let him intimidate her, and took a step farther into the chamber. She came to an abrupt halt, however, when she felt something crunch under the toe of her slipper. Looking down, she saw the shards of a crystal snifter littering the floor and realized that this was the source of the crash she had heard just before she had entered the study. The mental picture of him hurling it at the door in the grip of some dark emotion was enough to remind her of the anguish he must be suffering, and she immediately softened.

"Royce, please," she beseeched him. "I know how much Balthazar meant to you and I know you must be hurting. You shouldn't be alone right now."

His grating laugh held a wealth of cynicism and very little humor. "Ah, but that's where you're wrong. I am better off alone. It's best for everyone."

"No one is better off alone."

"Really?" Royce arched a brow at Aimee's adamant assertion. "Well, you are entitled to your opinion, I suppose, but I'm afraid I am forced to disagree."

Pivoting on his booted heel, he strode over to the mahogany sideboard, where he dashed a liberal dose of scotch into another snifter and tossed it back before glancing at her over his shoulder.

"You know," he drawled, one corner of his mouth curling mockingly, "this is the second time since you came to stay at Stonecliff that you have sought me out dressed in your nightclothes." His deliberately salacious gaze roamed over her from head to toe, lingering in a blatant fashion on every curve and hollow in between. "A person could be excused for thinking that my accusation the other night wasn't so far off the mark after all."

Aimee crossed her arms and glared at him. Even though she was well aware of what game he was playing, she couldn't contain the heated little shiver that raced through her at his lustful stare. "If you are trying to make me take offense so I will go storming off and leave you to your own devices, you may as well give up now. It isn't going to work."

"Ah, but if at first you don't succeed . . ."

Brushing aside Royce's taunting words, she advanced toward him, closing the distance that separated them until she stood close enough to look up into his sardonic visage.

"Please," she whispered. "You don't have to pretend with me. Let me help you."

For just an instant, she thought she caught a glimpse of something haunted in the depths of his eyes before he slammed the empty snifter down on the sideboard and whirled away from her with a muttered imprecation.

"Take my word for it, Aimee," he growled, his hands fisting at his sides as he started to prowl restlessly around the edges of the room. "You don't want to help me. It's never a good idea to champion a lost cause. Just look at poor Balthazar. I tried to help him, and you see what happened."

"You're not a lost cause, and Balthazar's death wasn't your fault. You did everything you could to save him, but you heard the doctor. There was nothing more to be done."

Royce raked unsteady fingers through his hair. "It was a mistake to get so attached," he said bitterly. "To let myself care. You'd think I'd know better by now, but—" His mouth snapped closed and tightened into a grim line, and when his gaze met Aimee's once more, there was a savagery in his expression that reminded her of a caged animal. "If you have any sense of self-preservation at all, Kitten, you'll run away right now and count it a lucky escape."

The edge of finality in his last statement gave her a vaguely uneasy feeling, for she could sense a mounting tension in him, rising up to charge the very air around him. Like lightning before a storm.

"What is that supposed to mean?" she demanded to know, planting her hands on her hips.

"It means that I want you to get out." Stalking back across the study to the sideboard in a few lengthy strides, he reached for the bottle of scotch again, a wildness blazing in his eyes that frightened her. "If I'm going to drink myself into oblivion, I would rather do it in peace."

When she neither moved nor spoke, but continued to stand there, watching him apprehensively, he jerked his head in her direction and cast her a savage glare. "Did you hear me?" he spat. "I said get out."

She hesitated as her mind worked at a frantic pace. Perhaps it was a mistake to push him now, but she couldn't quite bring herself to walk away and leave him like this. So, despite the trembling of her slender frame, she lifted her chin and faced him defiantly. "No."

And that was when the wildness exploded.

"Bloody hell!" Rearing back, his teeth bared in an almost feral snarl, Royce hurled the bottle of scotch at the wall as hard as he could. It fragmented into a thousand pieces, its contents spraying across the plaster in an amber tide of liquid. The sound of shattering glass made Aimee flinch as it rained down onto the floor.

Then, before she even had a chance to recover from her shock or react in any way, he lunged toward the desk in the corner, sweeping everything off its surface and sending books, papers, and office implements flying as he overturned the massive piece of furniture with one mighty heave.

"Damn it, what will it take to make you go away?" he thundered, rounding on her, his features suffused with a primitive rage. "Now do you see why you have to stay away from me?"

Stunned, stricken, Aimee knew she should probably be terrified at his show of violence. She had never seen him like this before, and it was chilling to behold. But something raw and tortured just beneath the surface of his fury called out to her, holding her there even as her head urged her to flee. Somehow, no matter how out of control he appeared to be, she couldn't believe that he would ever hurt her.

So, taking a deep breath and shaking off her trepidation, she hurried forward just as he made another restive motion, as if he were considering smashing something else.

"Stop, Royce!" she cried, seizing his wrist, hoping to prevent any further destruction. "Stop trying to scare me away. This isn't you."

He froze, his chest heaving with his labored breathing, and she could feel the tension thrumming through him as he fixed his feverishly glittering stare on her. Finally, after a long, drawn-out moment in which she began to wonder about the wisdom of her actions, he seemed to exert a tremendous effort and regain some semblance of control over his temper. Slowly but surely, one breath at a time, the anger gradually seeped out of him.

Extricating himself from her hold, he took a step away from her, his shoulders slumping as he peered down at the damage he had wrought with a fatalistic expression. "Don't fool yourself, Aimee," he said hoarsely. "This is the *real* me. The man you think you know doesn't exist. It's a disguise I wear to hide the truth."

"Then what is the truth?" Not about to let him

turn his back on her now, Aimee pursued him, reaching out to grab his sleeve. "Tell me. Please, Royce. Make me understand."

"I tried to tell you the other night." He brushed her off again and dropped into the chair next to the wreckage of his desk, reaching up to scrub at his face with a shaking hand. "There's something inside me. A darkness so full of anger and desolation that I can barely contain it." He spread his arms in a gesture that encompassed not just their immediate surroundings, but Stonecliff itself. "Look around you. I no longer have a normal life. I've had to isolate myself, seclude myself, because every moment I am in the company of other people, I can feel it clawing at my insides like some slavering beast, fighting to escape. And each time it takes over, someone else gets hurt. Someone I care about."

Aimee sank to her knees before him, trying to make some sort of sense of his words. She had heard of men who returned from war forever changed, their minds altered by what they had witnessed in battle. Could he have been affected in the same way?

"Royce, listen to me," she began diffidently. "I know what you experienced at Waterloo must have been a nightmare for you. And I know that men are forced to do terrible things in war that—"

"No," he interrupted her, shaking his head.

"This isn't because of Waterloo. Oh, it's certainly grown stronger and harder to control since then, but this has been with me forever. Since I was born, I think."

Letting his gaze travel past her in the direction of the fireplace, he contemplated the mesmerizing flicker of the flames with a faraway expression. "My mother died bringing me into this world, and my father always hated me for that. He never let me forget it. All of his attention and affection went to my elder brother, while I was treated like a piece of offal he had wiped off the bottom of his boot. He used to tell me that I was a hell-spawned little bastard who had been cursed from the second I was ripped from my mother's womb. That I was destined to bring nothing but pain and misery to everyone around me."

Aimee drew herself up in wrathful indignation, her blood simmering in her veins like lava. What sort of monster would say such unforgivable things to his own son?

She placed a gentle hand on Royce's knee. "I'm so sorry," she said softly. "He sounds like a horrible man who didn't deserve to have any children."

His mouth curved in a wry grimace. "I won't argue with that. But what he said about me was nothing but the truth."

"I don't believe that."

"I never wanted to believe it either, Aimee, but I can't deny that I was full of rage from the time

I was a child. I felt constantly driven to rebel, to strike out at the people around me, and there was very little I wouldn't do."

"You wanted your father's attention, Royce. That's all."

"Perhaps. It was more than that, however. I wanted to hurt him, and I eventually learned that the most effective way to do that was through Alex."

Aimee tilted her head, studying Royce quizzically. "Your brother?" she prompted.

Nodding, he got to his feet and wandered over to take up a stance before the hearth, the pain that marked his brooding countenance unmistakable. "Alex didn't deserve my ire. He never treated me with the same sort of cruel contempt as our father. We were even close for a time as lads. But I grew to resent the way he could do no wrong in our sire's eyes, and I became fiercely competitive with him." He glanced back at Aimee. "Of course, after our father passed away and Alex inherited the title, things settled down somewhat. We weren't the best of friends, to be sure, but without our father there to fan the flames of our rivalry, we were able to come to an understanding of sorts. And that's when Cordelia entered our lives."

The reverent way he spoke the woman's name, the genuine warmth that lit his eyes all too briefly, made it obvious that this Cordelia had meant a great deal to him.

"She was the daughter of the Earl of Sumter,

and she was truly beautiful," he went on. "Both inside and out. Always laughing and cheerful. Alex fell head over heels for her the instant they met and proposed to her soon afterward. And when he brought her back to Stonecliff to meet me, I couldn't help but be equally enchanted. Right away she sensed the strain between the two of us and started trying to mend fences, to bring us closer together as brothers. I'd never met anyone like her."

Aimee rose and moved to stand next to him. "You fell in love," she said quietly. It wasn't a question. Never before had she considered the possibility that Royce might have given his heart to someone else, and she felt an unwanted pang of jealousy.

"I thought I was in love at the time. Looking back now, however, I can see that it was just boyish infatuation. I was young, only twenty, and I'm afraid that my resentment toward Alex hadn't been completely buried. Suddenly I started to look around at all that he had—the title, Stonecliff, Cordelia—and I decided that I wanted something for myself."

"So you seduced her." Again, it wasn't a question, and Royce responded to Aimee's flatly uttered statement with a scowl.

"I'm not proud of it," he grated. "However, in my defense, she certainly didn't discourage my attentions. I would even venture to say that it was a mutual seduction. But Cordelia regretted it almost immediately. She told me that she loved Alex and always would. That what had happened between us could never happen again.

"And that's when the darkness inside me rose up, stronger than ever. That angry, all-consuming need to strike out at everyone. Especially Alex. It was like a sickness, prodding me to bait him at every turn, until I'm sure he was quite prepared to throttle me. But no matter how angry I was, I never intended—I didn't want—"

When Royce stumbled to a halt and swallowed visibly, Aimee knew that he had come to the most important part of the tale, and she reached up to touch his arm in a gesture of comfort.

"What happened?" she prodded gently.

Bracing his hands on the mantel before him, he gripped the edge so tightly that she could see his knuckles turning white. "I was out riding one afternoon when I encountered Alex and Cordelia, out for a drive in Alex's phaeton, and just the sight of her sitting next to him so complacently was enough to bring my temper roaring to the surface. As usual, I was deliberately snide and insulting, and some heated words were exchanged. Before I knew it, I was issuing a challenge: a race back to the house, with the winner to receive a kiss from Cordelia.

"Of course, I knew Alex would accept. He was never one to back down from a dare, and he seemed particularly primed to best me. Perhaps he had some inkling as to what had passed between myself and Cordelia, but I suppose I'll never know now. Halfway to our destination, he took a bend in the trail too swiftly and the phaeton overturned, slamming into a tree."

He paused, and when he continued, his voice sounded thick and guttural, as if the words were being wrested from him against his will. "Cordelia was killed instantly, her neck broken. Alex's legs were pinned beneath the wreckage and he was left a cripple."

Horrified, Aimee stared up at the man next to her, her heart aching for him. Though his face was impassive, she could sense the overwhelming guilt and grief hovering over him like tangible entities.

Her nails digging into the material of his shirt, she willed him to look at her, to see the sincerity in her eyes. "Royce, you can't blame yourself. It was an unfortunate accident, but you didn't *make* it happen. It wasn't your fault."

When his gaze finally swung about to lock with hers, she could barely stifle a gasp at the wrenching agony that swirled within those gray irises. "Alex certainly thought it was. I can remember him attacking me at Cordelia's funeral, accusing me of being a blight on the family name. He told me that everything Father had said about me was true and that anyone who cared for me was doomed to a tragic end."

"I'm sure he didn't mean it."

"And I'm sure he did. I had just killed the woman he loved, Aimee."

Before she could voice the protest hovering on her lips, Royce pulled away from her and moved back toward his desk, where he stooped down to retrieve a heavy glass paperweight from the mess on the floor.

"In any case, I couldn't bear to remain at Stonecliff and witness his pain, day in and day out," he continued. He was hefting the faceted object in his palm, examining it as if he had never seen it before, as if he needed something else to focus on besides the story he was relating. "I packed up and left to accept my military commission, like any dutiful second son. At that point, I was so driven by the darkness, so full of rage and self-contempt that I didn't care what happened to me, and I can recall actually being eager for battle. As it happened, it wasn't long before I got my wish."

"At Waterloo?" Aimee surmised as she watched him turn to place the paperweight on a nearby table.

He inclined his head in acknowledgment. "At Waterloo. I was an inexperienced officer among an inexperienced regiment under the command of the Earl of Uxbridge, and when he gave us the order to charge that day in support of the infantry, I didn't hesitate. I threw myself into the fray recklessly, without a second thought. I think I wanted to die.

"Everything passed by in a blur, and I don't remember much of the actual battle except for the sound of cannon fire. I was in the thick of things when a French soldier appeared from out of the smoke and knocked me from my horse." Lifting his hand, he traced the scar that snaked down his cheek. "You saw what he did to Balthazar. The same thing he did to my face before he poised his weapon over my heart. I thought the end I had sought had finally arrived."

"But you didn't die." Aimee wrapped her arms around her midriff, struggling to repress the urge to wrap them around him instead. She was very much afraid that if she did so, he would push her away and bring an abrupt end to the conversation. "You survived."

"Not because of anything I did to save myself," Royce told her flatly. "One of the soldiers in my regiment was a young man by the name of Benton Garvey. I had a passing acquaintance with him, as we had attended Eton together, but we had never been bosom chums. For some reason, he had decided to latch on to me, and though I tried to keep a distance between us, the blasted fool wouldn't be dissuaded. The last thing I saw before I passed out from the pain was him throwing himself at the enemy standing over me."

His jaw worked furiously and he closed his eyes, as if trying to ward off the memories that were assailing him. "When I returned to consciousness, I was lying on the battlefield, bleeding but alive. Alive while so many around me were dead. Including Garvey. And to add to my guilt, I came home to discover that Alex was gone as well. A belated victim of the accident I caused."

"So you see," he concluded, confronting Aimee with an almost resigned air, "that was when I knew that Father had been right all along. I am cursed. And while I appreciate your concern, Kitten, if you value your life, you are much better off far away from me."

Aimee let several seconds of silence tick by before replying.

"I don't think," she finally said, slowly and quite deliberately, "that I have ever heard such a pile of rubbish in my life."

Chapter 17

Royce gawked at Aimee in utter stupefaction, his mouth agape. He couldn't possibly have heard her correctly. He had just finished confiding in her all the sordid details of his bleak and anguish-ridden past, and her response was to call it a pile of rubbish?

"I beg your pardon?" he drew out slowly, his eyes narrowing to dangerous slits.

Her own eyes were sparking with militant ire as she met him glare for glare. "You heard me. What rot! You are no more cursed than I am."

Her tart retort had Royce stiffening in outraged affront. "Did you pay the slightest bit of attention to anything I just said?" he ground out from between clenched teeth, trying desperately to hang on to what was left of his patience. "This is not a joke, nor is it an exaggeration on my part. People *die* around me."

"But not *because* of you. They were accidents. Surely you must see that." When he failed to answer, she made a sound of frustration and stamped her foot, her small frame practically vibrating with the force of her indignation. "I wish I had your father in front of me right now. That . . . that . . . *monster* should be shot for ever putting such an idea in your head in the first place."

Her display of righteous fury on his behalf surprised Royce, and some of his irritation subsided. It had been a quite a while since anyone had championed him, and her show of loyalty warmed him way down deep in a place that had been cold and empty for a very long time.

Stepping forward, he rested his palms on her rigid shoulders before addressing her in a carefully controlled tone. "Aimee, I appreciate that you want to help, but there isn't anything you can do for me. You saw what I'm capable of, and it gets worse. I was able to tamp it back down this time, but next time . . ." He paused, his gaze holding hers solemnly. "I'm not always in my right mind when it happens, and I don't want to hurt you."

"Nonsense," she said with quiet confidence. "I've said it before, and I'll say it again. You would never hurt me. Yes, you apparently have a formidable temper. That doesn't mean that you deserve to be locked away from the light of day and shunned for all eternity. And I personally think it says a great deal for your character that in all of the years I've known you, you've never displayed the more volatile side of your nature in front of me until now."

Bloody hell, there was no getting through to t
obstinate woman, Royce thought with a grima
Releasing her, he whirled away from her, racki
his brain for some means to make her see reaso
but she followed, circling around him until s
was looking up into his face once again.

"Royce, please," she murmured, her expressi
troubled. "You must see how ridiculous this
Tell me you don't honestly believe that you ha
really been cursed."

Avoiding her probing gaze, he gave a fatalis
shrug. "In the literal sense? Perhaps not. But the
is something wrong with me, Aimee. I'm dar
aged somehow. Whether because of my fath
or the people I've lost, or the war, or some oth
worldly curse, I don't know. What I do know
that I cannot and will not expose anybody else
this demon that torments me."

He started to move past her again, but this ti
she stopped him by the simple expedient of sl
ing her fragile hand into his. The trusting way s
twined their fingers together brought a lump
his throat, temporarily rendering him speechle

"Royce, believe me when I say that I und
stand what it's like to be so haunted by your p
that you let it affect every aspect of your life." F
voice was soft and steady. "For years I've felt as
were lacking somehow. As if I were inadequate
so many ways. I was convinced that no one cou
ever want me, and the thought of offering mys

to someone, only to be rejected, was terrifying. It was far easier to hide behind my walls and pretend I was content to be a dowdy spinster for the rest of my life than it was for me to take a chance."

A wave of self-loathing washed over Royce at her words. "You see," he grated. "And that's my fault as well."

She shook her head. "No! It wasn't until my memories began to return that I realized it all goes back to the night my mother was killed. I know now that Mama didn't mean any of the things she said to Lord Stratton, that it was all an attempt to distract him, to keep him from hurting me. Back then, however, when I heard her tell him that she was unhappy with her life, that she wanted to leave with him, I was devastated by it. I genuinely believed that my sisters and I weren't important enough for her to stay. That *I* wasn't important enough."

Her countenance was so sorrowful that Royce couldn't resist the urge to lift their linked hands to his lips and press a tender kiss to her knuckles. "Never doubt your importance, Kitten. I know she loved you."

"Yes, she did. But looking back, I see how her words that night have affected my sense of self-worth for years, even though I didn't consciously remember any of it. And when you add on the responsibility that I felt over Lord Stratton pulling the trigger . . . Well, you can imagine."

"That wasn't your fault. You were just a child who wanted to hold on to her mother."

"Maybe, but I can't help but wonder what would have happened if I had simply let her go. She might still be alive if I hadn't interfered."

Incensed that she would take such a burden onto her own shoulders, Royce leveled Aimee with a stern frown. "Don't do this to yourself," he told her firmly. "Stratton may have wavered for an instant, but the man was insane and would have probably shot her anyway. There is nothing you could have done any differently to change the outcome."

She bit her lip. "I want to believe that," she whispered.

"Then believe it." Letting go of her hand, he reached up to cup her chin in his palm. "And you can believe this as well. There is nothing wrong with you. I said it the other night and I meant it. Everything about you is incredibly right."

A tide of hot color washed into her cheeks at his compliment. "I think you're beginning to convince me of that. Knowing that you desire me makes all the difference in the world." She gave him a tentative smile. "You know, you've always been one of the few people in my life besides my father and sisters who never treated me as if I weren't good enough. I can't tell you how much that meant to me and how much I valued our friendship. I . . . missed you when you were gone."

Royce winced. Never before had he truly appreciated the full extent of the damage he had done to her vulnerable heart with his defection. But he did now, and the guilt and regret was staggering. "I'm so sorry that I left you without an explanation, Aimee," he rasped. "I was trying to do the right thing."

"I thought it was because my declaration of love had revolted you. That it was your way of rejecting me." She cast a brief glance in the direction of the overturned desk and the mess surrounding it. "But this is why you did it, isn't it? Because of this curse you are so certain is hanging over you."

At the reminder of a subject he had no desire to revisit, he dropped his hand and moved back from her, removing himself from her tantalizing proximity. "I told you before it had nothing to do with you. I did—I do—want you. But I couldn't let myself get any further involved with you than I already was. It was getting more and more difficult to resist the pull between us, and I knew if I kept coming around to visit you and your father, sooner or later I would give in."

A speculative look entered her eyes, and she took a step forward, immediately closing the distance he had just put between them. "You don't seem to be having any trouble resisting me right now," she murmured, her lashes lowering in a surprisingly provocative fashion. "Perhaps I should see if I can do something about that."

Going up on tiptoe, she startled him by running a finger along the line of his jaw, and he couldn't help but wonder if the little minx was actually attempting to seduce him. If so, she was remarkably skilled at it for an innocent. He was frozen in place, held prisoner by the gentleness of her touch and the warmth in her eyes.

But when her finger skimmed upward, making unexpected contact with the jagged edge of his scar, he flinched and quickly ensnared her wrist. "Don't."

"Why?"

"Because it's a mark of the ugliness inside of me."

"There is no ugliness inside of you. When I look at you, I don't see it at all."

"Aimee, please." Her nearness was scattering his thoughts like leaves on the wind, making it impossible for him to remember all the reasons he shouldn't touch her. "I don't think this is a good idea."

She shifted closer, the soft curves of her breasts just brushing his chest. "Oh, I happen to think it's a very good idea," she breathed.

Then, leaning forward, she pressed her lips to his scar in a tender benediction.

And that was all it took. Suddenly, the desire he felt for her was more than he could contain, and he could no longer summon the will to try and fight it.

With a savage growl, he wrapped his arms around her and seized her lips with his.

Aimee felt the thrill of elation sweep through her as Royce's mouth came down on hers, hard and seeking. She had never played the role of temptress before, hadn't even been sure she was capable of it, and it was a strangely addictive pleasure. What a heady feeling, to know that this powerful man was just as susceptible to the sensual spell that held them in its thrall as she was.

Tangling her fingers in the shaggy hair at his nape, she reveled in the way his strong arms tightened around her waist, locking her against him. The way his lips caressed hers over and over, as if he couldn't get enough of her. He tasted of the most erotic of fantasies, his rich and spicy flavor intoxicating to her senses, and an intense heat began to unfurl inside her, consuming her. All she could think about was getting even closer to him, making him see that what was between them could no longer be denied.

This feels so right, she thought dimly. *As if it were meant to be. Surely he can feel it too.*

As if in response to her thoughts, Royce suddenly took the kiss deeper, his tongue parting her lips to delve into the moist warmth of her mouth and tangle with hers. A moan vibrating in the back of her throat, she met his invasion with an equal hunger, swept away by their mutual ardor.

The next thing she knew, she was lying on the hearth rug and he was looming over her, quickly divesting himself of his lawn shirt. His fingers were dexterous on the buttons, and when he stripped the garment off and tossed it aside, she was barely able to stifle a gasp at his muscular perfection. The firelight glinted off the sculpted planes of his chest and bathed his bronzed skin with a molten glow.

He was like some Greek statue come to life, Apollo or Adonis in the flesh, and she could hardly believe he wanted her. But there could be no denying the evidence of his desire as he shed his breeches. His manhood sprang free, thick and swollen with his arousal.

"Royce," she murmured, lifting her arms, anxious to feel him against her again. "I need you."

"Shhh." He lowered himself to her and pressed another kiss to the tip of her nose, the flickering flames illuminating the unscarred portion of his face and revealing the secret smile that curved his mouth. "I want this to be perfect for you, Kitten, and I have every intention of taking my time. Patience, hmmm?"

Her lashes fluttered closed on a soft sigh as he swept her hair aside so he could smooth his lips down the column of her throat, leaving a burning trail in his wake. It was enough to wring a shiver from her, even as his teeth nipped delicately at the racing pulse just above her collarbone.

"Please," she entreated, not quite sure what she was begging him for. Clutching at his shoulders, she arched her neck to give him better access, awash in sensations that frightened her even as they exhilarated her. Already she was damp and aching between her thighs, desperate for something she instinctively knew only he could give her.

And he was well aware of how he was affecting her. "I *will* please you, sweetheart," he crooned close to her ear, his breath tickling her cheek and stirring the tendrils of hair at her temple. "I promise."

His long, lean fingers went to work, and somehow her nightclothes seemed to melt away, one diaphanous layer at a time. When he finally had her naked before him, he reared back and let his heated gaze travel over every inch of her, from the curves of her small, pink-tipped breasts, to her slender hips, to the golden-brown thatch of hair that guarded the entrance to her feminine core.

"You're beautiful, Aimee," he rasped, his features taut with a raw and savage hunger. "Don't ever doubt it again."

And as he moved to cover her body with his once more, his mouth capturing her lips for another long, drugging kiss, she genuinely *felt* beautiful for the first time in her life.

It was at that point that every rational thought

seemed to fly from Aimee's head, and she lost herself to the passionate loving of the man she now knew without a shadow of a doubt held her heart.

With a single-minded thoroughness, Royce set about bringing every nerve ending she possessed to tingling life. With lips, hands, and tongue, he explored her curves and hollows, lavishing his ardent attention on her breasts, belly, and thighs. The damp heat of his mouth drove her to heights of ecstasy she hadn't imagined existed as he sucked the pebbled peaks of her nipples until she was writhing beneath him.

But just as he cupped her hips and fit himself against her in the most intimate way possible, she was assailed by a wave of self-doubt.

Pressing her hands against his chest, she held him off, staring up at him uncertainly. "Royce, wait."

Her words brought him to an immediate halt, and he lifted his head to look down at her in concern. "What is it?" he asked.

"I don't know. It's just . . ." She sank her teeth into her lower lip, hesitating as she studied his compelling visage. He had seen so much more of the world than she had. Had no doubt shared what he was about to share with her with many other women through the years, and the thought made all her insecurities come rushing back to the surface. "I don't want you to be disappointed."

The tension that had seized his powerful frame seemed to dissipate as she spoke, and he gave her a tender look. "You could never disappoint me."

"But I'm so woefully inexperienced, Royce. I know there must have been women in your past who knew how to please you, but I—"

He silenced her with a kiss. "There have been women, though not as many as you might think." Lifting his hand, he traced his scar in an almost absent fashion. "Most of the females I meet are put off by this, I'm afraid. And I swear to you that not one of them ever affected me the way you do."

The question spilled forth before Aimee could call it back. "Not even Cordelia?"

There was a deafening hush. Then, his eyes burning with a fierce light, Royce cupped her face in his hands and met her gaze unwaveringly. "Not even Cordelia."

The rough assurance in his husky voice succeeded in allaying her fears, and she finally pulled him back down to her, silently urging him to take up where he had left off.

And he did. Between renewed kisses and caresses, he parted her thighs, his fingers finding the entrance to her feminine portal and sliding gently within, attempting to widen it in readiness for his possession. She gasped at the liquid rush of warmth that gushed forth when the rigid length of his manhood nestled against her soft nest of curls, and he used the slickness of her juices to ease his penetration as he pressed himself into her velvety depths and broke through the barrier of her innocence.

At first, Aimee was conscious of nothing but a burning fullness that had her nails digging into his muscled flanks in reaction. But with a smooth, rocking glide, he began to move within her, each stroke lessening her discomfort until she was panting at the force of her swiftly escalating pleasure. Her body seemingly beyond her control, she clenched around his driving shaft, milking him in an effort to increase the titillating friction, and he responded by lifting her legs higher along his hips and plunging deeper, picking up the tempo of his thrusts.

Suddenly, with a harsh groan, he went rigid above her and shuddered convulsively, the scalding heat of his release tightening her womb and sending her plummeting over the edge into her own shattering orgasm.

Afterward, limp and replete, they both lay cuddled together, their bodies still entwined. More content than she had ever been in her life, Aimee could feel herself floating on a blissful cloud, pictures of the future she could have with this man flitting through her mind.

"I love you, Royce."

She hadn't meant to let it slip out, but the admission escaped her without her volition. And just as he had the last time she had whispered those words to him, Royce abruptly stiffened before he disengaged himself from her and rolled away.

With troubled eyes, she watched him as he dressed, praying she hadn't ruined everything with her hasty declaration. "What is it, Royce?" she murmured, even though she knew the answer. "What's wrong?"

Slipping into his shirt, he glanced back at her over his shoulder. "Don't love me, Aimee," he rasped, his eyes cold. "I'll only end up destroying you in the end, and I refuse to let that happen. There are no happily-ever-afters with me."

With that, he turned and strode from the room, leaving her curled cold and alone by the fire.

Chapter 18

The rest of the night passed with agonizing slowness for Aimee once she had returned to her own chamber. Tossing and turning in her bed, unable to drift off, she had spent most of the time going over everything that had happened and wondering if there was anything she could have said or done to convince Royce of the fallacy of his thinking.

The blasted man was so stubborn, she fumed. So set on believing the worst of himself. But then, he hadn't really had any reason to believe otherwise. Losing the few people in his life who had truly mattered to him must have only reinforced every bitter and vindictive indictment his father had once hurled at his head.

O'Keefe had been right. The late viscount had been a demon, and she hoped he was burning in the fires of perdition. Because of his father's irrational hatred of him and the tragedy that had shadowed him from birth, Royce was honestly convinced that he was a danger to anyone who got too close, and he was determined to turn his back on her and everything they could have together in order to save her from some nonexistent curse.

But she wasn't giving up that easily. This evening she had finally bid farewell to all her reservations and inhibitions and had placed her heart as well as her body in Royce's keeping. She was in love with him. It was as simple—and as terrifying—as that, and she had no intention of letting him push her away. Not after what they had shared.

Her cheeks heated as she recalled the way they had come together. He had made love to her so tenderly, so exquisitely. It had been everything she had ever dreamed of and more. Just as Jillian had predicted, she had been swept off her feet, and by the very man she had always secretly longed for. The one man who saw through her shy and mousy demeanor to the woman she truly was underneath.

No matter what he said, no matter how resolute he was in his decision to keep her at a distance, she had to make him see that letting himself love her wasn't a mistake.

Finally, after what seemed like hours spent wrestling with her thoughts, attempting to sleep without success, Aimee conceded defeat and got out of bed with a sigh. Making sure to stay as quiet as possible so as not to wake her still slumbering chaperone, she struggled to button herself into her rose-colored morning gown, wincing at the twinges of soreness in places that she had never before been aware of. But the discomfort was just another reminder of Royce's lovemaking, and a self-satisfied smile curved her mouth as she let herself out of the room.

This early in the day, no one appeared to be about, not even a servant. The hallways were peaceful and deserted. Deciding that a brisk walk was just what she needed to clear her head, she retrieved her cloak and bonnet, then descended the rear stairs, where she could hear the staff just starting to bustle about in the kitchens. The sound of her passage was muffled by the rattle of pots and pans as she let herself out into the rosy light of dawn.

It wasn't a surprise to her to find Edmundson already at his post. Regardless of the hour, Tolliver's men were ever vigilant. After offering the guard a pleasant good morning and informing him of her plans, she set off with his stalwart form shadowing her every step, as usual. From the direction of the stables, O'Keefe lifted a hand in greeting as she passed, and she waved back, but didn't stop. The wounds from the day before were still far too fresh for her to want to be anywhere near Balthazar's empty stall.

Instead, she left the courtyard, following the winding drive that snaked around the side of the house before sloping steeply downward to meet the path that their carriage had traversed on the day of their arrival. As she strolled along, gazing unseeingly out at the panoramic view of the sea, the sun climbed higher in the sky and she lost all track of time.

When she finally came back to herself enough to notice her surroundings, she realized that she had reached the bend in the road where it veered sharply away from the cliffs and entered a dense grove of trees. If she recalled correctly, the estate's towering entrance gates loomed just on the other side.

"Perhaps we should turn back, my lady," Edmundson suggested from behind her, sounding vaguely disapproving.

He was probably right, Aimee conceded, biting her lip as she contemplated the matter. They were out in the open here and quite some distance from the house, not to mention that Theodosia would soon be wondering what had become of her. But after being cooped up for so long, she was far from ready to return to the oppressive atmosphere at Stonecliff. It felt too liberating to be out in the fresh air with no walls to confine her.

"It's all right," she assured the guard, tilting back the brim of her bonnet so she could send him a disarming smile. "We'll head back shortly. But it's too nice a day not to seize the opportunity to enjoy it while I can."

Glancing around, she took note of a large, flat-topped boulder just off to the side of the path, perched on a wide ledge overlooking the water. It was shaded by a single tree and several scrub bushes and looked to be the perfect place to relax and mull over the troubles that plagued her.

She gestured toward it. "I'm just going to sit down for a little while and catch my breath. I promise I won't be long."

Though he didn't look happy at her decision, Edmundson made no objection. He merely trailed her over to the rock and took up an alert stance next to the tree, his watchful gaze constantly moving over their surroundings, searching the shadows for any sign of hidden danger.

Settling herself with a sigh, Aimee turned her back to him and let her eyes drink in the spectacular vista before her. From this vantage point, she could see for miles. Far to the right, the imposing outline of Stonecliff stood out against the surrounding cliffs, nestled on its craggy promontory.

It was so peaceful, with the blue sky arching overhead and the frothing water far below, it was hard to remember that there might be someone out there who wanted her dead. She felt safe here and far removed from everything that had occurred in London, especially since her nightmares seemed to have deserted her.

How she wanted to believe that her dreams could have played her false. Wanted to believe that even now a message from her father was on its way to Cornwall, bearing the news that the man who had accosted her had been captured. That the law's assertion that the incident had been nothing more than a burglary attempt gone awry had proven correct. Perhaps then she could finally learn to accept that her memories of her mother's death were gone forever and concentrate on the one thing that seemed to have taken over her thoughts to the exclusion of all else.

A life with Royce.

Aimee let her head fall back and her lashes drift shut, savoring the possibility of a future with the man she loved at her side. Together they would stand against the snide comments of the ton, would put to rest the ghosts of their tragic pasts.

It was such a lovely fantasy, and she basked in the warm glow of it for several long minutes. In fact, so caught up was she in the images playing out in her head that she was aware of nothing else, until a scuffling noise from behind and a loud thump had her scrambling up off the boulder in startled haste.

Before she could turn around, however, something rammed into her with stunning force, knocking her off balance and sending her tottering forward, dangerously close to the edge of the cliff. And as she tried in vain to regain her footing, another shove sent her plummeting over the side with a choked cry.

She was falling, plunging with frightening speed through empty air. With only a split second in which to save herself, she reached out desperately and just managed to grab hold of the ledge with both hands, pulling herself to a teeth-jarring halt.

Clinging with all her might, she dug her fingers into the crevices in the rock in a painful grip, her slippers scrambling for a toehold, though she was hampered by her heavy skirts. Dislodged stones from above pelted her head and shoulders, and she flinched as they struck her, but didn't let go. There was no need to glance downward to remind herself of what her fate would be should she slip. It was a sheer drop, and she would be dashed to pieces on the sharp rocks in the water beneath her.

Suddenly a dark shadow loomed over her as someone bent down at the edge of the cliff, squinting over the ledge into her shocked eyes.

It was a man. Tall, cadaverously thin, and dressed in ill-fitting clothes, he had a pale face and pinched features that gave him a vaguely foxy appearance. The menacing glint in his gimlet eyes sent a shiver up her spine.

"Why, 'ello there, m'lady," he greeted her in a

gravelly voice, a smirk twisting one corner of his cruel mouth. "Recognize me?"

She most certainly did, and she went icy cold all over with fear and dread. She might not have seen his face that night, but she recognized his build and the fetid odor of his unwashed body. It was the very man her father and Tolliver were combing London for right now.

Her mysterious assailant.

If she'd had the breath to do so, she would have laughed hysterically. And here she'd just been thinking that she'd been imagining the danger that had hounded her steps these past weeks. But she'd been wrong. She had become too complacent as far as her safety was concerned, and now it seemed she would pay for her foolhardiness with her life.

"You're rather 'ard to kill, y'know," the man told her almost matter-of-factly, leaning in closer. "Like a bloomin' cat wiv nine lives. Niver thought it would be so difficult to off some spoiled young miss."

"Please," she whispered, her shoulders and arms burning under the strain of holding her body weight suspended. The jagged stone cut into her fingers, and she felt the warm trickle of blood across her palm as she once again scrabbled for a toehold, and once again failed to find one. "Please don't."

He shook his head at her. "It's nothing personal,

y'understand. But I 'ave a job to do and I've come all this way to finish it. Me employer won't be pleased if I fail again, and that means I won't get paid." He reached down to pat one of her hands where it curved over the rock shelf, in a gesture of mock sympathy. "Sorry, m'lady. But a man 'as to make a livin', don't 'e?"

The next thing she knew, he was prying at her fingers, attempting to break her frantic grasp. Screaming, she felt her nails tear, felt herself slipping as she tried valiantly to hang on despite his efforts.

Dear God, I'm really going to die here, she thought wildly. She would never see her family again. Never have the future with Royce she had been daydreaming of. This monster was going to kill her, and there was nothing she could do to stop it.

Then, as abruptly as the man had appeared, he was gone.

Through the buzzing in her ears, Aimee heard a muffled curse, followed by shouting and several dull thuds. And before she could even begin to wonder what was going on, someone else took her attacker's place on the ledge.

Royce.

His face taut and his eyes burning with a fierce light, he was lying on his stomach, one strong hand extended toward her, palm upward.

"Give me your hand, Aimee," he instructed, his

tone firm and unwavering. "I can pull you up, but you'll have to grab on to me first."

She hesitated, certain she would plunge to her death if she loosened her hold for even an instant. But his encouraging gaze gave her the strength she needed to overcome her fear. Sucking in a steadying gust of air, she muttered a quick prayer and grabbed for his hand.

He caught her, his fingers twining with hers, then reached down to grip her forearm with his other hand. With a mighty heave, he pulled her back up over the edge onto solid ground . . . and into his arms.

For long minutes, neither of them moved or spoke. They stayed kneeling on the ledge, locked in each other's embrace. Trembling from exertion, Aimee fisted her hands in Royce's shirt and buried her face against his neck with a soft sob of relief, the sudden dampness of her lashes wetting the starched material of his cravat. She was afraid to let go of him. Afraid that if she did, she would lose whatever tenuous control she still possessed over her turbulent emotions.

He held her just as tightly, his mouth pressed to her head, his fingers stroking through her hair, and she realized rather inanely as she savored his comforting touch that she had lost her bonnet. Crushed against him as she was, she could feel his heart beating with the same rapid and erratic rhythm as it had that night in her sister's guest chamber. The night he had saved her from this very same man.

"Are you all right?" he finally murmured, holding her at arm's length from him so he could examine her for any signs of injury.

She gave a slightly jerky nod. "I'm fine."

"God, when I think what could have happened . . ." Bowing his head, he pressed a kiss to her scraped and bleeding fingers, his agonized expression clearly revealing that he had been far more frightened for her than he had first let on. "If the dowager duchess hadn't sent me to look for you . . . If O'Keefe hadn't seen you come this way—"

She silenced him by laying a finger over his lips. "It will take more than a little tumble off a cliff to get rid of me," she reassured him with a faint smile, a bit of her spark returning now that the shock was wearing off. "I keep trying to tell you that I'm stronger than you think."

Glancing over his shoulder, she caught sight of a dazed-looking Edmundson leaning against the nearby tree, the pallor of his skin and the wicked gash just above his right ear offering mute testimony as to why he had been unable to come to her rescue. Not far away, another of Tolliver's men held her attacker with his arms pinioned behind his back and a pistol aimed at his temple.

The mental vision of that gaunt face leering down at her over the edge of the cliff had Aimee shivering despite the warmth of the sun, and scooting closer to Royce.

"He's the one," she said, fighting to keep her voice steady and calm. She would not let the odious little toad have the satisfaction of knowing how much he had terrified her. "The one who attacked me at Maura and Hawksley's town house."

She felt Royce tense next to her, and when she turned her head to look at him again, it was to discover that his countenance had hardened into a mask of menacing fury.

"Is that so?" he growled, getting slowly to his feet, his enraged glare promising retribution as it focused on their scowling captive.

"No, Royce!" Clinging to his arm, Aimee managed to stand as well, though a residual weakness made her less than steady. "You can't hurt him. Someone hired him. He admitted it. We have to get him to tell us who it was or this will never be over."

His eyebrows lowered, and he took a step forward, dragging her along with him. "Is that true?" he demanded, his hands clenching at his sides, as if he were barely resisting the urge to lash out with his fists.

The man tightened his mouth into a mutinous line, refusing to speak.

"I asked you if what she said was true. Did someone hire you?"

Still no reply.

"Damn you!" Before Aimee could stop him, Royce lunged at the man, seizing him by the lapels of his dirt-stained coat and giving him a ferocious shake. "Perhaps I left you with the mistaken impression that you have a choice as to whether or not you're going to answer my questions. Let me assure you that you do not. I want to know who hired you and I want to know now."

A cackling laugh escaped the man and his lips curled into an evil grin, revealing several missing and rotten teeth. "What will you promise me if I tell you?"

"You slimy little bastard, I'll promise not to tear you apart—"

"Royce, please." Galvanized into motion by the murderous intent written on his face, Aimee clutched at Royce's arm, desperate to get through to him before he strangled the one person who could give them the answers they sought. "Listen to me. He's not worth it. Let Tolliver's men question him."

He didn't even glance in her direction. "He would have killed you," he gritted out, the words vibrating with the force of his ire.

"But he didn't. It's over with and I'm fine. Please let him go."

It seemed her entreaty had made an impression, for he finally looked over at her, his jaw working furiously. Then, with a savage curse, he released the man and backed away, raking a hand through his hair.

"Get him out of here," he barked.

The guard who was restraining their prisoner immediately complied, turning and using the butt of the pistol to prod the man toward two horses that had been left tethered next to the path a few yards away.

All too aware of Royce's still seething temper, Aimee tentatively squeezed his arm, drawing his attention back to her once more. His eyes when they locked with hers were as gray and volatile as the sky during a thunderstorm.

"It's better this way," she said softly, injecting a note of quiet conviction into her tone. "You'll see. Tolliver's men will get to the bottom of things."

Royce didn't look convinced, and he had just opened his mouth to no doubt express his skeptical opinion on the subject when it happened.

Halfway to the horses, Aimee's attacker unexpectedly wrenched free from his captor with a surprising strength, knocking the guard off balance and sending the pistol flying. Then, whirling about, he reached down and yanked out a knife that had been secreted in the top of his boot before facing Aimee and Royce with deadly purpose.

"Time to finish things, m'lady," he rasped.

From that point on, events unfolded almost as if in slow motion for Aimee. He lurched toward her, his weapon upraised, a maniacal glint in his eye. At the same time, Royce let out a shout and threw his body in front of hers, his arms going around her, shielding her from the oncoming threat.

Images of her mother doing exactly the same thing on the night Lord Stratton had pointed his pistol at her raced through her head with blinding speed. Merciful God, Royce was going to die for her! She couldn't let him! She wouldn't!

But even as she fought to push him away, to break free from his protective embrace, a shot rang out.

Craning her neck to peer around Royce's considerable bulk, Aimee saw the man jerk to a halt, his eyes rolling back in his head and the knife slipping from his grasp. Just beyond his swaying figure, she could see Edmundson, who was now standing with one hand braced against the trunk of the tree he'd been sitting beneath earlier. In his other hand, he held a still smoking pistol.

In numb disbelief, she watched as the man gave one last spasmodic twitch and then went as limp as a rag doll, slumping to the ground to lie with his lifeless eyes staring up at the sky.

He was dead. And he had taken with him whatever knowledge he possessed regarding the identity of the person who had hired him to kill her.

Chapter 19

And here she was, left to her own devices once again.

Pacing furiously at the foot of her bed, Aimee gnashed her teeth and cast an annoyed glance in the direction of the chamber door. For hours she'd been quietly seething, fighting the urge to snatch up the closest knickknack to hand and hurl it at the panel in a childish display of temper. How many times throughout the long afternoon and evening had she mentally willed it to open? How many times had she been tempted to fling it open herself and storm out into the hallway, demanding to know where the master of Stonecliff had disappeared to?

But she had stayed where she was. And the door had remained tightly closed.

It was enough to make her want to scream in vexation.

Upon returning to the house after the incident on the cliffs earlier that day, Royce had deposited her in her room and had left her there with the stern admonition that she was not to leave it for any reason. She had not seen him since, and she had no idea what was going on or what he was planning to do next.

Obviously her father would have to be informed of what had occurred, she reasoned. They couldn't let the marquis and Tolliver continue to waste their time searching for a man who was dead. And after her close call today, they would no doubt have to decide whether it was safer for her to remain here or return to London.

In either case, Aimee couldn't help but feel that she should be involved in the decision-making process. After all, it was her life that was at stake, and she was tired of being relegated to the background while others determined her fate.

With a frustrated huff, she sank down onto the edge of her mattress and stared at her bandaged hands. The cuts were minor and hadn't required a physician's attention, though it had taken all of Aimee's persuasive abilities to convince Royce he didn't need to summon one. The maid who had delivered her supper tray had helped her to tend to them, and the healing tincture that had been applied kept her discomfort to a minimum.

Drat Royce's stubbornness! Why did he insist on shutting her out? The man who had held her so tenderly on the cliff after her ordeal had all but vanished once they had made it back to Stonecliff. His walls were once more firmly in place, and he seemed as set as ever on keeping her at a distance.

So here she was, alone again, with no one to share her fears and uncertainties with. She couldn't even talk to Theodosia about any of it. As much as she had longed to tell the dowager duchess the truth about everything, she had kept the news of the attempt on her life to herself, explaining away her injuries by saying that she had tripped and taken a bit of a tumble during her walk. Though the elderly woman had eyed her a trifle suspiciously, she had made no comment.

From somewhere out in the hallway, a clock struck the midnight hour, making Aimee eye her pillow yearningly. Despite her weariness, she knew there would be no losing herself in the sweet oblivion of sleep. She had taken a short nap earlier in the afternoon, but she was feeling much too restless right now to even consider lying down.

Just how long was she expected to go on like this? she wondered angrily, ignoring the stinging sensation in her fingers as she fisted her hands in her lap. How long was she to continue hiding while the people around her decided what was best for her? Perhaps once she might have been content with such a sheltered and isolated existence, but not anymore. She had changed, and going back to being the timid little mouse she had been before was no longer an option.

You are more like Elise than you think . . .

Theodosia's words rang in her head as she got to her feet with an air of purposeful intent. She was not going to cower in her room. She was going to find Royce and let him know in no uncertain terms that she didn't appreciate being kept in the dark when it came to matters that concerned her, and she wasn't going to put up with it any longer.

There were still things that needed to be settled between them, whether he knew it or not, and he was about to find out that she could be every bit as stubborn as he was.

Damnation!

With a vicious swipe of his quill, Royce crossed out the sentence he had just spent a quarter of an hour trying to compose and glared down at the parchment before him. The rest of the page was filled with similarly marked-out passages that were all beginning to blur and run together in a meaningless jumble, swimming before his bleary eyes. After several hours and numerous false starts, he was no closer to finishing this blasted letter than he had been when he first sat down to write it. The right words just weren't coming, no matter how hard he racked his brain.

But then, how was he to find the words to tell a man he admired as much as he admired the Marquis of Albright that he had bungled things so very badly? That he had failed to do the one thing the marquis had ever asked him to do?

Keep his daughter safe.

For a brief instant, Royce was flung back to that heart-stopping moment when he had thrown himself down at the cliff's edge and had peered over the side to find Aimee looking up at him with wide and frightened eyes. Seeing her there, dangling over the pounding waves and sharpened rocks so far below, had turned his blood to ice in his veins. Never before had he been so afraid for another person, and it made his stomach churn to realize that if he had arrived on the scene just a second or two later, he might have been too late to rescue her. Too late to prevent her from plunging to her death.

Shoving away the terrible images of Aimee's body, lying still and broken at the base of the cliff, he balled up the sheet of parchment with a muttered imprecation. He would have to finish penning his missive to the marquis first thing in the morning and hope that the appropriate words would come a little easier after a good night's sleep. Once he knew that his message was safely on its way to Lord Albright in the hands of one of Tolliver's men, he could turn his attention to getting Aimee and the dowager duchess packed and ready for the return trip to London as soon as possible. If nothing else, the incident on the cliffs had proven that she would be far better off under the protection of her family than she would ever be with him.

No doubt Aimee would agree with that assessment, he thought as he pushed back his chair and got to his feet with a weary exhalation. What with his continued bad temper during the last week and her ordeal this morning, she was bound to be happier away from him and Stonecliff, and he couldn't blame her. He had let his determination to avoid her and his grief over Balthazar distract him from the threat that hung over her head. And though he had wasted no time in taking Tolliver's men to task for the lapse in vigilance that had allowed her assailant to slip onto the estate grounds, in the end he knew that he was truly the one to blame.

God, he never should have given in to his need for her, never should have allowed himself to touch her when she had come to him last night. The pain over Balthazar's death had weakened his resistance to the point where he couldn't have pushed her away if he had tried. She had felt so right in his arms, so perfect underneath him, and he didn't think he would ever be able to forget the feel of her silken skin or the sense of coming home that had washed over him as he had pressed deep inside her. Making love to her had been everything he had dreamed of and more.

But it had been a mistake. One that might have exposed her to the ever-growing darkness that surrounded him and that seemed so intent on claiming everyone he had ever been close to.

At that moment, a knock at his door jerked him from his ruminations, and he frowned in irritation. It was well after midnight, and he couldn't imagine why anyone would seek him out in his bedchamber at such a late hour. Unless . . .

Unless there had been another attempt on Aimee's life.

The dread-inducing possibility had all sorts of nightmarish visions flooding his mind and sent him striding across the room to fling open the door.

Only to find Aimee herself on the other side.

"I need to speak with you," she said rather abruptly, her chin raised at a belligerent angle. She gave him no chance to reply, but came barreling across the threshold, obviously in high dudgeon.

Surprised by her unexpected appearance, Royce did his best to conceal his disconcertment as he closed the door in her wake. Crossing his arms and leaning back against the panel, he surveyed her with a deliberately bland expression, praying that the hunger for her that had been his constant companion ever since she had come to stay at Stonecliff didn't show in his gaze.

"I thought I told you to stay in your room," he said, his tone cold and distant.

She whirled to face him, not at all put off by his less than effusive welcome. "You tell me to do a lot of things," she informed him with some asperity. "But I've decided that doesn't mean I have to listen to you."

Her tart response had him stifling the sudden urge to chuckle despite the seriousness of the situation. It appeared that she was set on confronting him, and nothing he could say was going to dissuade her. He supposed he could only be grateful that she was at least fully clothed this time. He didn't know if he could have withstood the temptation if she had shown up in her wispy nightgown again.

Memories of the way she had looked spread out before him, her creamy skin gleaming in the firelight, her delicate curves outlined by the sheer fabric of her nightdress, sent a bolt of pure desire shooting through him from head to toe. But he brushed it aside with an effort and pushed away from the door to move past her into the room, where he came to a halt at the foot of his bed.

"I don't suppose it occurred to you," he began, addressing her without turning around, "to consider what could happen should your chaperone awaken and find you gone?"

"She won't." Aimee's statement held an unwavering note of certainty. "Theodosia sleeps like the dead. And I would have been quite happy to have this conversation at a more appropriate time and place, but that would have been difficult to do since you spent most of the day avoiding me."

He glanced at her over his shoulder, one eyebrow winging upward in a deceptively lazy manner that belied his inner turmoil. "And why would you think that I'm avoiding you?"

She glared at him. "Oh, perhaps the fact that you confined me to my room like a recalcitrant child and then left me there to worry over what was happening. You must have known I would have questions, that I would want to know what you planned to do next now that my attacker is no longer a threat, yet you gave me not a second thought."

Now what could he possibly say to that? he wondered, contemplating her in brooding silence. While he couldn't deny that he had made a conscious choice to stay away from her, it wasn't true that he hadn't thought about her. To the contrary, she had rarely left his mind all day.

He had no intention of confessing this to her, however, so he gave a careless shrug. "There is nothing to tell. At this point, I think the only option is to write to your father and let him know I am bringing you home."

Propping her hands on her hips, she straightened her spine and took a step toward him. "What if I don't want to go home?" she inquired defiantly.

"Don't be absurd. Only a little over a week ago, you were insisting that you didn't want to accompany me here to Stonecliff."

"That was before."

"Before what?"

"Before we made love, you infuriating, insensitive dolt!"

Struck speechless, Royce stared at Aimee, caught off guard by the vehemence of her ire-filled outburst. And she looked more than a trifle bemused herself, as if she couldn't quite believe that she had not only said the words aloud, but had shouted them at the top of her lungs. Her cheeks reddened self-consciously, but she didn't back down. She merely returned his gaze, fierce and unflinching.

Once again, a mental picture of the two of them entwined flashed behind his eyes, but he slammed a curtain shut on the arousing images and finally managed to speak in a gravelly rasp. "I told you it would be best if we both forgot about that."

"Well, I don't agree." She moved another step closer to him, and he could see that her eyes had subtly softened. The amber depths held an entreaty that it took all his willpower to resist giving in to. "I can't forget. And I don't understand how you can pretend that it meant nothing to you."

Gripping the bedpost with one white-knuckled hand, he gritted his teeth against the desire for her that coursed through him, wishing desperately that she would cease her badgering and go. Having her so near when he couldn't touch her, couldn't hold her, was almost a physical ache.

Why couldn't she see that he was doing this for her own good? Why did she have to make everything so bloody difficult? "Damn it, did you hear nothing I said to you last night?"

"Oh, I heard. But none of it made the slightest bit of difference to me."

"How could it not? My God, Aimee, you almost died this morning! Surely you must see now that everything I told you was true!"

She blinked at his agonized exclamation. "Is that what this is all about? You think that your curse had something to do with what happened out there on the cliffs?"

Before Royce knew what she was going to do, she had crossed the remaining distance between them and reached out to seize him by the crisp folds of his shirtfront. "Listen to me," she enunciated slowly, clearly, as if trying to communicate with someone who was particularly dull-witted. "I am the one to blame for what happened today, and no one else. I was the one who decided to walk so far without a thought for my safety. I was the one who refused to listen when Edmundson suggested we turn back. I acted rashly, convinced myself that there was no danger, and I put myself at risk."

He opened his mouth to argue the point, but she cut him off, her flushed countenance reflecting her frustration.

"No. You might as well save your breath, because I refuse to let you twist this around so that it is somehow your fault. Someone was trying to kill me long before we ever made love. Your fictional curse had nothing to do with my attack. And even if I were foolish enough to believe that it did, it's all over now and I'm fine. So you see, no matter what your father said, not everyone you allow yourself to care for is destined to die some horrible death."

The first faint traces of a headache had begun to throb at Royce's temples, and his increasing exhaustion was only further impeding his ability to think with any sort of coherence. He could feel Aimee's fingers burning through the fabric of his shirt, straight to his skin, even as her impassioned efforts to reason with him were tearing at his defenses, weakening his resolve not to give in to his need for her.

Struggling to keep his mask of reserve in place, he disentangled himself from her discomfiting grip and set her from him. "You and I both know that you are not out of danger yet," he told her, his mouth tightening into a grim line. "It's quite possible that whoever hired your assailant will simply hire someone else once he learns you are still alive. And next time it could turn out differently."

"Yes, it could," she agreed without hesitation. "But I'm not willing to go on hiding in my room, just in case it does."

"Well, I'm afraid I'm not willing to take a chance

with your life, simply to soothe your sense of indignation at having been ignored."

His harsh retort was a deliberate attempt to rile her, to force her to pull back from him, and it succeeded. Throwing up her hands in a gesture of exasperated fury, she began to pace before him, her eyes narrowed.

"This is not just some childish tantrum, and I resent your implication that I would waste my time indulging in one," she fumed, leveling him with a glacial look. "Why is it that everyone insists on treating me as if I am still that terrified nine-year-old girl who witnessed Mama's murder? As if I am in need of constant shielding and completely incapable of even a modicum of intelligence?"

The mixture of hurt and bewilderment that resonated in her voice affected Royce in spite of himself, making it impossible for him to maintain his implacable demeanor. "No one treats you that way, Aimee," he said quietly, his tone gentling.

"Don't they?" She jerked to a halt and swung toward him once again. "It's *my* life that's at stake, Royce. My memories of the night my mother died that brought this on. Don't you think I deserve to be a part of this?" The beseeching way she gazed up at him all too easily penetrated the barricades that he had tried to erect between them, to tug at his heart. "Don't I deserve the chance to prove that I can contribute something useful to the investigation? That I can be just as strong as my sisters?"

Before he could stop himself, he had reached up to cup her cheek, skimming his thumb across her soft skin in a feathery caress. "You don't need to prove anything to me. I already know how strong you are."

"Then maybe I need to prove it to myself. Maybe I'm finally ready to put the past behind me and move forward with my life, the way Jilly and Maura have been urging me to for months." She paused, swallowing visibly before finishing in a rush, "And maybe I want to do it with you."

God, how he yearned to seize what she was offering and never look back. To cast aside the fetters of his tragic past and have faith that all would be well. But how could he when he had already come far too close today to discovering what the world would be like without Aimee in it? As much as he wanted her, wanted to be with her, he could not let her suffer the same fate as the others who had once been close to him.

He dropped his hand and stepped away, already feeling the crushing weight of her loss, pressing down on him like an anvil. "I'm sorry, Aimee. I can't."

The light in her eyes flickered and died, and she quickly ducked her head. "Of course not. How silly of me. I guess I just assumed that our love-making the other night meant as much to you as it did to me." She lifted a shoulder, attempting an indifferent shrug that she couldn't quite carry off. "Obviously I was wrong."

"I—"

"No. Please don't feel as if you owe me any explanations. I am humiliated enough as it is. Let us just say that once was enough for you and leave it at that, shall we?"

Aimee pivoted on her heel and marched toward the door, and as he watched her go, Royce became aware of an aching emptiness in the vicinity of his chest. A gaping maw of darkness and despair that grew bigger with every step she took away from him.

"Once could never be enough for me!"

The words burst from his lips without volition, echoing in the stillness of the chamber and freezing Aimee in her tracks.

A stunned hush followed.

Several tense seconds ticked by, and when it became obvious that she wasn't going to speak or turn around, he went on in a husky voice.

"I know you don't understand, Aimee. That you think it's all in my head. But whether you believe I'm cursed or not, I have too much blood on my hands to pretend that it's merely coincidence. I would never forgive myself if being with me endangered your life."

There was another short span of silence, and when Aimee finally glanced back at him, her face was rigidly composed, completely devoid of any emotion.

"I told you I love you last night, Royce," she said softly, solemnly, "and I meant it. Curse or no curse. But I'm not going to hover in the background, waiting in vain for the day when you finally decide that being with me is worth taking a risk."

Balling his hands into impotent fists, he barely contained the overwhelming urge to pound one against his bedpost in frustration. "Bloody hell, can't you see that I'm trying to protect you?"

"Are you? Or are you trying to protect yourself?"

Her accusation hit him like a physical blow, leaving him gaping at her. She didn't give him a chance to recover, however. She simply kept talking, as if a dam had broken and she was determined to unburden herself of everything she had been wanting to say to him.

"Lately I've realized that I truly do want a family of my own someday. A husband and children. A real life. And I honestly believed that you were the man I was destined to have that with. But if you don't want that too, I have to learn to resign myself to it and find a way to go on without you."

She stared into his eyes, the faint glitter of tears shining like a sprinkling of miniature diamonds on her lashes. "I love you. But I can't—I won't—live the rest of my life alone."

With that, she gave him one last tremulous smile and started for the door once again.

He should let her go, Royce thought numbly, his gaze locked on her retreating back. Let her get on with her life without him and wish her well. But just visualizing Aimee in the arms of another man, loving him and letting him love her, giving him children . . . It was like a knife thrust to his heart, and he could not bear the agony.

"Aimee, wait!"

Stalking after her, he caught up with her just as she placed her hand on the doorknob and manacled her wrist, not quite sure what he hoped to accomplish by holding her here, only knowing he was desperate to do so. She tensed at his touch, then turned her head by slow degrees to look up at him, tracks from the tears she had finally allowed to spill over staining her cheeks.

And the next thing he knew, they were locked together in a torrid embrace, kissing each other as if they could never get enough.

For Royce, everything around him melted away, and he was instantly lost. Nothing else mattered. This was what he needed, and he couldn't believe that he had fought it for so long. With an untamed urgency, he devoured Aimee's lips, and she met him eagerly, kiss for kiss, their mouths clinging moistly and their tongues entwining. Her intoxicating flavor heated his blood, even as the feel of her soft curves pressed up against him made him long to strip away the barrier of her clothing, to expose her silken skin to his hands and mouth.

His passion spiraling out of control, he swept her up into his arms and carried her to the bed, where he pushed aside the tasseled hangings and deposited her on the high, firm mattress. She lounged there against the plump pillows and blue satin sheets, observing him through heavy-lidded eyes as he divested himself of his shirt and breeches, her amber eyes aglow. And if he'd had any doubts at all that she wanted this as much as he did, they were instantly dispelled when she reached for him and drew him down to her, her lips curving into a beatific smile.

"Love me, Royce," she murmured.

And love her he did. Wildly, thoroughly, and with a fervent intensity that he had never before known he was capable of. Peeling away her gown and layers of undergarments until she was bare and trembling before him, he skimmed his lips over every inch of creamy flesh he uncovered, leaving not a curve or hollow of her body unexplored. Each kiss, each caress stoked the flames of their mutual ardor ever higher, ever hotter. And when they finally came together, the culmination of their joining was so powerful, so cataclysmic that it swept all before it, leaving them both shattered and utterly spent.

In the aftermath, as a slumbering Aimee lay cuddled against his chest, Royce stared down into her delicate face and wondered what he had ever done to deserve her unshakable faith in him. She made him want to believe in fairy tales and happily-ever-afters when he had stopped believing in such things long ago.

I told you I love you last night, Royce, and I meant it . . .

Hearing those words spilling from her lips had filled him with a fierce sense of elation, even as it had set off all his inner alarm bells. He had never really let himself examine his own feelings for Aimee too closely, had never wanted to put a name to the powerful emotions she stirred within him. He knew he wanted her more than he had ever wanted anyone else in his life, but admitting to feeling anything stronger than desire had always seemed like it would be tempting fate, especially when he knew that nothing could come of it. For how could he ever take a chance on building any sort of future with her when he would constantly be wondering when she would be snatched away from him?

When he knew that if he gave her his heart, only to lose her, it would destroy him?

He stared off into the dimness of the room, and it was a very long time before he slept.

Chapter 20

*O*h God, Mama was dead!

 The knowledge hit Aimee like a sledgehammer blow to the chest, robbing her of breath and freezing her in place as she watched her mother's body slump to the ground before her, limp and lifeless. The report of the pistol still reverberated in the stillness of the chamber, still echoed in her ears, even as the coinciding rumble of thunder from outside gradually faded away into nothingness.

 In a state of shock and petrified with fear, she wrapped her trembling arms around herself and tore her disbelieving gaze away from the still form of the marchioness, to look up at the man towering over her, expecting him to turn his deadly wrath on her at any second.

 To her confusion, her mother's murderer appeared to be just as stunned as she was. His eyes wild, he let his smoking weapon fall from his hand and collapsed at Lady Albright's side, shivering as if he had just been doused with frigid water.

"No," he moaned, the word little more than a whisper. Reaching out, he gripped the marchioness by the shoulder and gave her a shake, as if unable to bring himself to believe that she was really gone. But when her head lolled listlessly and her eyes remained wide open and glazed, a sound like a strangled sob escaped him. "No. She was going to leave with me. We were going to be together."

Racked by an unrelenting mixture of pain and grief, Aimee knew she should be screaming at the top of her lungs, should be calling out for someone to help her, but her vocal cords were just as paralyzed as the rest of her. And before she could manage to find her voice, the man's crazed stare fell on her.

"This is your fault, you little bitch!" he spat with savage ferocity, his face mottled and almost animalistic in his fury. "This didn't have to happen. She was coming with me, but you ruined everything. You made me kill her!"

Aimee shook her head and shrank away from him, covering her ears with her hands. She didn't want to hear what he was saying, but she couldn't seem to block it out. The same way she couldn't block out what she had just seen. Couldn't block out the truth.

Mama was dead.

It was at that moment, as the enormity of what had just occurred washed over her and silent tears spilled down her cheeks, that a flash of lightning lit up the room once again. In the silver-white glow, she caught sight of something at the French doors where she had thought *she'd seen a flash of movement earlier, just as the man had pulled the trigger. A face, pressed up against the glass, peering in at them through the pouring rain.*

The man, oblivious to the fact that they were being observed, had lunged to his feet to seize her by the arms and was continuing to rant and rave in a rather disjointed manner, his voice an indecipherable mutter in the background, droning on and on. And even though something was prodding at the edges of Aimee's consciousness, telling her that she needed to listen to what he was saying, that his words were important, her attention had been completely arrested by the appearance of that pale, familiar visage framed in the window.

A pale, familiar, feminine *visage that suddenly swam sharply into focus . . .*

Aimee jerked awake with a choked gasp to find herself wrapped in Royce's strong arms, one of his hands stroking her tangled hair back from her face while he murmured soothingly in her ear.

"Shhh. It's all right, Kitten. You're safe, and I'm right here."

As the minutes ticked by and she clung to him, grateful for his solid, comforting presence, the lingering effects of the dream began to wear off and she slowly relaxed, her heartbeat returning to a more normal rhythm. Giving herself an extra second or two to compose her rattled nerves, she took a steadying breath, then another, before drawing back to meet his anxious gaze.

"Was it another nightmare?" he asked with a concerned expression.

She nodded jerkily. "Yes. And this time . . . Oh, Royce, this time I recognized her."

He lifted a brow, appearing momentarily puzzled by her statement. "Recognized who?"

"The person who stood outside in the rain the night of Mama's murder." She paused, and her stomach heaved as an image of that pallid countenance flashed through her mind. She could still picture those cold blue eyes, staring in at her through the fogged glass, narrowed with malevolent satisfaction. Could still recall the way the wet strands of light brown hair, coming loose from its chignon, had been plastered to the high, sharply carved cheekbones of a face she knew all too well. Even now, it was hard for her to accept what her dream had revealed, but there was no denying what she had seen with her own eyes.

"It was my aunt," she finally whispered, the admission spilling from her lips in a pain-filled rush. "Aunt Olivia."

Thirty minutes later, fully dressed and curled up on the silk-cushioned chaise longue next to the bed, Aimee watched as Royce paced before her, his hands clasped behind his back and his forehead furrowed in an intent frown.

"And you're positive it was your aunt?" he prompted for the second time in as many minutes, casting her an inscrutable glance over his shoulder.

"Yes, I'm positive," she told him, her tone holding an edge of weary impatience. She had just finished relating to him all the details of her nightmare, and the experience had left her feeling drained and listless. Every word out of her mouth had been like physically reliving the ordeal, and she had no wish to go over it all again.

But apparently Royce was unaware of her increasing agitation, for he came to a halt and turned to face her, his piercing stare unwavering as he continued his line of questioning. "There's no chance you are mistaken or that you could have imagined—"

She cut him off with a shake of her head. "No. I saw her face far too clearly this time." Hugging herself against the chill that had hovered over her like a shroud ever since she had awakened, she rose and wandered over to the window, where she stared out into the darkness with unseeing eyes. "It was Aunt Olivia. No mistake."

Dear God, how she wished she *was* mistaken, she thought desperately, her fingers digging into the velvet draperies in a convulsive grip. She felt as if her whole world had been yanked out from under her feet and she had been left floundering with nothing to cling to. No matter that she had never been all that close to her aunt, that the woman had never shown her even the slightest hint of warmth or kindness. It hurt to know that a member of her very own family—someone who was supposed to love her—could hate her enough to want to see her dead.

And poor Papa! He was going to be devastated when he found out that Olivia had not only had a hand in the murder of his wife, but might also be behind the attacks on his youngest daughter.

"All these years she's lived under my father's roof," she said hoarsely without turning around, the words tasting bitter on her tongue. "Pretending that she was there to help raise me and my sisters, and it was a lie. She was only there because she wanted to keep track of me. To make sure I never remembered her presence there that night."

There was a short span of silence before Royce spoke up from behind her. "You know, just because she was there doesn't necessarily mean that she was involved in your mother's death. Or that she hired your attacker."

"But it makes sense, doesn't it?" She spun about to glare at him. "Aunt Olivia always hated my mother. Hated the fact that she married my father and brought all sorts of scandal down upon the family name. And she was in the garden the night of the dinner party too. She could have overheard us discussing my dreams just as easily as Baron Bedford or the Duke of Maitland."

"True. However, that doesn't completely eliminate everyone else from the list of suspects."

Somehow, Royce's cool rationality managed to cut straight through the anger that was driving Aimee and take the starch out of her spine, deflating her as effectively as a pinprick. Her shoulders slumping, she dropped into the armchair by the window with a shuddering sigh.

"I suppose not," she conceded, unable to keep her voice from quavering as she looked up at him helplessly. "But even if she wasn't directly involved, she was there, Royce. She saw what happened, and she didn't lift a finger to come to my aid. She just walked away and left me there with a madman."

For a fleeting instant, she could have sworn she saw a trace of some volatile emotion she couldn't quite put a name to glittering in the depths of his gray eyes, and he made an abrupt movement, as though he would reach for her. But to her disappointment, he merely tore his gaze away from hers and raked a hand back through his already tousled hair instead, his features tight and expressionless.

Biting her lip at his withdrawal, she bowed her head and tried to fend off the despair that churned within her, threatening to take over. The sense of betrayal she felt over her aunt's perfidy was staggering, and she had never needed Royce's arms around her more, but that was a wish that seemed destined to go unfulfilled. Though she had no idea why, he had been retreating from her little by little ever since she had told him about her dream, re-erecting the walls of defense between them until they were higher and more impenetrable than ever.

On top of everything else and after all they had shared, his frosty indifference was almost more than she could bear, but she forced herself to tamp down her feelings of hurt and focus on the matter at hand.

"We'll have to let your father know what's happened," Royce was saying, arms crossed as he regarded her in a sober manner from under lowered brows. "I was going to send a message ahead with one of Tolliver's men—"

"No," she interrupted decisively. "Papa deserves to hear this face to face, and I don't want to be miles away from him when he finds out. I want to be the one to tell him." She paused, her eyes holding his, alight with resolve. "And I want to be the one who confronts my aunt with what I've remembered."

A muscle leaped in his jaw. "I don't think that's such a good idea."

"Why not?" Fisting her hands on the arms of her chair, she leaned toward him, determined not to let him talk her out of doing what she had to do. "We discussed this earlier, Royce. After everything I've been through, I have the right to look her in the eye and make her admit what she's done. And I want her to know that I have no intention of letting her get away with it."

After a minute's hesitation, he stalked forward, and this time he did reach for her, though not to pull her into his arms. He seized her by the shoulders and yanked her to her feet, scowling down at her with a ferocity that would have quailed a less hardy soul than she.

"Listen to me." His voice was a low, rough growl. "We don't know what she'll do or how she'll react if she's cornered. Obviously the woman is desperate. If she is capable of hiring someone to kill her own niece, then she's capable of anything."

"Maybe I don't care."

"Well, maybe I do."

Aimee jerked away from him, her temper rising to the fore once again, even as angry tears clouded her vision. How dare he affect concern for her now!

"Do you really?" she hissed. "Because I certainly see no sign of it. If you truly cared for me, you wouldn't be distancing yourself from me again just when I need you the most. And I wouldn't be standing here, feeling as if I'm talking to a stranger right now."

Royce took a step back from her, his narrowed eyes darkening like turbulent storm clouds. "This isn't the time for us to be having this conversation."

"I think it is. Not much more than an hour ago, the two of us were making love. And now you're acting as if it never even happened. Why?"

"Damn it, Aimee, I've told you all the reasons why!" The words exploded from him with the forceful impact of cannon fire, bursting from his lips as if they had been pent up inside him for too long and he could no longer hold them back. "Making love didn't wipe those reasons away, no matter how much I might wish circumstances were different. God, I should be shot for touching you again, but lately I seem to have no self-control where you're concerned." He shook his head and scrubbed at his face with one hand, visibly shaken. "Nothing has changed. I'm still the wrong man for you. I'm too—"

"Yes, I've heard it all before." Aimee brushed aside his explanation with a dismissive gesture. "You're too damaged to have a normal life, a normal relationship. Everyone you care for is fated to die. Have I missed anything?" Her tone bordered on caustic, but she couldn't seem to muster the energy to care. She was far too tired and hurt to be sympathetic or understanding right now. "You know, as much as you loathed your father, he's provided you with a very convenient excuse, hasn't he?"

He stiffened, a hectic flush staining his high cheekbones. "What does that mean?" he ground out.

"It means that as long as you believe that everything he said about you is the truth, you can continue to justify your decision to isolate yourself from the people around you. You use your father's words as a shield and tell yourself that you're doing what's best for everyone else when you're really doing what's best for yourself."

"Now wait just a minute—"

"No, you wait." She marched forward, crossing the distance that separated them until she stood boldly before him. "You know it's true," she said, her gaze never wavering from his. "It's easier for you to push everyone away than it is to take a chance on loving and losing again, isn't it?"

His face hardened and he opened his mouth to speak, but she didn't give him time to rebuke her. She plunged ahead, intent on making him see the folly of his reasoning. "Royce, I'm sorrier than I can say that Cordelia and Garvey died. And I'm sorry that you lost Alex before you had the opportunity to put things right between you. But you're not the only one in the world who has lost people you love and suffered because of it."

Reaching up, she touched his cheek, her fingers just grazing the jagged line of his scar. "You are not the monster you think you are. I could tell you that the darkness that torments you is nothing more than the pain and rage of a confused, neglected little boy who locked his emotions away inside of himself long ago and refused to let himself feel. That there is no curse and never was." She shook her head sadly, and her hand fell away.

"But unless you are ready to let yourself believe that, I'd simply be wasting my breath."

He stared down at her, his eyes holding an aching vulnerability that he very rarely let her see. "You don't understand."

"I do understand, Royce. Love makes us vulnerable, and there are no guarantees for any of us. But I sincerely believe that being with you is worth taking the risk. And if you ever come to that same conclusion, you know where to find me."

Backing away, she smoothed down her skirts with damp palms. "In the meantime, it will be dawn soon. I'll inform the dowager of our imminent departure so that we can begin packing." She gave him a tremulous smile. "Just let me know when you are ready to leave. I'll be waiting."

In more ways than one, she added silently, forcing herself not to look back as she swept out of the room, her heart heavy in her chest. She had done all that she could. Now she could only pray that Royce would realize how much he stood to lose before it was too late.

Chapter 21

By the time their carriage finally turned off Park Lane and rolled to a halt in the curving drive in front of Maitland House several days later, Aimee was no closer to solving her dilemma than she had been on the night she had argued with Stonehurst. In fact, he seemed farther away from her than ever. The defenses he had once erected between them, the defenses that she had been certain had collapsed with their lovemaking, were back in place, stronger and higher than ever, and she had no idea how to go about tearing them down for good.

Drat the man's stubborn hide!

Royce had set a breakneck pace on the return trip to London, limiting the number of stops along the way, and there had been no chance to confront him again on the subject of their relationship. She suspected he had planned it that way. Instead of traveling in the carriage with her, he had spent most of his time during their journey on horseback, riding alongside Tolliver's men. And on the few occasions when he had retired to the confines of the coach, their conversation had been restricted due to the presence of the dowager duchess.

Reminded of her elderly companion, Aimee glanced over at Theodosia now. The woman was ensconced in the opposite corner of the carriage, her hands folded on the head of her cane and her face turned in profile as she gazed out the window at the imposing brick edifice of her home. Her expression was unreadable and very far away, almost as if she were lost in her ruminations.

Strangely enough, the dowager herself had been uncharacteristically silent ever since they had set off from Stonecliff. Other than eyeing Aimee speculatively at the announcement that they would be leaving for London earlier than scheduled, she had made no comment on their hasty departure from the viscount's estate or the increased tension that hovered in the air. Aimee couldn't help but wonder what she must be thinking, for the woman was far too perceptive not to be aware that something was afoot.

At that moment, the squeak of the carriage door swinging open had her looking up to see Royce looming in the aperture, his large frame silhouetted by the hazy afternoon sunlight behind him. Though his countenance was cast in shadow, she could just make out the harsh set of his features as he lifted his hand to assist the dowager in alighting before reaching in for Aimee.

She reared back from him. "What are you doing?" she hissed under her breath. "I'm not staying here. I told you I want—"

"I know what you told me, but it isn't going to happen." His voice was a deep, menacing growl, and he leaned toward her so that Theodosia couldn't overhear from outside the coach. "And you *are* staying here, if I have to toss you over my shoulder and carry you into the house. Is that really what you want?"

He would too. The warning in his eyes told her in no uncertain terms that he wouldn't hesitate to humiliate her by lugging her inside like a sack of potatoes right in front of the dowager and the rest of the pedestrians on Park Lane, should she continue to argue. So she leveled him with an impotent glare and grudgingly allowed him to help her climb down.

Tucking the dowager's arm through his and keeping his hand at Aimee's elbow, he proceeded to guide them up the marble steps to the front door, even as several footmen rushed forward, intent on unloading Theodosia's baggage from the coach.

"Your Grace!" Fielding, the dowager's balding and stoop-shouldered butler, waited to bow them into the entrance foyer. Obviously flustered by his mistress's unexpected appearance, he hurried to aid her in removing her dusty traveling cloak. "I had no idea that you were planning on returning today. I was under the impression that you would be staying in Cornwall for quite some time."

"So was I, Fielding." Glancing back over her shoulder at Aimee, Theodosia's eyes narrowed shrewdly. "I would have sent a message ahead to inform you of my arrival, but apparently there was some need for speed and a great deal of secrecy."

Aimee flinched at that penetrating stare. She had known that the dowager wasn't oblivious to the fact that something was going on, and it appeared that the woman wasn't about to let her evade the issue any longer. But how could she possibly ever find the words to explain?

Before she could even begin to rack her brain for the answer to that question, however, Royce spoke up, his tone firm and authoritative. "Fielding, as of this moment, no one is to be admitted to the house until I return. Not for any reason. Should anyone come to the door, you are to inform them that the dowager duchess is exhausted from her journey and isn't receiving visitors today. I also want you to gather a few servants and direct them to make sure that all of the doors and windows are locked up tight. I want every possible means of entry checked and double-checked. I'm assuming that Maitland isn't here?"

The butler blinked, as if dazed by the abrupt query after such a litany of instructions, then shook his head. "No, my lord. I believe His Grace is attending some sort of gathering at the home of Lord and Lady Braverhampton and I do not expect him back until late."

"Good. That's one less person we shall have to make explanations to right now. In any case—"

"I beg your pardon, Stonehurst." Theodosia's peremptory voice cut across Royce's words, drawing all attention to her. She was leaning on her cane, a frown of distinct displeasure marring her forehead. "I don't suppose you would care to tell me why you are ordering my staff about as if they were under your command. You make it sound as if we are under siege."

He turned to face her, his expression carefully blank as he inclined his head in a deferential manner. "I do apologize, Your Grace, for usurping your authority. I would have asked for your permission to issue these instructions, but as you said before, time is of the essence. I promise you, all will be explained shortly."

Without waiting for a reply, he seized Aimee by the wrist and pulled her with him toward the door, just out of earshot of their companions.

"Listen to me," he began, his gaze holding hers with a grave intensity. "I am leaving two of Tolliver's men here with you while I head over to your father's town house. I sent a message ahead so he should be awaiting me there along with Tolliver. Hopefully before this day is over we'll be able to get to the bottom of things." He gave her a little shake and his jaw suddenly tightened, a muscle jumping just beneath the surface of his taut skin. "You are not to venture out of this house under any circumstances. Do you understand? No matter who our culprit is, we have no way of knowing whether he has had a chance to hire someone else to get rid of you. You'll be safer here until we do."

"But—"

"No buts, Aimee. I don't have time to argue with you about this, and I need to know that you are going to use your head and not do anything rash, like try to slip out and follow me once I've left."

Aimee's spine stiffened. Of course she had been planning to do exactly that, and it was frustrating in the extreme to know that he could read her so easily. "I don't suppose it has occurred to you that I could be of some use," she said with wounded asperity, straightening her shoulders. "After all, I do possess a modicum of intelligence on occasion."

Releasing her wrists, Royce wound his fingers through hers and pulled her a step closer to him, his eyes warming and softening in a way that stole her breath. "I know that. Believe it or not, I did hear what you said the other night, and you were right. To a certain extent. If your aunt did play a part in all you've suffered for the past ten years, then you deserve the chance to confront her. To demand some answers from her. But you need to let me assess the situation first. We have no idea how she will react to our accusations or who could be helping her if she is guilty. We're walking into this blind, and if anything were to happen to you—"

He jerked to a halt and bowed his head for a second, then cleared his throat and went on with quiet assurance. "If it's truly what you want, I promise you will have a chance to face her once we have everything under control and we know what we are dealing with. I'll make sure of it. For now, I have to know you are safe."

Aimee felt her heart melt into a puddle in her slippers. Here she was, inwardly cursing him for his overprotective and autocratic nature, and he had to turn around and look at her like that, as if she was all that mattered to him. Had to say something in that caring and solemn tone that made her anger dissipate like the morning mist. Every time she was ready to throw up her hands and walk away from him, he did or said something that gave her hope that all was not lost for the two of them.

Closing her eyes for the briefest instant, she recalled the last words O'Keefe had whispered to her before they had all climbed aboard the carriage on the morning they had departed Stonecliff.

Please don't give up on him, my lady. I sincerely believe that he cares very deeply for you, no matter how much he tries to deny it. He's not nearly as harsh or as indifferent to his solitary existence as he pretends to be, and he needs someone in his life. Someone who understands the wounds he has suffered in the past and who is patient enough to stand her ground and give as good as she gets. Someone like you . . .

No, she couldn't—wouldn't—give up on Royce, for she loved him too much to ever do that. Lady Aimee Daventry had never been the sort of person to fight for what she wanted before, but that was about to change. Once they had solved the mystery behind the attempts on her life and the culprit was finally in custody, she planned on turning her attention to coming up with a way to make this man see once and for all that the two of them belonged together. Curse or no curse.

Swallowing back the lump in her throat, she gave a reluctant nod, her fingers tightening around his. "All right. I'll stay here. But please promise me you will let me know as soon as you find out anything."

"I will. In the meantime, I suspect you will have your hands full explaining it all to the dowager duchess. Something tells me she won't let you leave out the smallest detail." With a wry quirk of his lips, Royce freed himself from her grip and strode over to Fielding to mutter a few words in the butler's ear, then moved back toward the door.

When he hesitated next to her again, Aimee bit her lip and peered up at him anxiously. She was well aware that her heart was in her eyes, and she didn't care. She wanted him to see. Wanted him to know how much he meant to her.

"Be careful," she whispered.

His gaze burning into hers, he lifted a hand and caressed her cheek. Just a fleeting, feather-light caress, but it sent a shiver through her nonetheless.

And then he was gone.

The door had barely closed behind him when the sound of a throat being cleared had Aimee jerking her head in Theodosia's direction. The dowager was watching her, her lips pursed and her brows lowered in a fierce scowl.

"So," the elderly woman drew out crisply, lifting her cane off the floor to point it at Aimee in stern rebuke. "I was wondering when someone was finally going to get around to telling me the truth about our little jaunt to Cornwall. Start at the beginning, my gel, and don't leave anything out."

As Royce cantered his horse through the streets of Mayfair toward the Albright town house on Belgrave Square, his mind kept going back to those last few moments with Aimee. To the look on her face as he had walked out the door and left her standing in the entrance foyer of Maitland House, staring forlornly after him. Her expression had been so full of apprehension and sadness that he had longed to turn around and gather her into his arms. To hold her close and never let her go. But how could he when there were still so many issues left unresolved between them?

Whenever he recalled the way he had treated her after they made love on the evening before they had set off for London, he couldn't contain a guilty wince. He had been cold to the point of callousness, but it had been the only way he could think of to distance himself from her and gain some sort of rational perspective on their relationship. She made him feel too much, made him want things he knew were forever beyond his reach, and that was a dangerous proposition.

You are not the monster you think you are.

God, how he yearned to put his faith in Aimee's words. Wanted to believe that it was possible to have some sort of future with the woman he was quickly coming to realize would never release her hold on his heart. But her life would hang in the balance if he were selfish enough to try and keep her, and he knew beyond a shadow of a doubt that whatever pain he had already suffered would be as nothing compared to what he would suffer if he lost her. He would never survive it.

However, now was not the time to be thinking about that, he cautioned himself, brushing aside his weighty ruminations as he trotted his mount into the stable yard behind the Albright residence and swung down from the saddle. There were other, far more urgent matters to contend with at the moment.

Such as catching the person who seemed so intent on bringing an untimely and rather violent end to Aimee's life.

As specified in the message Royce had sent ahead to the town house, Lord Albright was awaiting his arrival in the library and immediately opened the French doors to admit him when he rapped lightly on the glass. Tolliver was there as well, seated in a wingback chair that had been drawn up to flank the large mahogany desk in the corner of the room.

"Stonehurst." Albright greeted him with a handshake before letting his gaze travel beyond Royce's shoulder, as if to ascertain whether anyone was accompanying him. "Where is Aimee?"

"I left her with the dowager duchess at Maitland House. It seemed safest for now."

"Your message said that you had some important news."

"Yes." Royce paused and studied the countenance of this man who had been so kind to him through the years. It was a sad fact that this was more than likely going to hurt Lord Albright every bit as much as it had hurt Aimee, if not more. But there was nothing else to be done. The marquis had to hear the truth and there was no avoiding it.

"I think," he finally said, indicating the empty

chairs next to the desk with a wave of his hand, "that it might be best if we were sitting down."

Thirty minutes later, he concluded his tale, only to be met by stunned silence. Both men were staring at him with jaws slack, apparently frozen to their chairs in utter incredulity.

"I don't believe it."

The words came from Lord Albright, cutting across the tension-fraught hush that had settled over the room with forceful denial. Lunging from his seat, he began to pace behind his desk, his expression haggard and almost desperate.

"I don't believe it," he said again. "It isn't possible."

Royce watched the marquis with hooded eyes, keeping his concern carefully veiled even as he replied in a calm and even tone. "I'm afraid it's very possible, according to Lady Aimee."

"She must be mistaken."

"She insists that she isn't. And while I agree that we must act cautiously and reserve judgment, I believe we must take her seriously."

"But my own sister?" Lord Albright stopped in his tracks and scrubbed his hands over his face. "She has lived under my roof for years. Has helped me to care for my daughters. How . . . ? Why . . . ? I cannot even fathom it."

Tolliver spoke up, his voice introspective, as if he were turning the possibility over in his mind. "I hate to say it, Albright, but it makes sense. Lady

Olivia has never made any secret of the fact that she hated your wife. The scenario seems entirely too plausible to me."

"Plausible or not, you are asking me to entertain the notion that my sister could be a murderess," the marquis snapped. "To believe that she teamed up with Stratton in a plot to kill my wife and then hired someone to rid herself of my daughter, all the while continuing to carry on as if nothing were out of the ordinary. It would take a monster to do something like that. It—"

"Must be considered, whether you like it or not," his friend interrupted him. "We cannot ignore this piece of the puzzle just because Lady Olivia is your sister."

Rising from his chair, Tolliver leaned forward and braced his hands on the desk, his gaze never wavering from Lord Albright's. "Come now, Philip. We have all but ruled Bedford out as a suspect, so who does that leave? Both Stonehurst and Lady Aimee saw her in the garden the night of the dinner party. And you were a witness to her reaction when we were discussing the return of Lady Aimee's dreams the morning after the attack at Hawksley's home. What do the clues tell you?"

"I don't know." The marquis shook his head wearily, looking older and more tired than Royce had ever seen him.

"I understand your hesitation, my lord," he ventured softly, getting up and moving to stand at the marquis's side. "I'm not suggesting that we haul her off to Newgate right this instant, but I think she should be questioned. Surely there is enough evidence to warrant that much. To deny it would be doing your daughter a disservice."

There was a moment of silence, then Lord Albright gave a weary sigh and moved to the door to call for a servant.

"Mrs. Bellows," he inquired of the housekeeper when she appeared, his voice edged with reluctance. "Do you happen to know where my sister is at present?"

"I believe she is in the parlor, visiting with the Baron Bedford, my lord."

"Please tell her that I need to see her in the library. At once."

The plump woman nodded and hurried away, and a few minutes later, Lady Olivia herself marched into the room.

"Really, Philip," she sniffed, her face drawn into a taut mask of displeasure. "I must say, I do not appreciate being summoned as if I were a lowly servant. And it is quite rude for you to insist that I leave my guest to entertain himself while—"

The marquis held up a hand, silencing her. "Olivia, I have something of grave importance that I need to discuss with you, and I think it might be best if you sit down."

Arching a haughty brow at his abrupt manner, she lowered herself into a nearby chair and smoothed out her skirts before giving him her full attention. "Very well. What is it?"

"I'm going to ask you a question, and I want you to promise me that you will answer me honestly."

"Of course."

"Were you here at the house on the night that Elise was killed?"

There was a lengthy hush as Lady Olivia blinked up at her brother, her countenance unreadable. "I don't understand," she finally said, her voice sounding far too tight and controlled. "Why on earth would you ask me something like that? You know I was not."

Royce took a step forward and spoke up, unable to remain silent despite the best of intentions. "Lady Aimee has remembered several more details of that evening. According to her, it was your face she saw that night at the window."

Something flashed in the depths of the woman's frosty blue eyes as she turned them in his direction, and the laugh that escaped her pinched lips sounded oddly shrill. "That is utterly preposterous!"

"Is it?"

"Yes, it is! The girl doesn't know what she is saying."

Lady Olivia's scornful tone set Royce's teeth on edge. He had never been able to stomach this vindictive harpy's contemptuous attitude toward

Aimee, and it would take very little provocation to push him over the edge into losing his temper with her. "Yet your niece claims that she is quite certain of what she saw. That she distinctly recalls your presence."

"Then she is lying!" Lifting her chin, Olivia glared at Royce before glancing over at her brother. "Philip, please. You know I couldn't have been here that night. I accompanied both you and Elise to the Briarwood ball and then I returned to Albright Hall and retired for the evening."

"Ah, but you *could* have been here that night, Olivia." The marquis was gazing down at her intently, a muscle flexing in the line of his jaw. "Albright Hall is naught but an hour's ride from London. And as much as I hate to even consider the possibility that you could have played a part in what happened to Elise, I cannot deny that all of the pieces are starting to fit."

Her eyes narrowed. "Are you actually accusing me of being involved in her murder?"

"Do you think that I want to believe that my own sister could be capable of something so vile? But Aimee would not lie about this, and you and I both know just how much you hated Elise."

"I had every right to!" Lady Olivia lunged from her seat, her face red with sudden rage and her hands fisted at her sides. "From the moment that woman came into our lives, she ruined every-thing! I was happy and in love and then she took it all away." A small, choked sound escaped her before the rest of the words burst forth. "She took Hawksley away."

And suddenly it all came together in Royce's mind. Bits and pieces of the conversation he'd had with Aimee regarding her aunt on the night of the dinner party drifted back to him and he stared at the woman in astonishment. "The man who jilted you. It was the late Lord Hawksley."

The revelation struck the room's other occupants with the force of a punch. Lord Albright gasped and staggered back a step, and even Tolliver's face blanched. But Olivia ignored their reaction and focused her feverishly glittering stare on Royce.

"Yes," she spat. "It was Hawksley. He told me that his family didn't approve of Philip's marriage to Elise and that he couldn't wed me, only to turn around years later and take up with Elise himself. As if our relationship never meant anything to him." The venom that laced her tone was unmistakable. "I couldn't bear it. Seeing the two of them together. Talking and laughing and whispering in corners. So on the evening of the Briarwood ball, I finally decided to confront him."

The marquis sank into a chair, his gaze never wavering from his sister. "And?" he prompted her quietly.

"And he claimed there was nothing of a romantic nature between them. That the rumors of their affair were untrue and that he had always loved me." She gave a stilted shrug. "I didn't believe him. And when I found the note, it seemed that I had good reason not to."

"What note?" The question came from Toll-iver, who had leaned forward in his seat and was eyeing her closely.

"The one asking him to meet Elise here at the town house after midnight. It fell from his pocket before he left the ball. Of course, I didn't realize at the time that it had been forged by Lord Strat-ton." In a sudden motion, she whirled about to face her brother. "There. I admit it. Yes, I was here that night, but I had nothing to do with the death of your wife. I was waiting outside for Hawksley to arrive in hopes of catching him and Elise in the midst of their planned tryst. When Lord Stratton showed up, I didn't know what to think. And then he pulled out a gun."

Lord Albright shook his head, looking pale and shaken. "You were a witness," he breathed, his expression one of dazed disbelief. "You saw it all. You knew from the very beginning that Lord Stratton killed Elise and that Hawksley was inno-cent, yet you remained silent."

"They were both dead. What good would it have done for me to come forward with what I knew? It wouldn't have brought them back."

"My God, Olivia, you let the real killer roam free! You stood back and watched while an innocent man's name was dragged through the mud for years!"

"He deserved it!" Lady Olivia hissed, her chin raised defiantly. There was not a spark of remorse in her cold eyes. "For the pain he caused me. For the heart he broke. He deserved to be repaid in equal measure."

Royce, who had been observing the proceedings and quietly seething this whole time, finally lost his patience. "And what about Aimee, my lady?" he drawled silkily, his voice dangerously soft. "Did she deserve it?"

There was a second of stunned silence as all heads whipped in his direction, but he was far too angry to pay any attention to the surprised stares. It was obvious this woman cared for nothing and no one but herself, and he was very close to wrapping his hands around her worthless neck and squeezing the life from her.

He prowled closer to her, his large frame practically vibrating with the force of his fury. "For years your niece has suffered because of what happened that night. Because of the loss of her memories. And you let it go on when you could have done something about it."

"I didn't—"

"You did!" Out of his peripheral vision, Royce was aware of the marquis gaping at him in astonishment, but he couldn't bring himself to stop. Not now that the dam had burst and everything he had ever wanted to say to this woman on Aimee's behalf was right there on the tip of his tongue. "But you didn't care, did you? You wanted to see her suffer. You enjoyed criticizing her, deriding her, because it was your way of punishing her. Of getting back at Lady Albright through her daughter. Wasn't it?"

"How dare you!" Lady Olivia snapped, drawing herself up huffily before she gave him her back and marched over to address her brother. "Why couldn't you listen to me, Philip, and leave well enough alone? You just had to go dredging up the past, investigating matters that are best left buried. I should have known that something was odd when the Duke of Maitland started asking me all of those questions about Aimee and the night Elise was killed, but I never thought you would set someone to spying on your own sister. This is an outrage, and I—"

"Olivia, if you do not cease your caterwauling right this instant, I swear I shall gag you and be done with it!"

The woman gasped and reeled backward, obviously stunned by her brother's rebuke, but Royce was too preoccupied to take any pleasure in her shock.

For some reason, her words had the hair on the back of his neck standing on end. It didn't make any sense. Why would the Duke of Maitland question Lady Olivia about Aimee? Neither the marquis nor Tolliver would have involved Maitland in the investigation, and Royce could think of no other reason for the duke's interest. Of course, the man's stepmother was serving as Aimee's chaperone, so it might have only been natural curiosity. Still, something didn't seem right about it . . .

A terrible sense of foreboding suddenly washed over him, and he went ice cold with fear from head to toe as he turned and raced for the door.

"Stonehurst, where the bloody hell are you going?"

Royce didn't stop to answer Tolliver's shouted query. He couldn't. All he could think about was getting to Maitland House as fast as he possibly could.

Dear God, had he spent all of this time pushing Aimee away, denying the all-consuming love he now knew without a shadow of a doubt that he felt for her, only to lose her anyway?

Chapter 22

"So Olivia has been behind it all from the beginning?"

Theodosia's shocked exclamation rang out in the stillness of the parlor, and Aimee restrained a wince as the dull headache that had begun to pound at her temples with Royce's departure gave a particularly vicious throb.

"It appears that way," she replied gravely. "I didn't want to believe it, but all the pieces seem to fit."

The dowager, who was seated on the settee across from Aimee's chair, shook her head dazedly. "I don't know why I'm so dumbfounded. No one hated your mother more than Olivia, and it would have suited her purposes to get rid of Elise if she could. But we were so sure that Stratton acted alone. There was no reason to suspect anyone else."

Restless, Aimee rose and wandered over to the window to gaze out at Park Lane. Just below, the guards Royce had left behind to keep watch paced along the perimeter of the drive, and she recognized one of them as Edmundson, a bandage covering his injury from that terrible day on the cliffs.

For several long minutes, she watched the two men unseeingly, her thoughts far away. Something was nagging at the back of her mind, but she couldn't quite put her finger on what it was, and her brain was far too muddled right now to try and figure it out.

"It's not right," she murmured aloud, her fingers digging into the polished wood of the window ledge until she was certain she would draw blood. "All of these years that my aunt has spent laughing at us while she carried on her charade. It makes me ill to think of her living in the same house with my family when she should have been in Newgate paying for her crimes."

"Well, I imagine she'll pay for it now," Theodosia spoke up from behind her. "I always knew the woman was a vicious and conniving little shrew, but I never imagined she could be so unspeakably evil. Newgate would be too good for her."

Aimee turned away from the window to meet the elderly lady's concerned gaze. "At least this nightmare is finally at an end. No more looking over my shoulder, wondering if someone is going to push me over a cliff or down a set of stairs."

The dowager's expression clearly reflected her

distress at the reminder of the danger that had plagued her young charge for the past few weeks. "Yes, that is one thing to be thankful for. I cannot believe that I was so completely unaware of what you were facing. When I think about you dangling over the edge of that cliff . . ." She shuddered. "You should have told me, child."

"I wanted to," Aimee assured her, feeling suitably chastened as she moved back toward her chair. "But Papa thought it would be best to keep it to ourselves. We didn't wish to frighten you or cause you any distress."

"Hmph. You should know by now that I don't frighten easily, gel. And it causes me more distress that you didn't share your troubles with me." A shrewd glint suddenly entered Theodosia's eyes and she leaned forward in her seat, bracing herself on her cane. "And here I was under the impression that our haste on the road from Cornwall was due to a rather urgent need for the posting of banns. After all, there is that little matter of you disappearing from your bed for several hours on the night before we left Stonecliff."

Caught off guard as she was sitting down, Aimee gasped and toppled backward, her rump hitting the cushions hard enough to knock the wind from her. Sucking in a gulp of air, she gaped at her companion in dismay.

"Well, you needn't gawk at me as if I have gone stark, raving mad," Theodosia said, waving her hand in an imperious manner. "I may be oblivious to some things, but not when it comes to young ladies sneaking out of their beds when they are supposed to be sound asleep. The only reason I haven't called you on it is because I happen to have a great deal of respect for Lord Stonehurst, and I know he cares for you. He is an honorable man, and if he has compromised you in any way, I'm certain he will do what is necessary to rectify the situation."

Tilting her head, she examined Aimee with an unnerving intensity. "There *is* a marriage proposal in the offing, isn't there?" The elderly woman's tone held an edge of razor sharpness. "I shall be most put out with that young man if he doesn't come up to scratch."

Before Aimee could recover from her discomposure enough to form some sort of coherent response, a voice boomed out from the direction of the doorway.

"What ho!"

His ruddy face wreathed in a cheerful smile, the Duke of Maitland strolled into the room, his sudden appearance startling them both.

"What a pleasant surprise, Stepmother," he called out jovially, closing the door behind him and crossing to the settee to lift Theodosia's hand to his lips in greeting. "I wasn't expecting to see you for several more days yet."

The dowager acknowledged his welcome with

a stiff inclination of the head. "Yes, I'm afraid there was a last-minute change of plans. An urgent matter came up that Lord Stonehurst needed to attend to here in town."

"I see." A slight frown marred the duke's thick-set features. "And would this 'urgent matter' have anything to do with the two armed gentlemen who are forbidding people access to my home?"

He sounded more than a trifle disgruntled at such an imposition, and Aimee shifted self-consciously in her seat before clearing her throat to reply. "I'm sorry, Your Grace," she ventured, her cheeks heating. "That would be my fault."

Puzzlement written on his florid countenance, he turned to face her. "I beg your pardon, my dear, but why would that be your fault?"

Aimee knew that he deserved an explanation, but she had no idea where to start, so she glanced over at Theodosia, mutely pleading for help.

And the dowager obliged, quickly relating the details of the attempts on Aimee's life and what she had remembered about the night of her mother's death. By the time she was done, the duke had lowered himself onto the settee, his expression one of stunned disbelief as he stared at Aimee.

"How astounding!" he exclaimed. "And you say Lady Olivia was responsible for all of this?"

Aimee nodded. "Unfortunately, yes. Lord Stonehurst is at my father's town house confronting her right now." She looked down at her hands folded in her lap as tears dampened her lashes. "I just don't understand it. I knew Aunt Olivia hated my mother, but to conspire to kill her? How could she do something like that?"

Theodosia sighed. "I'm afraid that in your aunt's eyes, your father's marriage to your mother and the accompanying scandal cost her everything that was of importance to her. Her family's good name, her standing among society, and the man she was in love with. Perhaps she thought it was the only way to regain what she had lost. Olivia was never very rational when it came to Elise."

"Yes, well, people do have a tendency to become rather irrational when they are threatened with losing everything that belongs to them."

This statement came from Maitland, and something about the way he spoke, the odd note in his voice, immediately arrested Aimee's attention. He was peering at her closely, his eyes glittering with a strange light that made her vaguely uneasy.

"Is that all you can recall about that night, my dear?" he prodded, his avid gaze never wavering from her face. "Did Stratton say anything to make you believe that someone besides Lady Olivia might have been involved?"

For some reason, the headache that had been pulsing at her temples gave another persistent throb at his query, then exploded into a fireball of agony that seared the inside of her skull like flaming knives. The pain was almost more than she could bear. Swaying in her seat, she let her lashes drift closed as the room began to blur around her.

Suddenly she was no longer in the parlor of Maitland House, but back in the darkened library of her nightmares, and Lord Stratton was shaking her, berating her, though it was impossible for her to make out what he was saying over the muffled buzzing in her ears. She knew if she were to look beyond his shoulder, she would see her aunt staring in at them through the rain-drenched glass of the French doors, but this time she forced herself to concentrate on Stratton instead, on his mottled countenance and enraged glare as his mouth formed words that she couldn't hear.

You must listen. It isn't over. It will never be over until you remember it all . . .

Her mother's warning echoed in her head, and everything finally snapped into place. Now it all made sense. It wasn't Lady Olivia's presence there that night that was important. It was whatever Lord Stratton had said. That's what Mama had been trying to tell her all along.

With that realization, the annoying buzz faded away as if it had never been, and her hearing returned with crystal clarity.

"You little bitch," Stratton *was snarling, spittle flying from his lips as his cruel grip tightened on her arms. "If you know what's good for you, you'll forget everything you saw here tonight. Everything. Because*

if you ever tell anyone, Maitland will send me back here to kill your precious papa and your sisters as well. You'll watch them die, just like you watched your mother die. So keep your trap shut."

Aimee jolted back to the present, her heart pounding against her rib cage with jarring force as her gaze focused on the duke, who was leaning forward on the settee, surveying her from beneath lowered brows.

"You've remembered something, haven't you?" he prompted softly, and for a brief instant he looked genuinely regretful. "How unfortunate. I suppose it was a mistake to keep probing, but I had to know, you see. I had to find out if that idiot Stratton had let anything slip that night that might incriminate me. He always swore that he hadn't, but I couldn't be sure." Getting to his feet, he withdrew a wicked-looking pistol from an inside pocket of his coat and leveled it on her with calm intent. "It appears I was right to be concerned."

Theodosia went rigid, scowling at her stepson in outraged indignation. "Maitland, have you lost your mind? What on earth are you doing?"

"Cleaning up a mess that I should have made Stratton take care of before he had the bad luck to go and get himself killed."

Aimee swallowed back the bile rising in her throat and clutched at the arms of her chair, unable to take her eyes off the barrel of the pistol that was still trained on her. "He's the one, Your

Grace," she whispered, fighting to keep her voice steady despite her fear. "He's the one who conspired with Lord Stratton, not Aunt Olivia."

"That isn't possible." The dowager's incredulous gaze whipped back and forth between the two of them before settling on the duke. "Warren, I don't know what you are attempting to prove, but tell the gel you wouldn't—"

"Oh, I assure you that I would and I did," he interrupted her, his expression deadly serious. "But I had no choice. I had to keep her from taking what was rightfully mine."

There was an oppressive silence, and when Theodosia addressed her stepson again, it was in a low and ragged-sounding rasp that was barely audible. "Randall told you, didn't he?"

Maitland jerked his head in her direction, studying her with obvious interest. "Ah. So you *did* know that Elise Marchand was Father's little bastard. I often wondered about that."

Aimee blinked, stunned and confused by what she had just heard. What sort of ploy was this? Was the man actually trying to say that . . . No, it couldn't be.

But even as she denied the possibility, the dowager was nodding grudgingly, her lips compressed into a thin, bloodless line. "Yes, I knew. Randall confided in me right before he became so ill, just as Elise was entering society as the new Marchioness of Albright."

The elderly lady's quiet confirmation yanked the ground out from under Aimee's feet, leaving her lost and floundering. Her mother had been the late Duke of Maitland's illegitimate daughter? It was too much for her to take in. And it was even harder for her to accept that Theodosia—one of the few people she had sincerely believed she could put her faith in—had been aware of that fact and had kept it a secret.

"Your Grace," she faltered, wrapping her arms about herself in a defensive posture, as if to ward off the staggering sense of betrayal that threatened to overwhelm her. "Is this true?"

The look Theodosia sent her was rife with sorrow and regret. "I'm afraid so, my dear," she admitted huskily. "I'm sorry, but Randall swore me to secrecy, and I had to abide by his wishes. You see, at the time he had just discovered who Elise was, and I don't think he had arrived at any firm decision as to what he should do about it."

"Oh, he had arrived at a decision, but I never gave him the chance to act on it."

Maitland's grim statement had his stepmother's eyes snapping back to him in suspicion. "What are you saying?" she gasped.

The duke gave a harsh bark of laughter that held no real amusement. "I'm saying that the old man summoned me to his bedchamber one evening soon after his illness had taken a turn for the worse. He suspected the time he had left to live was limited, and he wanted me to know about Elise. To know that he planned on acknowledging her publicly as his daughter and that he was going to make sure that she received her share of the Maitland wealth." He gestured angrily with his weapon. "Well, I couldn't let that happen, could I? Can you imagine the scandal that would have brought down on our family when he announced to the ton that London's most notorious stage actress was my bastard half sister?"

One corner of his mouth twisted into a smirk of malicious satisfaction. "So I kept it from happening."

The dowager paled and seemed to shrivel in on herself, slumping back against the cushions of the settee as if she was no longer capable of holding herself upright. "Warren, you didn't . . . Your father . . ." Clearly unable to finish, she gave a helpless shake of her head.

Maitland lifted a shoulder in a shrug that was all the more chilling for its utter indifference. "It was simple, really. He was struggling to breathe as it was, so all I had to do was press the pillow down over his face until he just . . . stopped. I did him a kindness by putting him out of his misery." At a faint moan from his stepmother, he shot her a fierce glare. "You shut up! Don't you see that I had to do it? Was I supposed to stand by and let him ruin our lives? Surrender part of my inheritance to some bloody trollop? Over my dead body!"

Aimee felt all the blood in her veins drain into her toes as she gaped up at this man she had known since she was a child. How could she have been so completely fooled by his affable demeanor? The duke was a monster who had murdered his own father before cold-bloodedly plotting the murder of her mother. He was responsible for hiring the assassin who had been terrorizing her for the past few weeks, and yet she had never even suspected.

"Of course, as long as Elise was alive, she was a threat," he went on coldly. "I couldn't take the risk that she might find out who she really was someday. That's when I ended up enlisting Stratton. He was already half mad and obsessed with her to the point of distraction, so it took very little prodding to convince him that she was a faithless jade who would keep leading men to their doom unless she was done away with. And the late Lord Hawksley was our convenient dupe."

His icy gaze focused on Aimee, piercing her with its hostility. "Things didn't go as planned, however, thanks to your interference. You witnessed everything, and Hawksley arrived before that idiot Stratton could finish the job. So you can imagine our immense relief when we learned that your memory of that night had somehow been eradicated. As the years passed and you showed no signs of recalling anything, we began to let down our guards, to believe that we were safe.

And when the part Stratton played in the crime was uncovered and he was killed without naming me as an accomplice, I believed that it was all over for good."

"But then you overheard me talking to Lord Stonehurst about my nightmares on the evening of the dinner party," Aimee surmised, able to guess how events had proceeded from there. "You panicked and pushed me down the stairs."

A muscle leaped in his jaw. "In that moment, I realized that I couldn't afford to allow you to live. Not without knowing what Stratton might have said or done to implicate me in front of you. Your fall down the stairs was an ill-conceived and desperate attempt on my part, I admit. And when you didn't break your neck as I had hoped, I came to the conclusion that it would be best to pay someone else to accomplish the deed."

"But the man you hired failed as well."

"To my extreme disappointment. It seems you can't find good help anymore. And now I have *two* people to rid myself of. Rather inconvenient, that."

"So what do you plan to do now?" snapped Theodosia. Apparently having recovered a bit of her starch, the dowager was glowering at her stepson, her matronly form trembling with the force of her ire. "It's not as if you can shoot us here, right under the noses of a houseful of servants."

"True," the duke conceded. "But I imagine they

would think nothing of it should I offer to take the two of you out for a carriage ride through the park. Just to get your mind off this unpleasant business with Lady Olivia, you understand. And when our coach is set upon by brigands and I am the lone survivor of the attack . . . Well, there will be no reason for anyone to suspect me. Not when Olivia has already been accused." He arched a brow, his mouth curving in a mocking smile. "I plan on taking every care to make sure that it looks as if I fought most valiantly to save you both. Bruises and cuts. Perhaps a bullet wound in my arm or leg. No one will doubt that I gave my all to defend my beloved stepmother and her innocent young charge."

Aimee took a deep breath, struggling to stay calm in the face of her swiftly growing fear. "You forget that Lord Stonehurst left two of Tolliver's men here to guard the house. You'll never get past them with us."

"Ah, but that's where you're wrong, my dear." Maitland lifted his free hand in a sharp motion, and the nearby French doors swung open, admitting Edmundson, who sauntered into the room as casually as if he belonged there.

"You see," the duke continued, gesturing toward the man with a flourish. "One of those guards has decided that he likes the color of my money much better than Mr. Tolliver's."

Aimee was struck speechless. Just when she

was certain that nothing else could surprise her, she was knocked off balance again. No wonder Maitland's hired assassin had been able to sneak up on them so easily the day she had been pushed off the cliff!

"What about the other guard?" Maitland was questioning Edmundson, his tone harsh and impatient.

"Taken care of," the man informed him with obvious relish. "Split his skull with a rock and dumped him in the bushes behind the house. I can guarantee that he won't be waking up."

"And my carriage?"

"Ready and waiting, as you requested. Your driver is taking a nice long nap in the loft of the carriage house. And don't worry. I made sure he didn't see who coshed him."

"Very good." Pivoting to face Aimee and Theodosia once more, the duke jabbed his pistol at them, then jerked his head toward the French doors. "Let's go. We're leaving."

Aimee exchanged an apprehensive glance with the dowager. Though she was tempted to refuse to cooperate, it would likely do little good. So she got to her feet and helped the elderly lady from her seat, her mind racing all the while. At this point, all they could do was pray that Stonehurst would return before too much longer and realize that something was wrong.

In the meantime, she would have to come up

with her own plan to get them out of this mess.

With the dowager clinging to her arm and Edmundson close at her heels, she followed the duke out the French doors and along the cobbled path that wound around the side of the building, her frantic gaze skimming over her surroundings as she went. Park Lane was relatively quiet and deserted at this time of day, and only a few pedestrians strolled along the sidewalks, much too far away for her to cry out to them for assistance.

The carriage was waiting for them at the bend in the drive, the horses harnessed and prancing. Hidden as they were by a tall row of hedges, it was highly unlikely that anyone would be able to see them from the house. Edmundson immediately swung up onto the driver's box, and Maitland whisked open the door, taking care to keep the butt of his weapon concealed by the overlapping edges of his coat, though the business end was still pointed straight at his intended victims.

"Get in," he ordered.

Theodosia leveled him with a haughty and hate-filled glare before climbing aboard with the aid of her cane, and Aimee slid in after her. Just as she settled herself onto the opposite seat, however, Maitland gave a vicious oath and practically threw himself into the coach, slamming the door behind him.

"It's that bloody Stonehurst!" he hissed.

A wave of relief washed over Aimee, and she

craned her neck so she could see out the window.
Sure enough, there was Royce cantering toward
them up the winding drive, like a white knight
on his faithful steed in her fairy tale dreams of
happily-ever-after.

But even as her heart rejoiced, Maitland reached
up to pound on the ceiling of the carriage. "Go,
you fool!" he bellowed at Edmundson. Then, as
the carriage rocked into motion, he leaned out
the window and sighted down the barrel of his
pistol.

Whether he actually planned to shoot Royce or
fire a warning shot or simply brandish it threat-
eningly, Aimee didn't know and she didn't care.
Just watching him aim at the man she loved made
something snap inside her, and a crimson haze
misted her vision. Because of this monster, she
had lost far more than any one person should ever
have to lose, and she was suddenly wildly, furiously angry.

It was time for the mouse to start fighting
back.

With a shout, she lunged at the duke, catching
him by the wrist and wrenching his arm upward
as hard as she could, slamming it against the
frame of the window in an effort to weaken his
grip on his weapon. At the same time, Theodosia
swung out with her cane, connecting solidly with
his shin. He cursed, and a shot rang out, the bullet
firing harmlessly into the air.

And the terrified horses harnessed to the carriage bolted.

Royce was still several yards away when he heard the echoing report of a pistol shot, and the blood froze in his veins as he urged his horse to gallop faster, harder. Though he couldn't see clearly enough to tell what was going on inside that coach, there could be no doubt that there was a struggle taking place, and he suspected that a certain kitten of his acquaintance had bared her claws with a vengeance. He could only pray that she hadn't been at the receiving end of that bullet.

The possibility filled him with a fear and a dread far beyond anything he had ever before known.

It soon became obvious that the shot had also managed to spook the carriage horses, for Royce could see the driver struggling to rein them in, to get them back under control. But it seemed the man was failing in that endeavor, for the conveyance suddenly veered off the driveway and took off across the wide expanse of parkland that separated Maitland House from the house next door, picking up speed as it went. Jouncing its way across the sloping lawn, it narrowly avoided a low stone wall and headed straight toward a pond that was surrounded by a small copse of trees.

No! Royce's mind roared, visions of his brother's phaeton overturning, of Cordelia's crushed and broken body, rising up behind his eyes. It was like living one of the worst days of his life over again, and there was no way he could reach them in time to stop what was going to happen.

In stunned horror, he watched as the horses shied, trying to swerve at the very last minute. But it was too late. The carriage crashed into the pond with a mighty splash, then flipped over onto its side, sending the driver tumbling from his perch.

A split second later, Royce was pulling up his mount a short distance away, barely coming to a complete stop before he flung himself from the saddle and raced toward the pond, shouting Aimee's name. He was only vaguely aware of the servants who had come racing from the direction of Maitland House, summoned by the sound of the gunshot.

Surveying the water for any sign of movement, he stripped off his coat and boots, praying as he hadn't prayed since he was a small child. The pond didn't look particularly deep, but it was enough to submerge most of the carriage, and anyone who was trapped in the wreckage or too injured to escape was in serious danger of drowning.

He didn't hesitate, but plunged in and struck out with long, steady strokes, intent on reaching the coach. All he could think about was getting to Aimee, and every second counted. But before he had gone very far, a small head broke the surface of the water close to the edge of the pond, coughing and sputtering. And when a pair of familiar amber eyes in a pale, streaming wet face turned toward him, he felt an overwhelming wave of relief.

Thank God!

Abruptly changing direction, he swam toward the small figure treading water, becoming aware only as he neared her that she was towing something behind her.

"Help me," Aimee gasped. "Theodosia."

The dowager was a deadweight in her grasp, dragging her down, and Royce immediately relieved her of her burden. Wrapping an arm around the elderly lady to hold her face above water, he set off for shore with Aimee keeping pace at his side, but it was slow going, and he was grateful when one of the Maitland House footmen waded out to help them onto dry land.

Once he had relinquished Theodosia to the servant's ministrations, he collapsed on the bank, cradling Aimee close against his chest. She was clearly weary and panting for breath, but miraculously free of injury, and he was so full of joy at having her back in his arms that he couldn't restrain the urge to tighten his grip on her.

"Th-Th—" Between chattering teeth, she struggled to form words and clutched at his wet shirt.

"Shhh," he murmured, pressing a kiss to her temple. "You're safe, sweetheart. Don't try to speak."

Author's Note

While doing research for this book, I came across the interesting historical fact that at a point in Napoleon's distinguished military career he was briefly imprisoned under suspicion of treason (August 9–20, 1794). Though promptly released, he fell out of favor with the then-ruling French regime. (His name was removed from the list of active army officers on September 15, 1795, and he did not return to government favor until he assisted in quashing an uprising of French moderates and royalists on October 5, 1795.)

This fact set my mind spinning. I wondered if someone who had met this twenty-six-year-old, down-on-his-heels French officer would ever have ventured that he'd soon seize power in France, later crown himself emperor, and then attempt to dominate Europe? What if that same someone had exposed a cherished secret *to* the young man, never guessing that Napoleon might soon become his greatest enemy? These musings led me to the idea for Evelyn Amherst's legacy from her father, and my story began to take shape. The wonder of fiction for me is all the more interesting if interlaced with fact. I hope you enjoyed my wild imaginings in bringing Evelyn's and Justin's story to life.

"But Theodosia—"

"Is fine. She's breathing, and her staff is taking care of her."

There was a small silence, then she spoke again, her voice a hoarse whisper. "I did it, Royce."

"What did you say, Kitten?

"I did it. I survived your curse. Now there are no more excuses."

He had no idea how to answer that, so he remained silent, watching as the servants lifted a badly mangled body from the depths of the carriage. It was obvious from its unnatural angle that Maitland's neck was broken, and he could only be grateful for small favors. If the bastard had still been alive, he would have killed him himself.

In his arms, Aimee suddenly made a restive motion, as if she were going to pull away, but he held fast to her, not ready to let her go. He didn't think he would ever be ready to let her go. Not after this.

"God, I almost lost you today," he breathed close to her ear, cupping her chin in his hand and lifting her face so he could gaze down into her eyes. Even wet and bedraggled, she had never looked more beautiful. "Please, Kitten, don't ever let me lose you."

And he pressed his lips to hers in a fiercely tender kiss, vowing that he would do his best from now on to make sure he never did.

Chapter 23

"**P**lease, Theodosia, you must be still. You know the doctor said you are not to exert yourself for any reason."

At Jillian's admonishment, the dowager slumped back against her pillows with a huff of irritation, her nostrils flaring in obvious displeasure. "Fustian. The man is a quack. I'm perfectly fine, and I don't need the lot of you hovering over me as if I am about to breathe my last."

She punctuated her declaration with a petulant glare for the small group of people gathered around her bedchamber—Aimee, her sisters, and their father—none of whom was especially put off by her grumbling.

"You almost drowned today, Your Grace," Lord Albright pointed out from where he stood at the foot of her bed. His arms were crossed and he was surveying her sternly. "You need to rest and regain your strength. And if you refuse to cooperate, I assure you that I will not hesitate to order your servants to tie you down."

Theodosia gave another soft huff, but she didn't argue any further. It was an indication of just how weak she was underneath all the bluster.

Seated in a chair next to the bed, Aimee examined the dowager's normally regal features with a concern she couldn't quite hide. Despite the woman's protests to the contrary, she looked tired and drawn. Her skin was pale and as thin as parchment, pulled tautly over the bones of her face, and there were dark circles under her eyes.

As she took note of Aimee's anxious expression, Theodosia's countenance softened. "Don't fret so, child," she murmured. "You know I'm more resilient than I look. And lest we forget, I wasn't the only one in that carriage."

"She's right, darling." Her father rounded the bed to place his hand on his youngest daughter's shoulder. "You've been through a great deal in the past few weeks, and the physician did say you needed your rest as well. When I think of all you've suffered—"

"I'm all right, Papa." She glanced up at him reassuringly. "Really."

"Still, we should go," Maura spoke up as she rose from her chair and got reluctantly to her feet. "Theodosia should be sleeping, and we—"

"Wait, please." The dowager stayed her with a

beseeching gesture, levering herself upright with a speed that belied her frailty. "Before you leave, I owe you an explanation. And I . . . I need to apologize."

Jillian, who was sitting on the edge of the bed, pressed her back down gently. "Don't be silly. You have nothing to apologize for."

"Yes, I do. I should have told you about my husband's tie to Elise long ago, but—" The elderly lady halted, biting her lip, then took a deep breath before continuing in a choked voice. "The year after his first wife's death, Randall had an affair with a young maid in his household. I make no excuses for him. He was much older than the girl and he knew very well that it was wrong to take advantage, but he was grieving, and I think her love made him forget his pain for a short time."

Aimee felt her father's hand tense on her shoulder. "Until she became pregnant," he concluded.

The dowager nodded sadly. "Randall would have taken responsibility for the child, but she never gave him the chance. Perhaps she believed that he would try to wrest the babe from her, or maybe she simply panicked. Whatever the reason, one day she just vanished. For years, he did everything he could to find her. Even after he married me, he kept looking, combing England and hiring investigators. And he was just beginning to give up hope when one of those investigators came forward with the information that the girl had died in childbirth."

She bowed her head for an instant, and when she looked up again, her eyes were sparkling with tears. "The babe was turned over to a foundling home, and from there she grew up to become a London stage actress and then went on to wed the Marquis of Albright."

"Mama," Aimee breathed.

"Yes. You can imagine Randall's shock when he found out. He didn't know what to do, where to turn. And that was when he confided in me. He asked me to befriend Elise, to take her under my wing and try to ease her way into society until he could decide the best way to handle things."

"But why didn't he just tell Mama?" Maura asked, moving closer to the bed. "Didn't he think she had the right to know?"

Theodosia gave her a tremulous smile. "Of course he did, my dear, but he didn't wish to disrupt her life. She'd grown up without him, and I think he was afraid that she would be angry or resent that in some way. That she wouldn't want him." A tear spilled over and rolled down her wrinkled cheek. "And then he became so ill, and everything ground to a halt. Obviously, he decided to claim her, to tell her that he was her father, but he never told me of his plans. He must have spoken to Warren first, and—"

She broke off, and Aimee couldn't stand it anymore. She stood and threw her arms around the elderly woman's neck. "You mustn't upset yourself so," she said, her own eyes filling with tears. "It's not your fault."

"It *is* my fault," the dowager insisted, the words rife with self-blame. "If I had been honest from the very beginning, I might have at least prevented Elise's death, if not Randall's. I knew that something wasn't quite right with Warren, but I never dreamed he was such a monster that he could kill his own father and half sister. How could I have harbored such a demon under my roof and not even be aware of it?"

"None of us was aware of it, Your Grace," the marquis reminded her. "He was very good at fooling people. My family included."

Theodosia held Aimee away from her and stared up at the three sisters crowded together at the side of her bed. "Can any of you ever forgive me? I thought I was doing the right thing, being a good wife by keeping Randall's secret. But I can see now that once he was gone I should have told Elise everything. Your mother was my very dear friend, and I never want you to ever doubt that."

Aimee exchanged quick glances with Jillian and Maura and answered for all of them. "Of course we forgive you. We love you, and we know that you love us. That's all that matters."

The dowager's gaze settled on Lord Albright. "Philip?"

He paused for a long moment, then spoke in a gruff tone. "You've done so much for our family,

Your Grace. If Elise were standing here right now, she would forgive you without a second's hesitation. How can I do any less?"

Theodosia's watery smile was full of gratitude.

"Now, I think the time has come for us to take our leave," the marquis announced, inclining his head toward the door. "It's well past midnight, and Fielding is out in the hallway scowling at us, even as I speak."

Sure enough, the wizened, stoop-shouldered butler was hovering on the threshold, peering in at them with a disapproving frown, and they all stifled a burst of laughter.

Aware that their father was right about the lateness of the hour, however, the sisters gave in gracefully and took turns bidding the dowager good night. And as Aimee leaned forward to press a kiss to the woman's forehead, her whispered "We love you, Grandmother" brought the renewed sheen of tears to Theodosia's eyes.

Only this time they were clearly tears of joy.

Once out in the corridor, the four members of the Daventry family turned and began to move toward the staircase at the other end, walking close together in weary silence while they mulled over everything that had happened that day.

"Do you really think it's over, Papa?" Maura asked as they started down the stairs. "For good this time?"

Lord Albright sighed. "It appears that way, darling.

And only the three of you could possibly understand how very thankful I am to be able to say that. We've been tormented by more than our share of nightmares for the last ten years, but I think we can finally let go of the past." He smiled down at Aimee at his side. "No more nightmares for any of us."

"But what about Aunt Olivia?" she ventured, studying him worriedly. She knew how much hearing the truth about his sister must have hurt him, and she yearned to offer him what comfort she could.

His expression hardened. "She is no longer welcome under my roof, and hopefully she will be packed and gone by the time we get home," he grated, his words resonating with the force of his anger. "Whether she was responsible for your mother's death or not, she was there that night and did nothing to intervene. She deliberately let an innocent man take the blame for a crime he didn't commit in order to appease her jealousy. Bedford is welcome to her if he is foolish enough to still want to wed her after this."

Stopping at the bottom of the steps, he turned to pull his youngest daughter into a fierce hug. "I'm so sorry, Aimee. I should have seen just how abominably Olivia was treating you, but it took Lord Stonehurst to rip my blinders away and force me to face what she has become. I don't think I'll ever be able to forgive myself for letting her make you so miserable."

"It's all right, Papa." Wrapping her arms around his waist, Aimee hugged him back, her heart aching for him. "I never blamed you for any of it. And it would take far more than Aunt Olivia's vicious tongue to tear a strip off me. I am Mama's daughter, after all."

One corner of Lord Albright's mouth quirked ruefully and he released her from his embrace, tucking her arm through his. "Ah, it seems that my little mouse grew up when I wasn't looking. It is no wonder my gray hairs have multiplied."

She laughed and allowed him to draw her with him as they followed Jillian and Maura across the entrance foyer and into the parlor, where Hawksley and Connor were waiting patiently for their wives. But as Aimee entered the room, she discovered that her sister's husbands weren't the only ones present. Lord Stonehurst immediately rose from his place on the settee, and all else faded away as she drank in the sight of him.

With his dark hair wildly mussed and his clothes wrinkled and stained from his dive into the pond earlier, he looked a bit worse for wear. But despite the exhaustion and strain that marked his face, she couldn't help but wonder at the wealth of emotion that simmered in those gray eyes when his gaze locked with hers.

For a brief instant, her mind flashed back to the moment when he had first pulled her from the water after the accident. If she closed her eyes, she could still recall the way he had looked at her. Could still feel the quaver in the strong arms that had cradled her so closely to him. And the words that he had whispered in her ear had the power to make her quiver even now . . .

Please, Kitten, don't ever let me lose you.

How she wanted to believe it had all meant something. That there was hope for the two of them. But she had been rejected by him far too many times already to be the one to make the first move.

It was Jillian who brought her back to the present. "He's the one, isn't he?" she prompted in a gentle tone, eyeing Aimee knowingly. "The right man."

When Aimee could only nod, her sister reached over to give her a hug. "Then grab hold of him and never let him go, darling. You deserve to be happy."

"She's right, sweetheart," her father spoke up from behind her. "He's a good man, and from what I witnessed today, I'd say he is very much in love with you." He kissed her temple. "I'll wait for you in the carriage. And do let Lord Stonehurst know that I'll be expecting a call from him very soon. There is a proper way to go about this matter of marriage, you know."

The next thing she knew, her father and sisters had vacated the room with Hawksley and Connor in tow, leaving her alone with the man who held her heart.

There was a short span of silence as they both stared at each other, then Royce cleared his throat and addressed her with obvious concern. "Are you all right?"

"All things considered, yes," she replied, feeling more than a trifle awkward. "I'm a bit tired, but otherwise I'm well."

"Are you sure? After finding out about Maitland and your mother's relationship to the late duke . . . It must have been a shock."

"Yes, but I'll survive. We all will. And there are some good things to have come of all of this. I've gained a grandmother in the bargain."

He gave a wry smile. "That's my kitten. Always seeing the good in a situation."

"Am I?" She paused, peering up at him through her lashes. "Still your kitten, I mean."

She wasn't certain who moved first, but the next thing she knew, they were in each other's arms, kissing as if they couldn't get enough of each other.

When Royce finally tore his lips from hers, it was to give a husky groan. "Oh, sweetheart, when I saw that carriage go into the water today, I wanted to die. I was certain I was going to lose you, and my heart just stopped."

"I know," she told him, cupping his beloved face in her hands. "But you didn't lose me. I'm here and I'm safe. So what does that tell you?"

For a brief instant, a rare twinkle of humor lit his gaze. "Like all felines, you have nine lives?"

"Very amusing." She rolled her eyes. "No, it should tell you that no curse is strong enough to take me away from you. That I'm here to stay, whether you want me or not."

"Oh, I definitely want you. And I . . ." He paused and took a deep breath before letting the words come bursting forth. "God, Aimee, how I love you. I love you so much."

Her heart sang at finally hearing the words that she had been longing to hear from him for so very long. She had hoped and prayed that he would come to the realization, but never had she dared dream it would happen this soon. "I love you too."

"I've tried to run from it, to deny it, but I realized today that it's too late to change the way I feel about you. And if I keep pushing you away, keep letting my fear of losing the people I care about prevent me from having a future with you, then my father wins. He gets what he wants. Me, alone for the rest of my life."

"It doesn't have to be that way, Royce," Aimee murmured. "I honestly think that Garvey and Cordelia and even your brother would want you to be happy. Alex was angry and bitter, and I don't believe for an instant he meant what he said to you. He probably regretted it the moment you were gone." She stroked her finger gently over the line of his scar. "If there truly is a darkness in you, we can face it together. And we can defeat it. That's what love does."

He shook his head. "I meant what I told you before. I can't live the normal life of a lord of the ton. There will be no balls or dinners or lavish soirees. Crowds suffocate me, and loud noises and conversations make me flash back to my time on the battlefield. I'll never really be comfortable anywhere except Stonecliff."

"Royce, you know I have never cared about any of that," she scolded him. "A quiet life at Stonecliff with you and our children sounds ideal to me."

"Children." He swept her into his arms, peering down at her stomach in shock. "Sweet Christ, I never even thought of . . . Do you think?"

"Anything is possible, darling. And you needn't look so terrified. You'll make a wonderful father." She brushed her lips teasingly against his cheek as he bore her toward the settee. "You know, after that daring rescue you performed this afternoon, I do believe you deserve a reward. And I seem to remember a certain wise man telling me once that in some cultures, when you save a life, it belongs to you."

"Then I suppose my life belongs to you, Kitten," he drawled silkily as he lowered her to the cushions. "Because *you* were the one who saved *me*."

And his lips melted into hers.

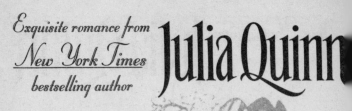

AVON

978-0-06-134024-6

978-0-06-087137-6

978-0-06-084798-2

978-0-06-124110-9

978-0-06-134039-0

978-0-06-111886-9